WHAT WOULD SCOTLAND YARD DO WITHOUT DEAR MRS. JEFFRIES?

Even Inspector Witherspoon himself doesn't know—because his secret weapon is as ladylike as she is clever. She's Mrs. Jeffries—the charming detective who stars in this unique Victorian mystery series. Enjoy them all . . .

The Inspector and Mrs. Jeffries
A doctor is found dead in his own office—and Mrs. Jeffries must scour the premises to find the prescription for murder.

Mrs. Jeffries Dusts for Clues
One case is solved and another is opened when the Inspector finds a missing brooch—pinned to a dead woman's gown. But Mrs. Jeffries never cleans a room without dusting under the bed—and never gives up on a case before every loose end is tightly tied.

The Ghost and Mrs. Jeffries
Death is unpredictable . . . but the murder of Mrs. Hodges was foreseen at a spooky séance. The practical-minded Mrs. Jeffries may not be able to see the future—but she can look into the past and put things in order to solve this haunting crime.

Mrs. Jeffries Takes Stock
A businessman has been murdered—and it could be because he cheated his stockholders. The housekeeper's interest is piqued . . . and when it comes to catching killers, the smart money's on Mrs. Jeffries.

continued . . .

Mrs. Jeffries on the Ball
A festive Jubilee celebration turns into a fatal affair—and Mrs. Jeffries must find the guilty party.

Mrs. Jeffries on the Trail
Why was Annie Shields out selling flowers so late on a foggy night? And more importantly, who killed her while she was doing it? It's up to Mrs. Jeffries to sniff out the clues.

Mrs. Jeffries Plays the Cook
Mrs. Jeffries finds herself doing double duty: cooking for the Inspector's household and trying to cook a killer's goose.

Mrs. Jeffries and the Missing Alibi
When Inspector Witherspoon becomes the main suspect in a murder, Scotland Yard refuses to let him investigate. But no one said anything about Mrs. Jeffries.

Mrs. Jeffries Stands Corrected
When a local publican is murdered, and Inspector Witherspoon botches the investigation, trouble starts to brew for Mrs. Jeffries.

Mrs. Jeffries Takes the Stage
After a theater critic is murdered, Mrs. Jeffries uncovers the victim's secret past: a real-life drama more compelling than any stage play.

Mrs. Jeffries Questions the Answers
Hannah Cameron was not well-liked. But were her friends or family the sort to stab her in the back? Mrs. Jeffries must find out.

Mrs. Jeffries Reveals Her Art
Mrs. Jeffries has to work double time to find a missing model *and* a killer. And she'll have to get her whole staff involved—before someone else becomes the next subject.

Mrs. Jeffries Takes the Cake

The evidence was all there: a dead body, two dessert plates, and a gun. As if Mr. Ashbury had been sharing cake with his own killer. Now Mrs. Jeffries will have to do some snooping around—to dish up clues.

Mrs. Jeffries Rocks the Boat

Mirabelle had traveled by boat all the way from Australia to visit her sister—only to wind up murdered. Now Mrs. Jeffries must solve the case—and it's sink or swim.

Mrs. Jeffries Weeds the Plot

Three attempts have been made on Annabeth Gentry's life. Is it due to her recent inheritance, or is it because her blood-hound dug up the body of a murdered thief? Mrs. Jeffries will have to sniff out some clues before the plot thickens.

Mrs. Jeffries Pinches the Post

Harrison Nye may have had some dubious business deal-ings, but no one ever expected him to be murdered. Now Mrs. Jeffries and her staff must root through the sins of his past to discover which one caught up with him.

Mrs. Jeffries Pleads Her Case

Harlan Westover's death was deemed a suicide by the mag-istrate. But Inspector Witherspoon is willing to risk his career to prove otherwise. And it's up to Mrs. Jeffries to ensure the good inspector remains afloat.

Mrs. Jeffries Sweeps the Chimney

A dead vicar has been found, propped against a church wall. And Inspector Witherspoon's only prayer is to seek the divinations of Mrs. Jeffries.

Mrs. Jeffries Stalks the Hunter

Puppy love turns to obsession, which leads to murder. Who better to get to the heart of the matter than Inspector With-erspoon's indomitable companion, Mrs. Jeffries.

continued . . .

Mrs. Jeffries and the Silent Knight
The yuletide murder of an elderly man is complicated by several suspects—none of whom were in the Christmas spirit.

Mrs. Jeffries Appeals the Verdict
Mrs. Jeffries and her belowstairs cohorts have their work cut out for them if they want to save an innocent man from the gallows.

Mrs. Jeffries and the Best Laid Plans
Banker Lawrence Boyd didn't waste his time making friends, which is why hardly anyone mourns his death. With a list of enemies including just about everyone the miser's ever met, it will take Mrs. Jeffries' shrewd eye to find the killer.

Mrs. Jeffries and the Feast of St. Stephen
'Tis the season for sleuthing when wealthy Stephen Whit-field is murdered during his holiday dinner party. It's up to Mrs. Jeffries to solve the case in time for Christmas.

Mrs. Jeffries Holds the Trump
A very-well-liked but very dead magnate is found floating down the river. Now Mrs. Jeffries and company will have to dive into a mystery that only grows more complex.

**Visit Emily Brightwell's website
at www.emilybrightwell.com.**

**Also available from Prime Crime:
The first three Mrs. Jeffries Mysteries in one volume
*Mrs. Jeffries Learns the Trade.***

MRS. JEFFRIES
IN THE NICK OF TIME

EMILY BRIGHTWELL

BERKLEY PRIME CRIME, NEW YORK

THE BERKLEY PUBLISHING GROUP
Published by the Penguin Group
Penguin Group (USA) Inc.
375 Hudson Street, New York, New York 10014, USA
Penguin Group (Canada), 90 Eglinton Avenue East, Suite 700, Toronto, Ontario M4P 2Y3, Canada
(a division of Pearson Penguin Canada Inc.)
Penguin Books Ltd., 80 Strand, London WC2R 0RL, England
Penguin Group Ireland, 25 St. Stephen's Green, Dublin 2, Ireland (a division of Penguin Books Ltd.)
Penguin Group (Australia), 250 Camberwell Road, Camberwell, Victoria 3124, Australia
(a division of Pearson Australia Group Pty. Ltd.)
Penguin Books India Pvt. Ltd., 11 Community Centre, Panchsheel Park, New Delhi—110 017, India
Penguin Group (NZ), 67 Apollo Drive, Rosedale, North Shore 0632, New Zealand
(a division of Pearson New Zealand Ltd.)
Penguin Books (South Africa) (Pty.) Ltd., 24 Sturdee Avenue, Rosebank, Johannesburg 2196,
South Africa

Penguin Books Ltd., Registered Offices: 80 Strand, London WC2R 0RL, England

This is a work of fiction. Names, characters, places, and incidents either are the product of the author's imagination or are used fictitiously, and any resemblance to actual persons, living or dead, business establishments, events, or locales is entirely coincidental. The publisher does not have any control over and does not assume any responsibility for author or third-party websites or their content.

MRS. JEFFRIES IN THE NICK OF TIME

A Berkley Prime Crime Book / published by arrangement with the author

PRINTING HISTORY
Berkley Prime Crime mass-market edition / March 2009

Copyright © 2009 by Cheryl Arguile.

ISBN: 978-0-425-22678-0

BERKLEY® PRIME CRIME
Berkley Prime Crime Books are published by The Berkley Publishing Group,
a division of Penguin Group (USA) Inc.,
375 Hudson Street, New York, New York 10014.
BERKLEY® PRIME CRIME and the PRIME CRIME logo are trademarks of Penguin Group
(USA) Inc.

PRINTED IN THE UNITED STATES OF AMERICA

10 9 8 7 6 5 4 3 2 1

*This book is dedicated to the congregation
of Irvine United Congregational Church.
A place which is proudly progressive, radically inclusive,
and where everyone is invited to the table.*

CHAPTER 1

—◆—

"Let's hope that the sight of Mr. Kirkland having tea with us doesn't send Uncle Francis into a fit when he finally decides to join us," Annabelle Prescott whispered to her cousin, Imogene Ross. They were sitting on the sofa in the drawing room and waiting for their uncle, Francis Humphreys, to come down and greet the guests he'd invited to tea.

"Mr. Kirkland said that Uncle was expecting him," Imogene murmured in reply. "Where is Uncle? Our guests are beginning to get restless. Mr. Eddington has cornered poor Mr. and Mrs. Brown and he's such a bore, they'll both soon be asleep. Honestly, I don't know why Uncle Francis has to invite him to every social function." She glanced in the direction of the closed double oak doors of the drawing room. "You'd think Uncle Francis would be down here promptly if for no other reason than to spare his guests from being forced to listen to Mr. Eddington's constant complaints about the Great Western Railway. Who would have thought a railroad could inspire such passion? It's all the man ever talks about."

Annabelle laughed softly. "Mrs. Brown just stifled a yawn. I expect Uncle Francis will be down momentarily. He's probably taking his time getting dressed and waiting for the 4:06 to pass."

"I thought he only cared about the 3:09 to Bristol? Still, it's not like him to be late. You know what a stickler he is for punctuality. Perhaps I ought to run upstairs." Imogene started to get up off the settee.

"Don't," Annabelle said sharply as she motioned Imogene back to her seat. "He was having trouble tying his cravat and you know how sensitive he's become lately. He hates people thinking he's too old and feeble to take care of his person. He'll not thank you for interrupting him."

"That's true." Imogene sank back down and smiled ruefully. "He got angry with me yesterday and all I did was mention that his waistcoat was unbuttoned. I didn't mean anything by the comment; I was merely trying to save him a bit of embarrassment. After all, he was on his way out. He was going to see his solicitor."

Francis Humphreys was their mutual uncle and the owner of the huge house where both women now resided. They were his nieces, but the circumstances of how the two cousins ended up living under the same roof were very different.

He had insisted Annabelle come live with him and play the role of the lady of the house when her husband had died two years ago. Imogene's invitation had been rather grudgingly given when she'd written from the railway hotel in Bristol that she'd just been sacked from her position as a governess.

Uncle Francis had very definite notions about family duty and obligations but that didn't mean he ever let her forget she had a roof over her head because he knew what was right and proper. Still, she oughtn't complain. She had a nice room and a small, but adequate quarterly allowance for her clothing and personal items. Nevertheless, she was looking for another position.

"He's not sensitive," a male voice said from behind Imogene. "He's senile and getting worse every day. If we don't do something quickly, he's going to spend every last farthing of my aunt Estelle's estate."

Annabelle twisted slightly and looked at the thin young man standing behind them. "Shh . . . someone will hear you," she warned.

Michael Collier shrugged, came around the sofa, and slipped into the empty spot next to her. He was perfectly dressed in a gray suit with a darker gray waistcoat underneath, red cravat, and white shirt. "I don't care who hears me. I'm simply saying what everyone else is thinking. Look over there at those two." He nodded toward a middle-aged couple sitting on the loveseat next to the fireplace. "They're both so worried about what he's going to do next that they came all the way up from Dorset just to have tea with the old man and make sure he hasn't gone completely bonkers."

"Be quiet, Michael," Imogene urged. "Uncle Francis will have a fit if someone repeats your words."

Collier raised an eyebrow. "I don't care if they give him a verbatim report. As a matter of fact, it might do him the world of good to know we're all concerned about his behavior."

"But he hasn't done anything yet," Imogene hissed. Like the rest of the family, she'd heard the rumors. "He's only talking about it."

"He's done more than talk," Michael muttered darkly. "He's been to see both the stockbroker and the solicitor. That means he's taking action. If we don't do something, we're all going to end up with nothing. Aunt Estelle may have left him all her money, but she meant for him to handle her estate wisely, not fritter it away on one nonsensical project after another."

"But she did leave it to him," Annabelle said bluntly. "Not to you."

"I get my share when he dies," Michael snapped. "And so do the rest of you, so get off your high horse, Annabelle. You're as concerned about this latest bit of nonsense as I am."

"Be careful," Imogene said softly. "Uncle Francis has ears everywhere." She glanced meaningfully around the huge drawing room. In one corner, Mr. and Mrs. Elliot, the distant relations from Dorset, were sipping tea and helping themselves to another slice of seedcake from the silver tray on the tea trolley. Another cousin, Pamela Bowden Humphreys, was sitting in the chair next to the Elliots and making no effort whatsoever to be sociable. She was staring morosely out the window, watching the falling rain.

Next to her sat Mr. and Mrs. Brown, the nice neighbors from the house closest to Humphreys House who were now stuck with listening to Robert Eddington drone on about the advantages of the broad-gauge track and how unfortunate it was that some railways had been coerced into converting to single gauge. Despite being old and white haired, Mr. Eddington had a voice that carried very distinctly. Sitting on a chair a few feet away was Joseph Leland Humphreys, another cousin. He was staring at Eddington with a sardonic, amused expression.

Leo Kirkland made up the last of the group. But he was sitting in an overstuffed chair on the far side of the fireplace, nursing a cup of tea and casting furtive glances toward the closed doors leading to the hallway.

Michael Collier rose to his feet. "Maybe we should see what's keeping Uncle Francis—" He stopped speaking as a loud, sharp noise boomed through the house.

"Good Lord, what was that?" Joseph leapt up.

"It sounded like someone dropped something." Annabelle put her cup down on the tabletop.

"That wasn't something being dropped." Imogene got up as well.

"It was a gunshot," Leo Kirkland said flatly. "Someone's shot off a gun and what's more, it was in the house."

Annabelle and Imogene looked at each other just as Joseph charged for the door. Michael Collier went flying after him.

Everyone else got to their feet. The relatives all ran for the staircase, leaving only Eddington and the Browns in the drawing room.

Joseph and Michael reached the first floor landing at the same time; the women were right on their heels. For a split second, they stood there. Then Annabelle pointed to Francis' room. "Look, his door is partially open. Oh goodness, you can see him. There's something wrong. He's not moving."

The two men charged into the room. Francis Humphreys was sitting at his desk. His head was slumped over as though he'd fallen asleep and he was leaning to his left.

Michael got to him first. He reached down and put his fingers under the man's chin. Then he gasped and hastily stepped back. Joseph impatiently shoved him aside. "What's wrong? What is it?" He lifted his uncle's chin so that everyone could see.

Blood dripped down from the small hole in Francis' forehead and his eyes were open, giving his plump face a rather surprised expression.

"He's been shot." Michael's voice was a shocked whisper.

"Oh, that's most definitely a gunshot," Leo Kirkland said calmly. He had entered the room quietly and come up to stand behind Annabelle.

"Oh my gracious," Imogene cried. Her lips quivered and her eyes filled with tears.

"I think the ladies ought to leave the room," Kirkland said softly.

"Is he dead?" Annabelle's voice trembled.

Joseph reached over and put his fingers on the pulse point on Francis' neck. After a few seconds, he moved his hand inside the man's jacket, placing his fingers over his chest. "I'm not a doctor, but I don't feel a pulse or a heartbeat. I'm afraid he's gone."

Kirkland sighed heavily. "You really must call the police."

"The police?" Pamela cried. "What are you talking about? Surely this was an accident."

"I didn't mean to upset you, Mrs. Humphreys." He smiled apologetically. "But it'll be up to a magistrate or a coroner's inquest to determine if this was an accident or murder."

"Murder?" Michael Collier snapped. "That's ridiculous. Who'd want to murder Uncle Francis? Maybe he did it to himself."

"Suicides don't usually shoot themselves in the forehead," Joseph muttered. "And I can think of any number of people who had cause to want our esteemed uncle dead." He looked pointedly at Michael.

"How dare you." Michael's eyes narrowed angrily. "That's rich, coming from you. Just last week you told me you thought the old man was losing his reason."

"I said that as well as a number of other things, but that's not the same as putting a bullet through his head. Unlike some in this family, I don't worship money."

"Gentlemen, please, this is no time for recriminations or accusations," Leo Kirkland said sharply.

Annabelle Prescott began to sob. Imogene put her arm

around her shoulders and led her toward the door. "Mr. Kirkland is right; this is no place for us. Come along, I'll take you to your room."

Annabelle smiled through her tears. "I can't stay here another moment."

"Neither can I," Pamela announced as she followed them out to the hall. "Let the men deal with this."

As soon as the women had gone, Kirkland looked at the two young men standing over the body. "Someone had better go fetch the police and do it quickly. In the meantime, I suggest you clear everyone else out of here and lock the door. The police will want the room preserved in case there's any evidence to be had."

The household of Inspector Gerald Witherspoon were finishing their afternoon tea. Mrs. Jeffries, the housekeeper, was at the head of the table. She was a short, plump woman of late middle years. Her dark auburn hair was streaked with wide gray strands, her complexion pale and there were freckles sprinkled across her nose. Deep laugh lines were etched around her brown eyes and her thin lips were usually turned up in a happy smile. As was her custom, she wore a brown bombazine dress that rustled nicely when she walked and sensible black shoes.

"How much longer do you think this rain is going to last?" Betsy, the pretty blonde-haired, blue-eyed maid commented as she reached for the teapot. "It seems like it's been pouring for days now."

"That's because it 'as," Wiggins, the footman, replied. He was a young man in his early twenties with round pink cheeks and brown hair that tended to curl in the damp. "All this wet is enough to drive a good man to drink."

"Stop your complainin'," Mrs. Goodge, the elderly, gray-haired cook interjected. "Wait till you get to be my age and then you'll feel the cold in every bone of your body. Besides, it's already March; spring will be here soon enough." She glanced at the carriage clock on the pine sideboard as the hour struck. "I do hope the inspector isn't going to be too late tonight. I've got a roast in the oven and it'll dry out if I leave it too long."

"Lucky for us we don't 'ave a case now," Smythe, the coachman, said. "Otherwise we'd 'ave to be out and about in this mess." He was a tall man in his late thirties. His hair was black, his features harsh, and his shoulders broad. He was engaged to Betsy and he loved her more than his own life. He grinned at her as he spoke, knowing his comment would provoke a reaction.

"I'd not mind the weather if we had a case." Betsy shot her fiancé an irritated glance and then lightly cuffed him on the arm when she saw his wicked grin. "You'd like it if we had a murder to investigate, too, admit it."

"We've all got umbrellas," Wiggins muttered. He still smarted from feeling just a bit guilty as he'd not worked as hard as the others on their last case. "And we've got boots. A bit of rain wouldn't be a bother if we was doin' somethin' important."

"We really mustn't wish for a murder just because it's wet and we've all been trapped inside," Mrs. Jeffries admonished them. "We should be glad there's been a few weeks of peace and quiet for Inspector Witherspoon. He deserves a bit of a rest." Gracious, even as the words left her mouth she felt a right old hypocrite. She was no better than the rest of them: She'd love it if they had a nice, interesting homicide to sink their teeth into.

Inspector Gerald Witherspoon had solved more crimes than anyone in the history of the Metropolitan Police Force. Considering that only a few short years ago, he was in charge of the Records Room, everyone, including the inspector, was somewhat amazed by his accomplishments. What very few people, including the inspector, didn't know was that he had substantial help from his household with each and every murder he solved.

It had all begun a few years back when Smythe had returned from Australia. He'd stopped in to pay his respects to his old employer, the inspector's late aunt, Euphemia Witherspoon. When he'd arrived at the house, he'd found her dying. She had a house full of servants, but the only one trying to take care of the poor woman had been a young footman, Wiggins.

Smythe had taken one look at the situation, fired everyone but Wiggins, and sent for a doctor. But even the best physician couldn't work miracles and Euphemia Witherspoon was too far gone to save. Before she died, she'd made Smythe promise to stay on in the house for a little while and look out for her only relative, her nephew, Gerald Witherspoon. She was leaving him this huge house and enough money so he'd never have to work another day in his life. Smythe, who'd made a huge fortune of his own in Australia, had agreed to stay and see the fellow decently settled with a competent staff.

The first one to be hired had been Mrs. Jeffries. She was the widow of a Yorkshire policeman. She'd come to London to take advantage of everything the city had to offer and had thought to do a bit of traveling. But after just a few short weeks, she'd tramped through every museum numerous times, attended a half dozen concerts, and seen every play in the West End. She was bored to tears. Then she'd spotted an advertisement as a housekeeper for a policeman. More curious than anything else, she'd gone to the address listed, interviewed with Inspector Witherspoon, and had been offered the position. She had had to remind him to check her references.

Mrs. Goodge had come along next and then Betsy had collapsed on their doorstep. When she'd recovered, she'd taken the position as the maid.

But even though it had started with his return, it had really been Mrs. Jeffries who had steered the household staff into helping the inspector. On their first case, she'd been very subtle and they'd not figured out what she was doing till the case was solved. The horrible Kensington High Street murders had gotten Witherspoon out of the Records Room and into a tiny office at the Ladbroke Road Police Station, where he was and remained to this day the only policeman of detective inspector rank. In the years that followed, Witherspoon solved one baffling case after another and owing to his amazing success, he was frequently called to Scotland Yard and other districts around the city when there was a particularly baffling homicide to be solved.

"We'll all get enough peace and quiet when we die," the cook responded tartly. "And that experience is coming sooner rather than later for some of us."

Mrs. Goodge had worked for some of the finest families in all of England before coming to the inspector's household. She had a vast network of old associates, colleagues, and friends whom she could call upon for information when they had a murder to solve. There was also the small army of delivery boys, rags and bones dealers, mush-fakers, laundrymen, and fruit vendors who trooped in and out of the house on a daily basis. She kept them well supplied with tea and treats while finding out everything there was to know about those who ended up as victims or suspects in the inspector's cases. She never had to even leave the kitchen to do her part in their investigations.

Mrs. Jeffries frowned at the cook. "You mustn't talk like that. You've plenty of good years left."

"And you're lots younger than Luty Belle," Wiggins

added. He was referring to their good friend, an elderly American eccentric named Luty Belle Crookshank. She and her butler, Hatchet, were special friends of the household and frequently helped on the inspector's cases.

"That's kind of you, lad. But there aren't that many years between the two of us old hens. Besides, Luty told me yesterday that if we didn't get another case soon, she'd have to shoot someone herself. Mind you, she was looking at Hatchet when she made that remark."

"She wasn't serious, though." Betsy laughed. "She would be lost without Hatchet. He's more than just her butler; he's her dearest friend."

Under the table, Smythe grabbed her hand and gave it a squeeze. He and Betsy had been through their own trials and troubles but come October, they'd be man and wife.

"Better a friend than a false sweetheart," Wiggins murmured, more to himself than the others. He'd had his heart trampled on during their last investigation and he was still hurting over the matter. One of the reasons he wanted another case was because he felt as if he'd let them all down. When everyone else in the household had been solving a double homicide, he wasted his time trailing after a deceitful young woman who was more interested in free lunches and teas than she'd been in him. It still smarted.

"What did you say, Wiggins?" Mrs. Goodge asked.

"Nothin'." He gave the cook a cheerful smile. He knew she'd been worrying about him and he wasn't having any more of that. At her age, the less aggravation there was in her life, the better and he wasn't going to be mooning about the place anymore, thank you very much.

Mrs. Jeffries looked toward the far wall. The kitchen of Upper Edmonton Gardens, like many kitchens in this part of London was built just below ground, so that the window literally faced out onto the pavement. Through the rain splattered pane, she saw the wheels of a hansom pull up in front of the house. "That might be Inspector Witherspoon." She got to her feet and headed for the back stairs.

But when she reached the front door, it wasn't the inspector but a constable she didn't recognize.

He nodded respectfully. "Mrs. Jeffries?"

"Yes."

"I'm Constable Wisden. Inspector Witherspoon asked me to stop by and let you know he'd be late coming home. He's been called out on a case and he didn't want his household to worry."

"Thank you, Constable. Would you care to come in for a cup of tea?" Witherspoon was rarely called out this late in the day unless it was serious so she was determined to find out what she could from this young man.

"No ma'am, I'm on my way to the Yard with some evidence, so I can't stop in, but I thank you for the invitation." He nodded again and started to turn.

"Did the inspector say what time he'd be home?" she asked quickly.

"No ma'am, but as it's a murder, I expect he'll be quite late."

"Oh dear, that's dreadful. I do hope he didn't have to go too far in this awful weather," she tried again.

"I'm afraid he did, ma'am." The constable smiled sympathetically. "He's been sent to Acton. Paddington Division has requested his help. He's gone to Humphreys House on Linton Road. Good day to you, ma'am."

"Good-bye, Constable, and thank you for delivering the message." She closed the door, charged down the hall, and raced down the staircase. For a woman of late middle age with both arthritis and a touch of rheumatism in her knees, she could move fast when the situation called for it.

Having heard her thundering down the stairs, the others rose to their feet as she burst into the kitchen. "We've a murder," she announced. "And it's bound to be an important one. It's out of our inspector's district."

Metropolitan police divisions were very competitive with one another and wouldn't have asked for Witherspoon's assistance unless someone had put pressure on them to make the request. That meant someone at Scotland Yard had wanted Witherspoon on the case.

"There's no time to lose," she continued. "The inspector is already on his way there, so you two"—she looked at Wiggins and Smythe—"had best get cracking."

Both of them were already moving toward the coat tree. "Where is it?" Smythe asked as he grabbed his heavy black overcoat and tossed it over his arm.

Wiggins slipped into his jacket, grabbed his hat, and reached into the brass stand for his umbrella. "Do I have time to put my boots on? They're just by the back door."

Smythe nodded. "Bring mine as well." He turned to Mrs. Jeffries. "Should I risk going to Howards for the carriage?" Howards was the livery where the inspector's carriage and horses were stabled.

"No, there isn't time." She didn't have to tell them what to do once they arrived at the murder site. They understood what needed to be done. "Take a hansom. Do you need any money?"

He grinned and shook his head. He knew that the housekeeper had only asked that question to keep up appearances. Wiggins and Mrs. Goodge thought he was just a simple coachman. He was rich as sin but the only people in the household who knew it were Mrs. Jeffries and Betsy. He'd never meant to keep the others in the dark; it's just that when he'd first come back from Australia he'd not planned on staying at the Witherspoon household very long. But everything had happened so quickly that by the time he should have gone, they'd started solving murders and he'd begun to hope that Betsy had feelings for him. By then, it was too late to tell them about his wealth.

He'd told Betsy about his money when they became engaged and Mrs. Jeffries had figured it out on her own. One day he'd tell Wiggins and Mrs. Goodge, but he'd wait until the right moment. Sometimes feelings were hurt if your friends thought you'd deliberately kept a secret from them.

"This is the house, sir." Constable Barnes deftly opened the umbrella and held it up as the inspector stepped down from the hansom cab. The constable was a craggy-faced veteran with over twenty-five years on the force. His complexion was florid, his posture rigid as a post, and beneath his helmet was a headful of curly gray hair. The rain had slowed to a light drizzle, but he kept the umbrella over them as he paid off the cab. He turned and stared at a six-story redbrick house. "It's huge."

"Of course it is." Witherspoon sighed heavily. "And no doubt it's owned by someone influential and rich." The inspector was a middle-aged man with thinning brown hair, a long, rather bony face, and deep-set hazel eyes.

"Plenty of property as well. It's set back from the road a goodly ways. That doesn't come cheap in any part of London," Barnes added.

Witherspoon stepped out from underneath the umbrella and started toward the house. "Right, we might as well get to it. At least the rain seems to be letting up."

As was both their habits, each of them surveyed the property as they made their way to the front door. Barnes lifted his hand to bang the knocker when the door opened and a young police constable stuck his head out. "Thank goodness you've arrived. We're having a hard time holding them." He held the door wide, stepped back, and waved them into the foyer.

The constable's words did not bode well, Witherspoon thought to himself. "I'm Inspector Witherspoon and this is Constable Barnes," he said as he continued his study of his surroundings. The house was as opulent inside as he'd thought it might be. The walls were painted in a pale peach shade with intricate white molding running along the top of the ceiling. A huge mirror with an ornate gold-painted frame hung on the wall and just beneath it was an over-sized fern resting on a white marble foyer table. The floor was polished oak and directly overhead was a huge three-armed amber glass chandelier. At the end of the long hallway, a carpeted staircase the same shade as the chandelier, curved up to the upper floors.

"Police Constable Bishop, sir," the policeman said quickly. "The body is upstairs sir, but the witnesses are all in there." He jerked his thumb toward a closed door farther down the hall.

"Witnesses," Witherspoon repeated hopefully. "You mean someone saw the killer?" Gracious, that would make his task so much easier. He'd never had a case where he had an actual eyewitness to murder.

"No sir." Constable Bishop smiled ruefully. "No one saw anything, but they did hear the fatal shots being fired. The house was full of guests when the incident happened and several of them are wanting to leave now. Naturally, I told them they had to wait until you arrived."

Witherspoon was bitterly disappointed and the struggle not to let the emotion show on his face resulted in his mind going completely blank for a few moments. He blinked and scratched his nose, hoping to buy himself a few seconds to think what to do next. Luckily, Constable Barnes had no such problem. "We'll have a quick word with the witnesses and then go up to see the body. Has the police surgeon been called?"

"Yes sir, but he's sent word back he may be delayed.

He's in surgery. He should be here before seven. I took the liberty of postponing the mortuary van until half past." He cast a quick glance at the inspector. "I hope that's all right with you, sir. But we've heard of your methods and we know you like the doctor to have a look at the body before it's moved."

Relieved that his brain appeared to be functioning again, Witherspoon nodded and started for the drawing room. "You did exactly right, Constable."

Witherspoon slid open the double doors and stepped inside. The conversation stopped as a dozen pair of eyes turned their gazes upon the two policemen. From the sofa, an attractive, blonde woman who appeared to be in her midthirties got up and came toward them. She smiled at Inspector Witherspoon and nodded at Barnes. "Hello, you must be the man in charge. I'm Annabelle Prescott. We've been waiting for you."

"We got here as quickly as we could, ma'am," Witherspoon replied apologetically. "I understand there's been a shooting?" Even as he introduced himself, he was studying the room. It was even more elaborate than the foyer. The floor was slats of oak parquet done in a diamond pattern, the ceiling a good twelve feet over his head, and the walls painted the palest shade of green he'd ever seen. Green and pink flowered curtains hung at the three long windows, a carved wooden mantel with an inlay of pink marble surrounded the fireplace, and the furniture was ornate French empire upholstered in shades of ivory, green, and pink.

"That's why we've sent for you, sir." A youngish man with dark hair stepped forward. "Our uncle Francis has been murdered. He was shot this afternoon while the rest of us were sitting here waiting for him to join us."

"What is your name, sir?" Barnes asked.

"Joseph Humphreys," he replied. "We were all here; we all heard the shot."

"What time would that have been?" Witherspoon directed the question to Annabelle Prescott.

"I didn't look at the clock," she replied. "So I don't know the precise time. Why? Is it important?"

"I do." A plump, brown-haired woman got up off a chair next to the fireplace and came over to stand next to the young man. "I looked at the clock just before we heard the shot. It was eight minutes past four. I'm Pamela Humphreys."

"Inspector, we were all sitting here when the shot was fired, so can't we just leave our names and addresses and go home?" The question was asked by a tired-looking elderly gentleman. "I'm Leo Kirkland. I'm no relation to Francis Humphreys. I'm merely a guest who was invited here to tea today and frankly this whole ordeal has exhausted me. I'd like to leave."

"All of you were here together when the shot was fired?" Witherspoon pressed. He didn't see any harm in acquiescing to their wishes. If they'd all been together here in the drawing room, they certainly couldn't have been murdering anyone. Unless, of course, all of them were in it together. He shuddered slightly and shoved that thought to the back of his mind. Conspiracies were dreadfully difficult to prove.

"Yes, Inspector." Annabelle Prescott smiled wearily. "We were all here waiting for Uncle Francis to come downstairs. Everyone in this room had been invited for tea but we heard the shot before any food was served. I imagine everyone here is both tired and hungry."

"Yes, I expect they are." He didn't really see any harm in letting people leave. He looked at their eager, expectant faces. "By all means, you must go home. Leave your names and addresses with the constable outside and you can go." He glanced at Barnes as he spoke, letting him know with a discreet nudge of his chin that he was to keep watch as the guests left and make sure no one departed without speaking to Bishop.

Barnes slipped into the hallway just before the first of the group came charging out, holding on to hats and coats and umbrellas as they crowded around the young constable. Bishop, scribbling furiously, wouldn't have had time to notice if half a dozen people had made for the door. But Barnes kept a close watch.

When the last of the guests had gone, Bishop put his pencil in his trouser pocket and shook his hand. "I don't think I've ever written so fast in my life."

"You'll get even faster the longer you stay on the force." Barnes smiled in amusement. "Have the house and the grounds been searched?"

"We searched both as soon as we arrived and saw the victim had been shot," Bishop said. "But we found nothing. Mind you, here in the house, it was a bit difficult."

"Difficult," Barnes repeated. "How was it difficult? What do you mean?"

Bishop shifted from one leg to the other. "We did our best but we kept stumbling over servants and guests. They were everywhere, sir. It was very awkward."

The constable's eyebrows drew together in a frown. "Awkward or not, I assume your search was thorough?"

Witherspoon came out of the drawing room. He smiled at the young constable. "I'm sure it was very thorough, wasn't it?"

Bishop smiled in relief and nodded vigorously. "Yes sir, it was."

Barnes resisted the urge to box the inspector's ears. Ye gods, now the lad would never own up to whether or not they'd actually conducted a rigorous search. Sometimes he wished Inspector Witherspoon wasn't quite so kind and decent.

"No sign of the weapon, I suppose," Witherspoon continued.

"None, sir."

Barnes, who was more than a little annoyed at his superior officer, said, "We'd best get upstairs to view the body, sir."

Witherspoon repressed a shudder and nodded, and the two policemen started up the stairs.

Another constable was standing guard in front of a closed door just off the first floor landing. He snapped to attention. "It's just here, sir." He opened the door and ushered them inside.

As he stepped over the threshold, Witherspoon took a deep breath. He hated dead bodies. Truth of the matter was that oftentimes some of the sights he'd seen had given him the worst nightmares. But he knew his duty, and no matter how unpleasant this might be, he'd do his job to the best of his ability.

He stopped and looked at his surroundings. The room was both a bedroom and a study. The ceiling was high and the walls painted a soothing shade of cream. A double bed with a carved wooden headboard and a maroon coverlet was on the left-hand side of the long room. Farther down and on the right was a large desk. Witherspoon quickly flicked his gaze past the body sitting propped up in the chair. Opposite the desk was a set of French doors.

Two brilliantly colored oriental rugs covered the dark wood floor. Shelves, tables, and bookcases lined the walls. On the far side of the room was a fireplace with a green marble mantel and just above it was a huge portrait of a steam engine.

Witherspoon blinked, sure his eyes must be playing tricks on him. But they weren't, the painting was a train all right. He saw that there were trains everywhere. Model trains cluttered the tops of tables and shelves, photographs of steam engines and railcars were on the walls, half a dozen timetable books were stacked in a heap on the rug, and a complete toy train set was spread out on the floor next to the desk.

Finally, the inspector focused his attention on the dead man. Francis Humphreys was slumped forward, looking for all the world like he'd just fallen asleep.

"We didn't move the body, sir," the constable said quietly from behind him. "We've all heard of your methods."

"Very good, Constable." Witherspoon took a deep breath and forced his legs to move. Constable Barnes reached the victim first. He lifted the man's chin and stared at the bullet hole in his forehead. "He hasn't bled much," he murmured. "That's odd. Usually head shots bleed like the very devil."

Witherspoon was glad his stomach was empty. "Yes, they usually do." He looked down at the desk. A copy of *Bradshaw's Monthly Railway Guide* was lying by the corpse's lifeless right hand. His left hand rested on a stack of papers and next to it was a notebook in dark green leather. "Perhaps Mr. Humphreys had sat down to have a look at the railway guide?"

"That's possible, sir. We'll ask the household if the victim was planning a trip anywhere." Barnes picked up the green leather notebook, opened the pages and scanned the contents. "This is a logbook. The last entry was yesterday at 3:09." He paused for a long moment as he read the contents. "Apparently, our victim was a real enthusiast, sir. He's noted every engine number for the 3:09 going back the past two years. Strange, isn't it, sir, what some people enjoy doing as a pastime."

Witherspoon was a bit of a train enthusiast himself. "Trains are very interesting."

Barnes tossed the logbook back on the desk and walked

to the double French doors. He tried the handle. "It's locked."

"Yes, but was it locked after the shooting or has it been locked all day?" Witherspoon murmured. "That's the question." He'd no idea what to think. The poor fellow was dead, the constables had searched the premises for the murder weapon and found nothing, and, except for the servants, everyone in the household had been downstairs.

"Should we do a house-to-house?" Barnes asked.

"Yes, perhaps we'll find a witness who saw or heard something."

"Too bad this property is so far away from the nearest neighbor." Barnes frowned. "Do you hear that, sir? It sounds like a train." He unlocked the door and stepped out onto the terrace.

Witherspoon followed him, coming outside into the cold evening air just as a freight train rattled past at the bottom of the long garden. "Good gracious, this house backs onto a railway line."

"The Great Western," Barnes muttered. "Now this is odd, sir. Why would someone as wealthy as Francis Humphreys want to build his house right next to the Great Western Railway Line? Most rich people get as far away from noise and inconvenience as possible."

"He liked trains." Witherspoon went back inside, stopping just on the other side of the door frame. "This is where the killer must have stood."

"Which means whoever did the murder must have been a good shot," Barnes said softly from behind him. "It's at least twenty-five feet between here and the victim. Most people aren't that accurate with a pistol, sir."

"Maybe the murder weapon wasn't a pistol," Witherspoon suggested. Immediately he wished he could take the comment back. "Oh yes, I see what you mean, a rifle or a shotgun would have blown the poor fellow's head off."

Constable Bishop stuck his head into the room. "Dr. Amalfi's hansom has just pulled up, sir?"

"We're through here, so we'll get out of his way. Do you know where the body will be taken once the surgeon has completed his examination?"

"St. Mary's in Paddington, sir," Bishop replied. "They've got the mortuary contract for this area."

"We may as well start taking statements, Constable," Witherspoon said. He gave the victim one last look as he walked toward the doorway to the hall. "There's nothing else we can do for this poor man except find his killer."

"Shall I start belowstairs, sir?" Barnes inquired as they came out onto the landing and started down the stairs. "I'd like to get the servants' statements while it's still fresh in their minds."

"Good idea, I'll just go along to the drawing room and see if I can find a family member—" He broke off as he saw Annabelle Prescott step into the hallway. "Miss Prescott," he began.

"It's Mrs. Prescott," she corrected softly.

"Oh dear, I am sorry. Mrs. Prescott, if it's not too dreadful for you, we'd like to take your statements. With your permission, Constable Barnes would like to have a word with the servants."

"Certainly. I'll have Imogene show him downstairs." She went back into the drawing room for a moment and came back with a younger, dark-haired woman. "This is Imogene Ross, my cousin. She'll take the constable downstairs to the kitchen."

Imogene inclined her head politely in acknowledgment of the introduction. "It's this way, Constable," she said as she moved off toward the far end of the hallway.

"Let's at least go sit down so we can be comfortable. This has been an awful day and I'm very tired." Annabelle smiled wanly as she led him back into the drawing room.

"Of course, ma'am." He followed after her. She sat down on the ivory empire couch and motioned for him to take the chair opposite. She waited for him to sit before saying, "What would you like to know?"

"Can you tell me what happened here this afternoon?"

She closed her eyes briefly before she spoke. "Uncle Francis had invited several people for tea today. That wasn't unusual—he often had people in for tea. He didn't like having dinner parties. He said they were too much trouble and kept him up past his bedtime."

"How many guests were here?" Witherspoon asked.

She thought for a moment. "From the family, there was myself and Imogene, we both reside here, our cousin by marriage, Pamela Humphreys, another cousin, Joseph Humphreys, and Michael Collier. Oh yes, the Elliots came up from Dorset. They're distant cousins. Then Mr. Kirkland was here and Mr. and Mrs. Brown from next door. Mr. Eddington was here as well. Let's see, that makes eleven of us. All of the guests arrived minutes before four o'clock."

"You had very punctual guests," Witherspoon observed. In his experience people were always late to social functions.

"Uncle Francis was well known for getting cross if people were late," she replied. "As a matter of fact, he was exceedingly concerned with punctuality in all things. He was a very kind man, but he has been known to fly into a rage when the train is late."

"Many people are like that," the inspector said softly. "Do go on, Mrs. Prescott."

"We sat down and the housekeeper wheeled in the tea trolley. I went ahead and poured. We waited for a few moments but no one got really concerned . . ."

"So your uncle's preoccupation with punctuality didn't extend to himself?" Witherspoon asked.

"He was always on time," Annabelle said. "But lately,

he's been showing his age, so when Imogene suggested someone go up and see what was keeping him, I simply thought he was having difficulties retying his cravat. In the past few months, he's had trouble doing ordinary, mundane tasks." Her eyes filled with tears and she blinked hard to hold them back. "But if I'd only listened to Imogene and sent someone upstairs, he might still be with us."

"If someone else had gone upstairs while the killer was here, that person might be dead as well," he said quickly. "You mustn't blame yourself."

"But I do, Inspector," she whispered. She dabbed at her eyes with a handkerchief. "I do. Uncle Francis has been so good to me. He took me in when my husband passed away and now he's gone, too." She took a deep breath. "But you want to know what happened next, don't you. As I was saying, we were drinking our tea and waiting for him to come downstairs when we heard a dreadful noise coming from upstairs. At first I'd no idea what it might be, but then one of the men yelled that it sounded like a shot—"

"Which man?" Witherspoon interrupted.

She thought for a moment. "I'm not certain, but I think it might have been Mr. Kirkland. Yes, yes, I'm sure it was Mr. Kirkland because he also said the shot was in the house."

"Mr. Kirkland was a friend of your uncle's?" Witherspoon asked.

"Oh no, as a matter of fact. We were quite surprised when Mr. Kirkland arrived this afternoon. You see, Inspector, he and Uncle Francis hated each other. One could almost say they were bitterest of enemies."

CHAPTER 2

———•———

Smythe stared down at the beer he'd been nursing for half an hour and wondered how a pub this empty could stay in business. He hoped that Wiggins was having better luck than he was. The two of them had made it to Acton just in time to see the inspector and Constable Barnes disappearing into a redbrick monster of a house. They'd ducked under the thin branches of an evergreen tree, but they hadn't dared stay in that spot as it was far too small to be a decent hiding place, and with each passing minute they'd risked being seen. But there'd been nary a doorway, stairwell, or garden shed that could conceal them from the eyes of any nosy neighbors or wandering policemen. So they'd split up. Each of them had set off in a different direction with the sole purpose of going into the first pub they came to and seeing if the news of the murder had made its way out into the community at large.

But the only customers in the White Lion Pub were himself and an old man sleeping in the corner. Even the

publican was of a morose nature, which might explain the
lack of custom in the place. Then again, despite being "on
the hunt," as it were, he wasn't feeling particularly cheerful
himself. He couldn't stop worrying about Betsy. She'd not
said that anything in particular was bothering her, but
twice now he'd come across her staring out the window
with a sad, wistful expression on her pretty face. Both
times, he'd asked it she was all right and both times she'd
assured him she was just fine. But he knew she wasn't. He
and Betsy were close. She'd trusted him with the secrets of
her past and he'd shared his with her. But he knew there
was something she wasn't telling him. Something important.

"You ready for another?" the barman asked.

"This will do me, thanks," Smythe replied. He glanced
at the door. It was firmly closed. No one, it appeared, was
in any hurry to come here for a pint. He'd give it another
ten minutes and then he'd head off to find Wiggins. On
such a gray and miserable day, he suspected the footman's
luck wasn't much better than his.

But he'd have been wrong. At the Boars Head Pub,
Wiggins motioned for the barman. "Can we 'ave another
one over 'ere." He pointed to his companion's empty glass.

"That's right nice of ya," the young man replied. His
name was Johnny Cooper and when he'd walked through
the door, he'd been white as a sheet.

One look at the frightened expression in the lad's eyes
had put Wiggins' instincts on full alert. This was someone
who'd been scared to death by something and the only really frightening incident that Wiggins knew of in the area
was a murder at Humphreys House. He'd waited till his
quarry had ordered a pint, noticed that he hadn't spoken to
anyone else in the pub, and then made his move.

Wiggins dug more coins out of his pocket as the barman slid another pint in front of Cooper, took the money, and then moved down the counter to serve another customer.

"I don't usually drink in the afternoons," Cooper said defensively. "But I tell ya, seein' the old man all slumped over like that was such a shock. The only dead body I've ever seen before was my old gran, but that was at her funeral. This was different. It was strange, if ya know what I mean. Especially when we heard they was sending for the police and that it was murder been done. None of us knew how to act or how we was supposed to feel."

"Were you the one that found 'im?" Wiggins asked.

"No, I only got a glimpse from the doorway, but that was enough." He shuddered slightly.

Wiggins took a sip of his beer and stared at Johnny over the rim of his glass. He was a lanky fellow with wispy blond hair and a long, narrow face. He claimed he was the gardener at Humphreys House, but Wiggins suspected Cooper was more a lad-of-all-work rather than a proper gardener. Even with the color back in his face, he didn't have that rough complexion that spoke of hours outside in the weather.

"Must 'ave been awful," Wiggins muttered. He wasn't sure how many questions to ask. He didn't want the lad accidentally telling the police that someone had shown an unnatural interest in a local murder. A bit of gossip was one thing, but asking too much could arouse suspicion. It was a fine line he walked. "But aren't you supposed to stay close and wait for the police when there's been a murder in the 'ouse?"

"No one said anything when I left and there was police hanging about everywhere," Cooper said defensively. "There were two constables standing right there on the back terrace when Mrs. Eames told me to go about my business and take the second coal cart down to Mrs. Bowden's house. If the police wanted me to stay on the premises, one of the coppers should have said something. I weren't hiding what I was doin'. It's a ruddy great cart and both them coppers watched me wheel it down the path and off the property. I've done nothin' wrong."

"Course you 'aven't," Wiggins assured him.

Cooper pursed his lips and glanced down at his drink. "Mind ya, I probably should have gone back to the house instead of comin' here. Mrs. Eames is goin' to have my guts for garters if I don't get back soon."

"Who's Mrs. Eames?"

"Who do ya think she is, she's the housekeeper." Cooper took another drink.

"If the police are still there, not even your Mrs. Eames will notice you've not come back," Wiggins retorted. The fear had faded from Cooper's eyes and his color was back. "'Ave another one. It's not often I get to talk to someone who's been close to a real live murder. It's ever so excitin'. Did ya hear the gun goin' off?"

"You'd had to have been deaf not to hear." Cooper relaxed. Wiggins could see he was starting to enjoy himself. "I'd just come out of the small shed at the back of the garden when there was a crackin' sound loud enough to raise the dead. Course I knew right away that it was a gunshot."

"Done a lot of shootin', 'ave you?" Wiggins smiled to take the sting out of the comment. But it was important to know if the lad was just talking or if he actually had known the noise was indeed from a weapon. Over the years, everyone in the Witherspoon household had learned that understanding the details was very important.

"I've never even touched a gun." Cooper looked horrified by the idea. "But I used to go with Mr. Humphreys when he went on his hunting trips to Scotland. He wasn't really much of a hunter. He told me once he didn't like killin' defenseless animals, but goin' to Scotland was a good excuse to drink fine whisky."

"Was your Mr. Humphreys killed with a huntin' rifle?" Wiggins asked. Cor blimey, if that was the case, no wonder the lad had headed for a pub.

"I don't think so." Cooper thought for a moment. "There weren't much blood. Besides, the shot I heard didn't sound like it come from a rifle. Like I said, I used to go with Mr. Humphreys, and even though he didn't hunt much he liked to practice shooting his Enfield when there was no one about."

"What's an Enfield?" Wiggins asked. He knew perfectly well what kind of gun an Enfield was, but he wanted to see how much Cooper knew about weapons.

"It's a revolver. Mr. Humphreys wasn't a very good shot, but he seemed to enjoy it. Poor fellow."

"Was he a good guv?"

"He was no better or worse than most." Cooper grinned. "Bit of a strange one, though. He always goin' on about the trains and worryin' about why they weren't runnin' on time. But for the most part, he treated the household decently." He swallowed the last of his beer and put his glass down on the counter. "Mind ya, I can't say the same for the way he treated his family."

"What do you mean?" Wiggins asked.

"He weren't mean or anything like that, but he could be right hard if he thought ya weren't livin' up to his expectations. He liked to lecture them about responsibility and obligations and behavin' properly."

"Did he have relations that didn't behave properly?"

"He thought so." Cooper laughed. "He had words with one of his nephews a couple of days ago because the fellow can't seem to hold on to a position, but he doesn't ever cut anyone off. He takes 'em all in but he makes 'em all dance to his tune and do what he says. None of 'em like it, but they put up with him. Guess havin' all that money buys a lot of forgiveness."

"He's a bit surly," Wiggins announced as he and Smythe came into the warm kitchen of Upper Edmonton Gardens. "He didn't 'ave much luck tonight."

"I'm not in a surly mood." The coachman shucked off his coat and hung it on the coat tree. "I'm cold and hungry, but I'm bloomin' well not surly."

Betsy giggled as she poured a cup of tea and put it on the table as he slid into his seat. "Drink this while I get your supper out of the warming oven."

Everyone had, of course, waited up for them. But no one started asking questions until both men were settled at the table with full plates in front of them.

"Was it a murder?" Mrs. Jeffries directed the question to the footman.

Wiggins nodded vigorously and swallowed his mouthful of cooked cabbage. "He was shot. I had a quick word with the gardener, not that I think he's a proper gardener, but the lad was there when it happened and heard the gun go off."

"I didn't 'ave a word with anyone except a right miserable publican," Smythe complained. "It's no wonder his pub is empty."

"You were at the same pub?" Mrs. Goodge asked, her expression confused.

"There was no place to hide near Humphreys House," Smythe explained. "So we each went off in different directions to the closest pub to see if the news had gotten around the neighborhood. Wiggins got lucky, I didn't." He glanced up and looked toward the window as they heard the distinctive rattle of a hansom cab pull up outside. "Cor blimey, looks like the inspector is home already."

"We'll continue this in the morning," Mrs. Jeffries said as she got up.

Betsy was already on her feet and moving toward the cooker. She grabbed a thick tea towel from the work table, opened the warming oven and took out the covered plate that held the inspector's dinner. She put the plate on the serving tray that the housekeeper had at the ready.

Mrs. Jeffries grabbed the tray and started for the back stairs. "Everyone go on up and get some sleep. Wiggins, you'll need to get up extra early to go fetch Luty and Hatchet. Tomorrow is going to be a busy day."

"Don't you stay up too late yourself," the cook called as Mrs. Jeffries disappeared up the stairs.

Inspector Witherspoon had already shed his coat and hat by the time she reached the front hallway. She stopped by the open dining room door. "Good evening, sir. I took the liberty of bringing your supper up, sir. I thought you might be hungry."

"Bless you, Mrs. Jeffries." Witherspoon smiled gratefully. "I'm famished. But I certainly didn't expect the household to wait up for me. I could have easily made myself a bite to eat." He took a deep breath, inhaling the rich aroma of the food as he came to the dining room and stepped inside.

Even though he was now a rich man with a huge house, he'd been raised in very modest circumstances and consequently treated his staff like human beings. "No need for that, sir. Mrs. Goodge has kept a lovely beef and cabbage stew in the warmer for you. Sit down and eat this while it's hot."

As soon as the inspector was tucked into his food, Mrs. Jeffries went to the drawing room and poured two glasses of sherry. She put them on a silver tray she'd brought up from the old butler's pantry earlier that evening. "I thought you might like a drink to ward off the chill," she said as she returned.

"Excellent, that's precisely what I need." Witherspoon speared a piece of beef onto his fork. "And I'm glad you brought a drink for yourself. Do sit down and keep me company."

"Thank you, sir, I will." She pulled out the chair, sat down, and took a sip of her sherry. She said nothing for a moment, giving him time to get some food in his stomach before she began asking questions. She knew he would willingly tell her about the day's events; from his very first homicide, she'd made sure that he'd gotten into the habit of discussing his cases with his very discreet and understanding housekeeper. He'd once told her that talking with her about his work helped him enormously. "It does so enable me to keep everything straight in my own mind," he'd said. She intended to do her best to insure that he continued to feel that way.

"Was it dreadful, sir," she asked sympathetically. She was one of the few that knew how squeamish he was about dead bodies.

"It wasn't pretty, the man was shot in the head. But as head wounds go, it wasn't as nasty as it could have been." He picked up his glass and took a quick sip. "The fatal wound was directly in the center of his forehead, but luckily there wasn't much blood."

"Really?" A faint, uneasy feeling tugged at her, but she pushed it to the back of her mind. She didn't know how much longer she could keep him up and chatting. It was late and the inspector was tired. "I thought head wounds bled profusely? Did the police surgeon have any idea why there was so little blood?"

"I didn't have time to ask him." Witherspoon speared a piece of potato. "There were people everywhere, and frankly we got too busy taking statements. I'll read his report tomorrow. He's doing the postmortem at St. Mary's in Paddington."

Drat. Mrs. Jeffries knew she had no right to be disappointed. But she had hoped their friend Dr. Bosworth would, by some miracle, be the one doing the postmortem. But Dr. Bosworth, who actually did know quite a bit about gunshots and the holes they made in human flesh, was assigned to another metropolitan police district and worked out of St. Thomas' Hospital. "I see. Who was the victim, sir?"

"An older man named Francis Humphreys. He was killed as he sat at the desk in his bedroom, and what's more, there was a houseful of witnesses but all they heard was the gunshot." He sighed heavily. "I don't think this is going to be an easy murder to solve."

"Was it a robbery?" she asked.

"I don't think so," he replied. "The housekeeper didn't see that anything was missing from his room and as I said, the house was swarming with people, the killer wouldn't have had time to do anything but shoot the poor man and then make a run for it."

"If the house was full of people, sir," she asked, "how did the killer get in and out without being seen?"

"We're not certain, but it was probably through the small terrace off his bedroom. It's up a floor from the ground, but there is a good sturdy trellis the assailant could have used to climb up and get into his room. As for getting out, there's half a dozen doors and lots of windows. It took a few moments for the rest of the household to get to his room when they heard the shot, so it's possible the killer could have used that time to his advantage."

She leaned back in her chair and listened as he continued with his meal. By the time his plate was clean, he'd given her every detail of the day. "Searching the house was rather awkward." He shoved his chair back and stood up.

"The constables had done a preliminary search as soon as they arrived, but Constable Barnes insisted it be done again under his direction. Odd, he usually trusts the lads to do things properly."

She got to her feet as well. Her mind was working furiously, taking in the few facts they had so far and trying to make sense of them. "Did you find anything useful, sir?"

"We found nothing." He yawned widely. "No open windows, no footprints, nothing that would point us in the direction of the killer. Frankly, finding the murder weapon would have been very helpful. But it's early days yet."

"Perhaps the killer managed to get the gun out of the house before the police arrived," she suggested as she began to clear the table. "It did take you some time to get there."

"That's possible, but the first officers were on the scene within minutes, and despite Barnes' insistence that the place be searched again, the constable in charge assured me they followed all the established procedures and secured the premises."

"Are you sure, sir?" She smiled wryly. "Sometimes the first constables on the scene don't realize how important it is to make sure that nothing gets taken away from the premises or that none of the witnesses leave. As you've said many times yourself, sir, often inexperienced police officers are very intimidated by the upper class."

"That's true. Tomorrow I'll have another word with them just to be doubly sure." He covered his mouth to hide another huge yawn. "Even though I do like to think 'my methods' have influenced how officers behave at a murder scene, the rule about leaving the body alone and not letting witnesses leave the premises, has actually been around for fifteen years. Gracious, Mrs. Jeffries, you must be as exhausted as I am. I suggest you leave that clearing up until tomorrow and we both retire for the night."

Upstairs on the third floor, Betsy stood at the window

of the bedroom that Mrs. Jeffries had recently converted into a cozy sitting room for the staff. The bed had been replaced by two old but comfortable armchairs they'd found in the attic and a blue velvet loveseat. In the darkened room, she stared out into the night.

She felt a small rush of air on her back as the door opened behind her. She knew who it was. "I'm all right, Smythe. I just came in to have a bit of a think before I went to bed."

"You're not all right, lass." He came up behind her and put his hands on her shoulders. "You're upset about somethin'. Tell me what's wrong? You know I'll keep badgerin' you till I get it out of you, so why don't you save us both a bit of time and talk to me."

She laughed softly and leaned back against him. "It's really nothing," she whispered. "But I was just wishing that I could find my sister. I'd do anything to have her at my wedding. She's the only family I've got."

"You were just a child when you saw her last, weren't you?" He chose his words carefully, knowing full well the awful circumstances that had led to the breakup of Betsy's small family.

"I was in my early teens. Norah was the oldest, but she was only eighteen when she married Leo and moved to Leeds. We kept in touch by letter until Mum and I got turned out of our room. I've not seen her since." Betsy sighed. "Once I got settled here, I sent off letters to the last address I had for her, but she never answered. I don't think she lives there anymore. I remember Mum getting a letter just before the baby died and we was turned out. Norah said she and Leo were thinking of immigrating either to Australia or Canada. But that's all I can remember. Oh, I know it's an impossible dream, but still, she's my sister and I'd love for her to know I was all right and marrying a good man."

He hugged her close. He'd go to any lengths to get her what she wanted. She asked so little from him and he loved her so much. She'd had it hard in life and he was determined she'd never want for anything again. But he'd not say anything yet. There was a chance that even with all his money, he'd not be able to find Norah and Leo Hanrahan in time for the wedding. "I'm glad you think I'm a good man."

"Of course I do, silly." She laughed. "Otherwise we'd not be getting married come October."

While the inspector and his household slept, less than two miles away in an elegant Georgian townhouse in Mayfair, Inspector Nigel Nivens made his way through the crowded room to say good night to his host, Lord Reese, who was also his godfather.

"I say, Uncle Nigel, can I have a word?" a voice said from behind him.

Nivens frowned irritably and turned around, plastering a smile on his face just as he made eye contact with his nephew, Lionel Gates. "Of course, Lionel. But do be quick about it. I'm on duty early tomorrow and it's already very late."

"I was wondering if you could do me a favor, Uncle." Lionel smiled broadly.

Nivens stared at him. Lionel had a round face with a red hue to his complexion, brown hair worn short and a sharp nose. He was the only son of Nivens' sister and like his uncle, he'd joined the police force upon leaving school. He was a constable at Potter's Bar in Y Division. At just five foot eight inches tall, he was lucky he'd joined the force when he did because now he wouldn't be allowed in under the new height requirements. For that matter, Nivens wouldn't be in, either. "What kind of favor?"

"There's been a murder at Acton and the victim is a

very prominent person, if you get my meaning." Lionel's smile faded and he contrived to look serious. "My sources tell me that three of the detectives in that division are out with flu and they are badly in need of help."

"Have good sources, do you?" Nivens regarded his nephew thoughtfully. The young man reminded him of himself at that age. He didn't like him very much.

"Of course." Lionel smiled proudly. "Every officer on the force ought to have sources. That was the first thing you told me when I joined."

"Then yours must not be too good," Nivens said. "Otherwise you'd know the problem of staffing has already been addressed. The chief inspector sent Inspector Witherspoon and Constable Barnes over to handle the Humphreys case."

"That's why I've come to you," Lionel exclaimed brightly. "You and Inspector Witherspoon are close colleagues and acquaintances. I was hoping you'd use your influence to let me go along and assist him."

Nivens couldn't believe it! He knew that Lionel was an aggressive little sod, but he didn't think the pup would have the gall to suggest something like this. Nivens was no admirer of Witherspoon and was the only one on the force who felt the fellow's reputation was decidedly exaggerated. But there wasn't a constable worth his salt that wouldn't give up a fortnight's holiday to work with the famous Witherspoon. "I'm afraid you give me too much credit. The inspector and I are acquaintances, nothing more. I've no influence on the man. Furthermore, he works exclusively with Constable Barnes."

"But if the inspector went to the chief and asked for me specifically," Lionel spoke slowly, as though he were speaking to a half wit. "I'm sure the chief wouldn't refuse his request."

"You impudent young pup, you've been on the force for

over three years now and you've done nothing to distin-
guish yourself," Nivens snapped. "Even if Witherspoon
and I were the best of friends, he'd hardly be likely to ask
for your help."

"That's not quite true, Uncle," Lionel said reasonably. "I
am the only one in my division that knows how to use the
typewriting machine." He wasn't offended. He'd learned
early in life that persistence was more important than
brains, talent, or courage. "And you're much more than just
a casual acquaintance to Inspector Witherspoon, you
helped him solve his last case." Lionel broke off and waved
to an old man across the room. "I know you don't like to
brag, but I overheard you telling Mama you'd given the
inspector the vital clue that led him to solve that murder of
the fellow they pulled out of the Thames."

Nivens silently cursed. That murder should have been
his case, not Witherspoon's. But he'd made one foolish
mistake, and instead of having a solved homicide to his
credit, he'd ended up in a situation that if Witherspoon had
been a nastier person he could have taken action that might
have cost Nivens his job. But Gerald Witherspoon was a
decent man and hadn't told anyone, least of all their superiors, about Nivens' lapse in judgment.

Nivens hated being obligated to anyone, especially
someone he didn't like. He was sure Witherspoon had help
in solving his cases. The man had an almost perfect record
and Nivens knew that no one was that brilliant a detective.
Nonetheless, he owed him. He certainly wasn't going to
repay Witherspoon by sticking him with Lionel. Ye gods,
the lad was his own flesh and blood and he could barely
stand the sight of him. "I did help solve that murder, but
you'll learn that you earn more respect by keeping your
accomplishments quiet than by bragging about them to all
and sundry. Besides, even if I could convince the inspector

to ask the chief inspector to put you on the case, you've no guarantee Barrows would do it. Not everyone thinks Gerald Witherspoon walks on water."

"Let me worry about that," Lionel interrupted. "Won't you at least speak to him? I could learn so much from an officer like him. He's well over twenty solved homicides to his credit. I know we're not supposed to think that such things matter, that keeping the peace in general is supposed to be reward enough, but we all know that's not true. Real advancement comes from solving the most serious cases. In other words, from solving murders."

Nivens had no intention of helping his nephew. "Sorry Lionel, but I really can't see my way clear to intervening on your behalf. Now if you'll excuse me, it's late and I'm on duty early tomorrow."

Lionel started to argue then seemed to think the better of it. He clamped his mouth shut. "Very well, Uncle. Good night." He turned and walked away.

Nivens' eyes narrowed as he watched Lionel make his way across the room. It wasn't like his nephew to give up so easily, but then again, perhaps this time he'd understood nagging or whining wasn't going to work.

Everyone in the inspector's household was up very early the next day. They wanted to get their household chores completed and be ready for their morning meeting as soon as the inspector had left the house. As was his habit, Constable Barnes had come to the house to accompany Witherspoon to the station before going on to the murder scene. But as Barnes had figured out a long time ago that the household helped in their employer's investigations, he'd stopped in the kitchen and had a quick word with Mrs. Jeffries before going upstairs to get the inspector.

The housekeeper was extremely grateful for Barnes'

assistance. Despite her best efforts in getting the details out of Witherspoon, there was often some information that Barnes was able to add.

As soon as the two men were out of the house, Mrs. Jeffries scooped up the wooden tray with the empty breakfast dishes on them and hurried downstairs. "He's gone," she announced as she hurried over to the counter by the sink and put down her burden. "What time will Luty and Hatchet be here?"

"It should be any moment now." Mrs. Goodge put a pot of fresh tea on the table. "Wiggins left to fetch them over an hour ago."

Betsy put clean cups on the table in front of the empty chairs. "They might have already had plans." From the corner of her eye, she saw Fred, the household's brown and white mongrel dog, leap to his feet and charge for the back door.

"Havin' plans wouldn't stop either of them," Smythe said with a laugh. He was trailing behind her with a pitcher of fresh milk. "Luty would send regrets to breakfast with the Queen rather than miss a murder."

"You're darned right I would," Luty Belle Crookshank said as she swept into the kitchen. She was an elderly, white-haired American woman with a love of bright colors and more money than most banks. Today she wore a peacock blue wool cape and a matching hat draped with what looked like yards of veiling. A sable-fur muff was tucked under her arm.

A tall, white-haired man dressed in an old-fashioned frock coat and carrying a black top hat trailed behind her. "Good morning, everyone." He put his hat on the chair and moved to help Luty with her cape.

Luty and Hatchet had become involved with the household during one of the inspector's earliest cases. They'd lived in the same neighborhood as the murder victim and

Luty had noticed the various members of the inspector's household asking questions and snooping about. After that case had been solved, Luty had come to them with a mystery of her own, and ever since, she and Hatchet had insisted on being part of all their cases. She was rich, eccentric, and a friend to politicians, financiers, and aristocrats. She used her connections to find out information. Hatchet, who had more than a hint of mystery about his own past, had his own sources.

Wiggins came in last, followed by a bouncing Fred who kept dancing around the footman in a bid for more attention. "We ready, then?" he asked as he stroked the animal's back before sitting down. "I made it to Luty's and back in record time." He was determined to do everything right and proper on this case. He'd not be shirking his duty for a pretty face.

"We were already dressed to go out." Hatchet sniffed disapprovingly. "Madam had a meeting with her solicitors, but she sent her regrets."

"Git off your high horse, Hatchet." Luty snorted and sat down in the chair her butler had pulled out for her. "You know as well as I do you'd rather be here than listening to a bunch of lawyers bore us both to tears."

"Oh dear." Mrs. Jeffries slipped into her spot at the head of the table. "I do hope we didn't interrupt some important business."

Luty laughed. "Don't be silly, Hepzibah. Nothing is more important than catching a killer."

Luty's lightly spoken words rang true. No matter how they'd ended up working for Gerald Witherspoon, all of them had been greatly changed by their experiences. What had started out as an alternative to the daily boredom of their ordinary chores and obligations had become a higher calling for each and every one of them. They weren't just alleviating the dullness of making beds, cooking meals, driving carriages, polishing brass, or meeting with solicitors—they had been called to work for justice.

"Well spoken, Luty," Mrs. Goodge said softly. Of all of them, she'd been the most changed. When she'd first arrived she'd been quite bitter; no family, no friends, and sacked from her previous position because of her age. Yet even with all that had befallen her, she'd never once questioned the fairness of a social system that could turf out an old woman without so much as a by-your-leave. She'd been a hidebound old snob, secure in the knowledge that people should stay in their place and sure that everyone in Her Majesty's prisons was guilty as sin. Then they'd started solving murders and that had shifted her world completely. In the twilight of her life, she'd learned that change was a good thing, everyone deserved justice, and a system that rewarded people solely on the basis of birth was ridiculous. She wasn't out to join any of those silly radical societies that were always having marches and demonstrations—she was too old for that—but she did send a bit of money from her quarterly wages to the London Society for Women's Suffrage. "Now let's get this meetin' started, I've a lot a baking to do today to feed my sources."

"An excellent suggestion," Mrs. Jeffries said. "To begin with, I'll tell what I found out from the inspector last night and from Constable Barnes this morning."

"What about me," Wiggins protested. "I never got to finish tellin' what I found out from that gardener, Johnny Cooper."

"I haven't forgotten you," she soothed. "But I thought that your information might make a bit more sense if we had a few more facts."

Wiggins nodded and she continued. "Apparently, the house was full of guests when the murder happened—"

"That'll give us lots of suspects," Luty interrupted eagerly.

"Sorry, but I'm afraid not. The house was full but everyone except the servants were all together in the drawing room when it happened. They were waiting for Francis Humphreys to come downstairs and join them."

"Well, nells bells," Luty muttered.

"Yes, I know, it is unfortunate that we've a houseful of people, but none of them appears to have been the killer." Mrs. Jeffries smiled ruefully and continued with her report.

They listened carefully, occasionally nodding or breaking in to ask the housekeeper to clarify a bit of information. When she'd finished, she looked at Wiggins. "Your turn. What did your young Mr. Cooper have to say?"

Wiggins looked a bit sheepish. "It really wasn't that much, but he did say that the gunshot was loud enough to wake the dead." As was his habit, after making that remark, he went on to give them almost a word-for-word recitation of his encounter with Johnny Cooper.

"Good gracious, that sounds like you remembered the entire conversation." Mrs. Goodge looked suitably impressed.

"Try my best not to forget anything." Wiggins smiled modestly.

"You've a good memory, Wiggins," Betsy agreed. "We all know that sometimes it's the smallest little thing that leads to finding the killer."

"I've worked hard to train myself to recall as much as possible." He reached for his tea mug. "It's hard work, but it's worth the effort." What he wasn't telling them was he'd also gotten in the habit of writing everything down so he wouldn't forget. He'd even bought a little brown notebook just like the one Constable Barnes used.

Smythe looked at Mrs. Jeffries. "So should we ignore all the people that were in the house when the murder happened?" he asked.

"Seems like we'd have to if they were all in the drawing room sippin' tea when Humphreys was shot," Mrs. Goodge complained.

"Actually, I don't think we ought to ignore anyone," Mrs. Jeffries said slowly. "I thought about it last night after the inspector retired. I don't know that I'm right, but it seems to me that considering the facts of the matter, there's always the chance that someone in the drawing room might have had some part in the crime."

"But the killer couldn't have shot him if he was with the others," Betsy pointed out. "And even though the inspector hasn't completed all the statements, the one thing you said they were sure of was that all of the guests were in the room together when they heard the shot."

"There might have been an accomplice." Hatchet looked at the housekeeper. "Is that what you think?"

Mrs. Jeffries didn't want to say too much. She'd learned to trust her instincts but even so, they had so few facts about the case. Still, there was something about the circumstances of the situation that struck her as odd. "I'm not sure what I mean," she finally admitted. "I've just got the strongest feeling that we shouldn't ignore anyone, even those that appear to have an alibi. I kept wondering why the killer would risk committing the crime when there were people everywhere. If the assailant crept onto the property and slipped into the house, he or she was taking a huge risk and could have been seen at any moment."

"But it was raining." Betsy poured herself another cup of tea. "Perhaps the killer counted on everyone being inside and in front of a warm fire."

"Not the servants," Wiggins argued. "They would 'ave been in and out doing their work. You don't stop fetchin' and carryin' just because there's a bit of wet. Any of them could 'ave seen the killer."

"Or the killer could have had someone in the house open a window or make sure a side door was unlocked," Betsy speculated.

"I've no idea what happened," Mrs. Jeffries said. "Either of those scenarios is certainly possible. I don't think we ought to rule out anyone, even those who have an alibi."

"There was half a dozen or more guests and almost as many family members," Smythe muttered. "That's going to take a bit of work."

"True, but we'll not let that discourage us. To begin with, I suggest we start on learning as much as we can about our victim and more importantly, about everyone who might benefit from his death."

Betsy was the first to get up. "I'll be off, then. Let's hope the local shopkeepers know something useful about the household."

"I'll see what my sources can tell me about Humphreys." Luty pushed back from the table and got to her feet.

"It would be useful to find out about his financial situation," Mrs. Jeffries suggested.

Luty picked up her muff. "That goes without sayin'."

"And I shall endeavor to find out what I can from my sources as well." Hatchet glanced at his employer and grinned. "Shall we have a small wager on who finds out the most information today, madam?" Though he was fiercely devoted to Luty, the two of them were very competitive when they were on a case.

Luty snorted, but before she could respond, Mrs. Jeffries leapt up and said, "Now, now, you're both too valuable for us to waste time on silly wagers." She didn't want this sort of thing to begin because she knew what would happen. The entire household would get competitive and they'd spend more time arguing over who'd learned the most or which piece of information was the more important than they did hunting clues. "Come on everyone, let's get to it. We've much to do today. We'll meet back here at our usual time this afternoon."

By nine o'clock that morning, Witherspoon and Barnes were back at Humphreys House. The constable was downstairs in the servants' hall while the inspector was in the dining room upstairs. They were taking statements.

He and Barnes had reported in at the Acton Police Station, but the postmortem report still hadn't arrived. A small contingent of constables had accompanied him to the victim's home and Witherspoon had sent them off to do a house-to-house. He was hoping that one of the neighbors had seen someone or something suspicious yesterday. Another group of constables were searching the grounds and he'd instructed them to look along the railway line as well.

The inspector rose politely as Imogene Ross came into the drawing room. "Mrs. Eames said you wished to speak to me?" she said.

"I just have a few questions for you, Miss Ross." He noticed her eyes were red rimmed from weeping and she was dressed in formal black mourning clothes.

"Yes, of course." She sighed heavily and sank onto the sofa.

"Please accept my condolences for your loss." Witherspoon sat down across from her. "I know this isn't pleasant, but it is necessary."

"I understand that, Inspector." She held herself stiffly, with her back ramrod straight and her hands neatly folded together on her lap. "But I don't know what you think I can tell you, I was down here when we heard the shot . . ." She broke off, her eyes filling with tears. "Sorry, please forgive me, but this has upset me dreadfully."

"You were close to your uncle." He smiled sympathetically.

"Oh no, I don't think anyone but Annabelle was ever close to him. He was genuinely fond of her. But Uncle Francis was very decent to me. He took me in when I lost my position and gave me allowance. He didn't deserve to be murdered."

"No one does," the inspector said softly. "How long have you lived here?"

"I came about three months ago." She gave him a sheepish smile. "As I said, I lost my position as a governess."

Witherspoon was in a quandary: He didn't wish to embarrass the lady, but he really did need to know the circumstances of how she came to lose her livelihood. "Er . . . uh."

"I was sacked, Inspector," Imogene said bluntly.

"May I know the reason why?"

"The mistress of the house wanted to give my job to an old school friend of hers." Imogene shrugged philosophically. "There was only one child and the family couldn't afford two governesses. It was very sudden. One moment I had a nice, comfortable position in a lovely house in Bristol, the next, I was at a hotel at the train station. I sent Uncle Francis a telegram asking if I could come to him. He replied straightaway that I was to take the next train to London. He met me at the station and told me I was to stay as long as I liked. I was family and I'd never be turned out."

"That must have been a great relief to you," the inspector replied.

"It was. I was very grateful." She paused. "But before you find it out from someone else, there's something else you ought to know. I'd been applying for other positions. I liked teaching children."

"You were looking for a position as a governess again?"

"I was applying for teaching posts as well," she said proudly. "I'm very qualified."

"Miss Ross, is there some reason you wanted me to hear this information from you?" Witherspoon had no idea why the question popped out of his mouth, but as he'd learned to trust his "inner voice," he was sure it must be important.

"You needed to hear it from me because I know you're going to hear all about it from someone else," she explained, "and I wanted to make sure you understood my side of the situation. You see, Uncle Francis didn't approve. I know he took me in and I know I should be grateful, which I was, but it was never enough for him."

"I see."

"No, you don't," she replied. "Uncle Francis didn't for a moment let me forget that I had a roof over my head because of his kindness and generosity." She took a deep breath. "Yesterday morning, Uncle Francis and I had a terrible row. He told me that if I persisted in my attempts to find a position, he'd stop giving me an allowance. It was a very ugly confrontation made all the uglier by my losing my temper." Her eyes filled with tears again. "I said terrible, terrible things to him and then he died before I could apologize."

Witherspoon hated it when women cried. He never quite knew what to do or say. "I'm sure it wasn't that terrible. Families have little quarrels all the time."

"It wasn't just a quarrel." She swiped at the tears falling down her cheeks. "I completely lost control of my tongue and said dreadful things to the poor man. After I'd come to my senses, I realized how horrid I must have sounded to him so I went to his room before tea to tell him how very sorry I was. But he was still so angry he didn't even reply when I knocked."

"What time was this?" the inspector asked.

"I'm not sure of the exact time, but it was a few minutes before I came down for tea and that was at four o'clock." She closed her eyes briefly. "I should never have spoken to him the way I did. Now it's too late. That's why I've been crying, I feel so guilty. I said the most horrible things to a decent old man who'd taken me into his home when I had no place to go. I told him he was being hateful and that everyone else in the family only put up with him because he controlled the money. I said that everyone was just waiting for him to die so they could get on with their lives without his interference. Then, God forgive me, a few hours later someone killed him."

CHAPTER 3

———

"I'm sure your uncle knew that you really didn't mean what you said. All families occasionally have harsh words with one another," Witherspoon said kindly, hoping she'd stop crying. But his comment had the opposite effect. She began to wail at the top of her lungs. Then she covered her face with her hands and rocked back and forth on the sofa.

Alarmed, Witherspoon leapt up. Ye gods, if she kept on like this, the poor woman was going to end up in a quivering, hysterical heap on the carpet. It was time to find the housekeeper or Mrs. Prescott. Just then, the door opened and Mrs. Eames stuck her head inside. "There's a constable here who insists he must speak with you, Inspector. Oh dear, Miss Ross, you mustn't go on so. You'll make yourself ill." She stepped into the room and hurried over to the wailing woman.

Witherspoon ran for the door and escaped into the hallway. A young constable standing by the staircase snapped to attention. "You wanted to see me," the inspector said to the lad.

"Yes sir, I'm sorry to interrupt, sir, but I've a message from Chief Inspector Barrows. He wants you and Constable Barnes to come to Scotland Yard right away."

"Now? But we're in the middle of a murder investigation, and I've not finished taking all the statements," Witherspoon protested. This was most odd; he could think of no reason why they would be called back to the Yard, not unless someone had confessed to the crime.

"We're to continue taking the statements, sir," the constable replied. "There's a hansom waiting for you—it's quicker than the trains."

An hour later, he and an equally puzzled Constable Barnes were standing in Chief Inspector Barrows' office on the third floor of the modern, redbrick building now housing Scotland Yard.

"You made very good time in getting here." Barrows smiled briefly. He was a tall, balding man with a pale complexion and a perpetually worried frown.

"The traffic was very light," the inspector replied. He thought the chief inspector seemed even more anxious than usual. Barrows' mouth was turned down, his shoulders hunched, and there were deep lines around his eyes. "Is everything all right, sir?"

Barrows sighed heavily. "I'm afraid not." He straightened up and looked at Barnes. "I've some unsettling news, Constable. I'm pulling you off this case. You're to report to Fulham for the time being."

Barnes stared at him impassively. He was surprised, but he was too wily an old fox to let anything show on his face until after he'd learned the facts. "Yes sir. Is that to be effective immediately?"

Witherspoon's jaw dropped in shock. He looked wildly

from the chief inspector to the constable. "Constable Barnes is being pulled off the case. But why? I don't understand. I can't lose the constable, his services are invaluable. I couldn't have solved any of my cases without his help. Has he done something wrong? Have we done something wrong?"

Barnes gave the inspector a brief, grateful glance. The reason the inspector was universally admired was because he always made sure the men working his cases got their fair share of the credit.

"No one has done anything wrong." Barrows shook his head and stood up. "The constable is one of our best men. His record is impeccable. The new assignment isn't a punishment."

"But then why am I losing him?" Witherspoon pressed. He couldn't imagine working on a homicide without his constable.

"Because I've no choice in the matter," Barrows admitted wearily. He turned and moved the short distance to the window, propped his hands on the sill and stared out at the Thames. "The transfer to Fulham isn't my idea. I know how well the two of you work together. Only a fool would break up one of the most successful homicide investigation teams in the history of this department. But there are plenty of fools about who have a great deal more power than I do, so there's nothing I can do but acquiesce." He turned back to face them. "If it's any comfort, Fulham is only a temporary reassignment."

"But if it wasn't your idea," Witherspoon asked, his expression confused, "whose was it?"

"The order has come from the very highest authority. Apparently, the home secretary thinks it's a good idea for some of our other young officers to have the benefit of working with you and learning your methods."

"But . . . but . . . my methods aren't in the least extraordinary, I can easily write them down—"

"It's all right, sir," Barnes interrupted. He knew when it was time to quit. There was nothing that any of the three men in this room could do except accept the situation. "We're police officers and we do what we're told."

Witherspoon's shoulders sagged. "Yes, of course. Who is going to work with me?"

Barrows cleared his throat. "A young constable from Fulham." He glanced at Barnes. "You'll be taking his place while he trains with Witherspoon."

"I'll report there straightaway, sir," the constable replied. The moment he'd heard where he was going, he'd known who was behind this change of duty. "Is the constable who I'm to replace by any chance Constable Lionel Gates?"

"How'd you guess?" Barrows' eyes narrowed. "Apparently, young Constable Gates isn't above using his family connections to get what he wants and what he wants is to work with the inspector on this murder." He glanced at Barnes and smiled briefly. "But I assure you, I'll not forget this, and one of these days this particular home secretary will not be around to help him."

Barnes grinned broadly but said nothing.

Witherspoon had some connections of his own and though he wasn't very good at the sort of machinations that were second nature to people like Gates, he'd do his best. The very idea of working a murder without Barnes was unthinkable, but he knew further arguments at this point would be futile, so he said, "When is Constable Gates to report to me?"

"Immediately. He went down to turn the transfer documents into the duty officer just a few moments before you two arrived. I expect he'll nab you before you make it out of the building, but if he doesn't he can make his own blooming way to Acton. You're not his nursemaid. Go on now." Barrows pointed to the door. "You're under no obligation to wait for the little sod."

As soon as they'd stepped into the hallway and closed Barrows' office door, Witherspoon said, "Constable, I'm going to do everything in my power to get you back on the case. Constable Gates isn't the only person with connections."

Barnes winced. There wasn't a polite way to point out that Witherspoon was such an innocent that any attempt he made to pull political strings was likely to result in a major disaster for both of them. "Of course not, sir, but—"

Witherspoon interrupted. "I rely on you too much to let this happen, I don't care what the home secretary says. I know I can do something. I'll have a word with—"

Now it was Barnes' turn to interrupt. "Don't have a word with anyone, sir. You don't want to be distracted when you're working on a case this complicated."

"But I don't think I can do it without you."

"You won't have to, sir," the constable said quickly. "Fulham is a quiet division, so I can easily stop in to see you in the mornings before I report in for my shift." He was thinking as he spoke, trying to come up with an idea that would keep Witherspoon's confidence up and more importantly, keep him from taking any actions that might ruin both their careers. "It'll be all right, sir. You'll see, I'll pop around in the evenings to see what's what and pass on any information I might have stumbled across about the Humphreys case . . ." He broke off as Inspector Nigel Nivens suddenly appeared at the top of the staircase. His face was red and was breathing hard, as though he'd been running.

"Thank goodness you're still here." Nivens slumped against the banister and tried to catch his breath. "I was afraid I'd missed you. I want you both to know," he panted, "that I had nothing to do with the chief inspector pulling

Constable Barnes off the Humphreys case." He straightened, pushed away from the staircase, and came toward them. "As a matter of fact, when my nephew asked me to use my influence for just that purpose, I flat out told him no."

Barnes wasn't sure he believed him. But he said nothing.

"I've no objection to training other officers in my methods," Witherspoon explained, "and I understand your nephew is very eager to learn, but an active murder investigation isn't the appropriate venue. Trainings are much better done in a classroom with lots of other young officers—"

"This wasn't my doing," Nivens interrupted. "You and I aren't the best of friends, but I am beholden to you from that last case."

"Of course this isn't your doing," Witherspoon assured him. "I believe you. I suppose what I'm asking is for you to use your influence with your nephew and . . . and . . ."

"Oh, there you are." Lionel Gates waved from the other end of the hallway.

"He must have come up the back staircase," Barnes muttered.

"Inspector Witherspoon, please wait for me," he yelled as he ran down the corridor and skidded to a halt in front of the three men. He nodded respectfully at his uncle before turning to the inspector. "I'm Constable Lionel Gates, sir. I'm at your service and very eager to get started." He thrust a packet of papers at Barnes. "Would you be so good as to give these to the roster officer at Fulham, that's a good man. Well now, shall we get started."

Wiggins raced across the train platform and into the carriage just as the train pulled out of the station. The young woman he'd followed from Humphreys House had taken the seat by the window. They were the only two people in the compartment so Wiggins, not wanting to frighten her, took the middle seat on the row across from her.

As he sat down, she shot him a quick glance. She had dark blonde hair tucked up under a brown hat, blue eyes, and a round face with a sprinkling of freckles across her nose. He gave her a friendly smile. She quirked her lips and then turned her attention back to the window.

He waited until the train pulled away from the platform before he spoke. "Excuse me, miss, but I couldn't help but notice you came out of Humphreys House."

Startled, her eyes widened. "How do you know where I've come from? Were you followin' me?"

"Oh no, miss, well, I was followin' you, but not on purpose." He stumbled over his words deliberately. "I just happened to be there and I saw you comin' out and well, I thought you'd not mind if I spoke to you about somethin' important."

"Well, I do mind." She put her nose in the air and turned back to the window.

"I'm awfully sorry, miss," he murmured softly. "I meant no 'arm." He made himself sound as pathetic as possible and then held his breath, hoping his ploy would work.

After a moment, she glanced at him and said, "What was so important that you had to follow me?"

He kept his gaze down, focusing on the tip of his shoe for a second, then looked up at her. "I 'eard there was a position available as a footman and I thought I'd apply for it," he said softly. "But a bloke passin' by told me there's been trouble there and they aren't 'irin'. When I saw you come out, I thought I'd just ask if it was true. I'm awfully sorry if you thought I was bein' forward."

"Why'd you waste your money on a train ticket into town if you're wantin' to apply for a position?" she asked, her expression suspicious.

Wiggins was ready for the question. "I live just off

Ealing Broadway and I've got an interview at an agency near Paddington station later this afternoon. But jobs is scarce these days and when I heard there might be a position at Humphreys House, it was close enough that I thought I'd just walk over and see if I could 'ave a word with the housekeeper or the butler. But I'd not want work in a house with trouble."

"Then you'll want to stay away. I didn't mean to sound rude, but the bloke who told you there was trouble was right." She leaned forward, her expression serious. "There's been a murder."

"Cor blimey, how awful for you."

She blinked, surprised by his concern for her. "It was, but it was worse for the master—he was the one that was killed. Shot right through the head, he was. We've had the police around asking all sorts of questions."

"Do they know who did it?" he asked.

She shook her head. "No, they've not caught anyone and I don't think they're goin' to, either."

"Why do you think that?"

"It happened right in the middle of the afternoon. The house was full of guests having tea. We all heard the shot, but by the time everyone got upstairs, the killer was gone. He must be very clever to murder someone in a houseful of people and get clean away with it."

"Maybe he was just lucky," Wiggins said hesitantly. "Maybe he used the confusion to get away."

She thought about it for a moment. "That's possible. All the relatives and even some of the guests were in poor Mr. Humphreys' room and we was all standin' about on the landing and the staircase. Even cook had come up out of the kitchen to see what all the fuss was about."

Wiggins wanted to know how much she'd actually seen. "Was there a lot of blood?"

"I don't know, I couldn't see all that much. I was too far away. It was right shockin', it was. We could hear the others from inside Mr. Humphreys' room, shoutin' and arguin' with one another. Then Miss Ross come out leadin' Mrs. Prescott off to her room and Mrs. Eames told us all to get about our business."

"What happened then?"

She shrugged. "Nothing, really. I went back up to the top floor to finish polishing the brass sconces on the lamps. But it was hard to concentrate on my work what with him lying down there dead, and then Mrs. Prescott pops her head up and orders me back downstairs to help Agnes clean up the tea things from the drawing room." She snorted derisively. "For someone who'd been bawlin' her eyes out only moments earlier, she recovered quickly enough. So I went back downstairs and Agnes and I cleared up the drawing room."

"I guess murder confuses things a bit." Wiggins gave her his kindest smile.

She looked out the window. "He wasn't a bad master. Truth of the matter is, we're all a bit worried about what's going to happen next. Even Mrs. Eames was concerned about whether or not we're all going to have our positions once he's buried and the will is read."

"Do you think you might be turned out?" Wiggins asked.

"I don't know." She bit her lip. "I hadn't even thought about it until I overheard Mrs. Eames talkin' with cook."

"What was she sayin' that upset you so much?" he asked sympathetically. He wasn't acting now; he was genuinely concerned for the poor girl. He knew what it was like to wonder if you were going to have a roof over your head and food to eat.

"She told cook that she thought Mr. Humphreys might

have mortgaged the house. She said she wasn't sure, but she knew he was wantin' to raise money and she knew he'd been to see both his banker and his solicitor right before he was murdered." She shrugged. "Then they walked away and I couldn't hear anything else." She suddenly looked at him with renewed interest. "What's the name of the agency you're goin' to see today? If I need work, maybe I'll try them?"

"Oh, it's Dalyrumple's Domestics on Praed Street," he lied. "But I'm sure you don't have anything to worry about. I mean, if your Mr. Humphreys just went to see his solicitor and his banker right before he died, there couldn't have been enough time for anything to happen. Doesn't that sort of thing take ages?"

"I suppose it does. Still, now that he's dead, none of us know what's goin' to happen."

The train slowed as it went through Royal Oak station and Wiggins had to decide if he ought to continue pursuing her. They'd be coming into Paddington in five minutes. "I've been ever so rude, miss. My name is John King."

"I'm Rachel Morgan." She smiled self-consciously. "I'm the upstairs maid."

He bobbed his head politely and said, "Miss Morgan, if I might make so bold, I'd be pleased if you'd have a cup of tea with me when we get to Paddington station. There's a very respectable café just off the platform."

"Don't you need to get to your interview?"

"It's not until later," he replied. "Truth is, that lodgin' house in Ealing isn't very friendly. You're about the first person I've met that's talked to me right and proper." Rachel Morgan worked in the dead man's house, and you didn't get much closer than that.

"I know what you mean," she replied softly. "Sometimes I feel the same way even though I'm in a house filled with people. I'd be pleased to have a cup of tea with you, Mr. King."

"I was surprised to hear you'd retired," Hatchet said to his old friend, Emery Richards. They were sitting in a window table at Corribani's Coffee House just off Bond Street. "But luckily, Daisy recognized me when I called at the Farringdon house to see you and gave me your new address. She said to give you her regards. I think they miss you."

Emery Richards was a small, slender man about the same age as Hatchet. He had a full head of iron gray hair, piercing blue eyes, and a long, straight nose. "Of course they do." He laughed. "I used to turn a blind eye to all their shenanigans. Truth of the matter is, I ought to have retired years ago. God knows I could have afforded it, but without a family or much else to keep me occupied, I thought I'd be bored."

"And are you bored?" Hatchet watched his old friend carefully, wanting to reassure himself that Emery was doing as well as he claimed. If he needed money, Hatchet would make sure he got it without damaging his pride.

He and Emery shared a long and interesting history. Years earlier when both of them had had more courage than brains, they'd been young, wild, thirsting for adventure, and very stupid. But despite their idiocy, they'd survived, seen quite a bit of the world, albeit on different continents for the most part, and then each of them had ended up as butlers. Emery had worked at a household that had figured prominently in one of the inspector's more recent cases.

"Not in the least." Emery gave him a knowing smile. "I'm fine, Hatchet. Despite the wild excesses of my youth, I'd saved my wages since returning to England and I've invested them prudently. When I left the Farringdons', I bought a nice little house just off Shepherds Bush. I've got lodgers and they give me a good bit of company."

"But what do you do with your time?" Hatchet asked curiously. He knew that at some point in his life, he might very well end up much like his friend.

Emery picked up his coffee cup and blew gently on the hot liquid. "I spend a lot of time reading and I help serve meals to the poor at St. Matthew's every Tuesday and Thursday lunchtime. As a matter of fact, I'm due there soon, so you'd best start asking your questions."

Emery had spent the last twenty years working for the rich and well connected in London. Always one to keep his eyes and ears open, he was an excellent source of information.

"Have you heard of a man named Francis Humphreys?" Hatchet sipped his coffee.

"You mean the man that was shot?"

"Yes. Inspector Witherspoon got the case," Hatchet replied. He wasn't in the least concerned that Emery knew about his activities. He was a man who could be trusted. He'd used him as a source on a half dozen of the inspector's previous cases.

"I've never met him. He didn't really travel in the same circles as the Farringdons or Lord Seaton," Emery replied, mentioning his previous two employers. "But I have heard of him. He was married to a rich American woman named Estelle Collier. She owned about half of every railway company in the United States. She died a few years ago and left him everything."

"Did they have children?"

"Not that I've ever heard about." Emery frowned. "I'm trying to remember something about them, now what was it? Oh yes, they used to have a huge flat just the other side of Hyde Park. But about ten years ago, he talked her into moving to some place a bit farther out of town. The gossip was that he wanted to be able to watch the trains go by or some such nonsense."

Inspector Nivens snatched the papers out of Lionel's hands as he handed them to Barnes. "You'll not speak to your betters in such a fashion," he snapped. "Constable Barnes is a senior officer and you'll treat him with respect. Furthermore, you'll take these documents"—he shook the papers under Lionel's nose—"to Fulham yourself and if you give me any argument about it, I'll go have a word with your mother. Do I make myself understood?"

Lionel stared at his uncle impassively for a moment and then tucked the pages under his arm. "I meant no disrespect to the constable. There's no need for you to get so angry. I was only excited to have the opportunity to work with Inspector Witherspoon." He looked at Barnes. "I apologize, sir." He then turned to Witherspoon. "If it's all the same to you, Inspector, I'll meet you at Humphreys House later this afternoon. What time shall I tell my superiors at Fulham to expect Constable Barnes?"

"He'll report there tomorrow morning," Nivens interjected. "And if anyone questions that, have them contact me directly."

Lionel bowed his head respectfully and started for the staircase. As soon as he was out of earshot, Nivens closed his eyes and sighed. "I'm sorry about this, Witherspoon. As God is my witness, I tried my best to get the transfer order rescinded, but it was impossible. My sister, Lionel's mother, has better connections to the home secretary than half the Queen's relatives." He sounded angry and bitter. "But at least I've got him out of your way for a few hours."

"I appreciate that, Inspector," Witherspoon said softly. "Now, if you'll excuse us, Constable Barnes and I need to get back to Humphreys House. We've still statements to take."

On the way back to Acton, Barnes did his best to reassure his inspector. "Not to worry, sir," he said with a confidence he didn't feel. "You'll soon have this case solved."

"I've never worked a murder case without you," Witherspoon admitted as the hansom pulled up in front of their destination. "I don't think I shall like it much. It'll be awkward working with a new person. Especially one that I'm not sure I can completely trust."

Barnes stepped out onto the road. "Constable Gates doesn't have the same reputation as his uncle." He paid the driver and the two men started up the long walkway to the house.

"That may be true, yet I find his behavior somewhat alarming," Witherspoon replied. They climbed up the steps to the door.

Barnes banged the brass knocker. "How so, sir?"

"He went to great lengths to get put on this case, Constable. Furthermore, he did it in a devious and rather backhanded manner."

"Some people will do whatever is necessary to get what they want," Barnes muttered. He was surprised by the inspector's comment. He generally gave everyone the benefit of the doubt. But now that the words had been said, the Constable found he agreed with them. "Watch your back, sir," he said as the door opened and Mrs. Eames ushered them into the house.

Annabelle Prescott was waiting for them in the drawing room. "I heard you were called away." She rose from the chair by the window and crossed the room, her black skirt rustling as she walked. "Mrs. Eames said you wanted to speak to me again."

Barnes slipped his little brown notebook out of his jacket pocket and flipped it open.

"We need to ask you a few more questions," Witherspoon said. "I'll try to make this as brief as possible."

"Then we might as well be comfortable." She gestured toward the furniture in front of the fireplace. "Please sit down," she said as she sank down on a chair.

Witherspoon took a spot at the end of the couch and Barnes sat on the loveseat, both of them now facing her.

"Mrs. Prescott, did your uncle own a gun?" the inspector asked.

Her brows drew together in surprise. "He owned a revolver. But what does that have to do with his death? He was murdered by an intruder. Surely you don't think someone broke in here, found Uncle Francis' weapon, and then shot him with it. The very idea is absurd. The house was full of people."

"That appears to be the case, however, we must be thorough in our investigation," the inspector responded calmly. "Do you know where he kept it?"

She sighed irritably. "He kept it in a hidden compartment at the bottom of his valise."

"May we see it, please?"

"It's in the storeroom on the third floor. I'll send one of the maids up to get it." She started to rise, but the constable was already on his feet.

"Don't trouble yourself, ma'am," he said. "I'll take care of it."

She eased back against the seat. "Mrs. Eames can show you where it is."

"Did you see any strangers hanging about the premises yesterday?" Witherspoon shifted into a more comfortable position.

"No, I saw no one." She crossed her arms in front of her and looked toward the window.

"Do you know of anyone who wished your uncle harm?" Witherspoon was asking the questions as they popped into his head.

"As far as I know, Uncle Francis had no real enemies." Her eyes filled with tears. "Or if he did, he certainly never mentioned anyone to me."

"What about Mr. Kirkland?" Witherspoon watched her carefully. "According to one member of your household, Mr. Kirkland and Mr. Humphreys hated one another."

She was taken aback, but recovered quickly. "You asked if I knew anyone who would want to harm Uncle Francis. His feud with Mr. Kirkland has gone on for years and even though there were bad feelings between them, I don't think Mr. Kirkland would wait over twenty years to commit murder."

"Why were the two gentlemen at odds?" Witherspoon asked.

She smiled wryly. "I don't know. My uncle wouldn't discuss the matter. All he ever said was that he loathed the man. That's why we were so surprised when Mr. Kirkland showed up at the house for tea. None of us had any idea he was coming, but he insisted Uncle Francis had invited him."

He made a mental note to speak to Leo Kirkland as soon as possible. "And you've no idea why your uncle invited Mr. Kirkland to tea?"

"None, Inspector. As I said, we were all surprised when Mr. Kirkland arrived, but he insisted he'd received an invitation so I could hardly refuse to let him in the house."

"How long have you resided here?" The inspector glanced at the clock on the fireplace and saw that it was already past three.

"Two years. My husband had just passed away and as Uncle Francis had recently become widowed himself, he invited me to come live here. The house is huge and though Mrs. Eames is perfectly competent as a housekeeper, he needed someone to take over the running of the house.

He's not very social, but even so, a man in his position needs someone to act as his hostess."

"Yes, of course." Witherspoon nodded. "I don't wish to distress you, Mrs. Prescott, but it would be most helpful if you tell me what happened yesterday. Was there anything odd or unusual that you noticed? Anything at all?"

"There was nothing, Inspector," she insisted. "It was a day like any other. The household arose at our usual time and had breakfast. Imogene commented that she needed to go into town to take care of some business so shortly there-after, she left the house. Uncle Francis left about half an hour later. I don't know where he went, but I assumed he had business to see to as well. I discussed the afternoon tea with Mrs. Eames. We had a number of guests coming and I wanted to make sure everything was ready. I spent the rest of the morning taking care of a few household duties and writing letters. Uncle Francis and Miss Ross arrived home in time for lunch. Mrs. Humphreys had been in-vited—"

"Mrs. Humphreys?" Witherspoon interrupted. "I un-derstood she was deceased."

"I mean Mrs. Yancy Osgood Humphreys, she's the widow of Uncle Francis' nephew. She lives just down the road. We have her to lunch quite often."

"Then what happened?"

"After lunch, Uncle Francis went into his room to work and I went upstairs to rest before tea."

Witherspoon said, "Did Mrs. Humphreys go home then?"

"She left, Inspector. I don't think she went home. She mentioned she was taking the train into London to do some shopping, but I don't know for a fact that's where she actually went." Annabelle frowned slightly.

"Why did you decide to have guests for tea?" the inspector

asked. Again, he had no idea why that question popped into his mind. But once it was there, he knew it was important.

"I don't understand what you're asking." She stared at him in confusion. "We have guests to tea for the same reason anyone does."

"Oh dear, I'm not phrasing this very well." He smiled apologetically. "What I meant to ask was if the tea was something you'd planned for a long time?" he explained. Mrs. Jeffries was right, he thought to himself. He really must learn to trust his "inner voice." What he was trying to learn was if the killer could have known of the tea in advance and used the occasion to his advantage.

"Uncle Francis had guests for tea at least once a fortnight," she replied. "So yes, I guess you could say it was planned in advance."

"Did he always invite the same guests?" Witherspoon leaned forward.

"Not always. Sometimes he invited other train enthusiasts like himself or sometimes he invited neighbors. It varied, Inspector."

"Mrs. Prescott, you were here all day yesterday, is that correct?" He shifted again.

"Yes, I've already told you that," she said impatiently.

"Did you hear Miss Ross and your uncle arguing?" He stared at her curiously. He couldn't help wondering why she hadn't volunteered this information herself.

She said nothing for a moment. "I didn't mention it because I didn't think it important," she said in a low voice.

"Mrs. Prescott, this is a murder investigation and someone having a nasty row with the victim only hours before he died is very important," Witherspoon insisted.

"Yes, I know, I'm sorry." She bit her lip and clasped her hands together. "But you can't possibly think Miss Ross had anything to do with Uncle Francis' death. She wouldn't hurt a fly. Oh, I know she's got a bit of a temper, but she was sitting with us in the drawing room when we heard the shot. She couldn't have had anything to do with such a wicked, wicked act."

"We're not saying she's responsible," Witherspoon answered. "But we really do need to know everything that happened yesterday."

"I've told you everything," she insisted. "Besides, I don't understand why you're bothering us with all these questions. Surely it is obvious what must have happened— Uncle Francis was murdered by someone from outside. We were all down here having tea. Why aren't you out looking for the person who shot him?"

"We're doing our best, Mrs. Prescott," he assured her. "Have you any idea why *anyone* would wish your uncle dead?" Someone with a motive would be useful, he thought.

"Uncle Francis wasn't an easy man to like, but no one that I can think of would want him dead. Not even Mr. Kirkland." She looked past him as the door opened and Constable Barnes stepped inside. "The gun is right where she said it would be," he said.

"Of course it is," Annabelle muttered.

Mrs. Eames came up behind him and he moved aside to let her through the door. "The vicar is here, Mrs. Prescott. He wants to speak to you about the service."

"Thank you, Mrs. Eames. Put him in the morning room and tell him I'll be right there." Annabelle got to her feet and started for the door. "You must excuse me, Inspector."

"Of course." The inspector nodded sympathetically. "If you've no objection, we'll continue interviewing your servants."

"Interview whoever you like. Mrs. Eames will be able to assist you," she said as she stepped out into the hall.

"You might want to move downstairs," Mrs. Eames

commented. "The servants won't be comfortable sitting in here and answering questions."

"Mr. Humphreys was a good customer. He doesn't skimp on food for his household like some around here," the grocery clerk said as she put a tin of Cadbury Drinking Chocolate down on the counter.

"He must have a big family," Betsy commented. She silently prayed no one would come into the grocery shop. She'd struck gold here. This clerk loved to gossip. All Betsy had to do to get her talking was to mention the man's name.

"He's no children and his wife is dead, but he's a couple of nieces that live in his house and he buys a lot of the provisions for another relation that lives just down the road from Humphreys House." She smiled at Betsy. "I wish I had a nice old uncle buying my food, don't you? Mind you, he's been feeding that household for as long as I can remember."

"He's feeding two households," Betsy exclaimed.

"He was." She laughed good-naturedly. "Mind you, Mr. Yancy Humphreys—that was his nephew—never earned much in his life despite all them contraptions he invented. Now I've heard that his widow, Mrs. Pamela Humphreys, has a small income of her own, but she's never marched in here and offered to buy her own provisions. Don't say that I blame her much, poor Mr. Francis has been paying the bills for so long it would be a bit of a shock to the woman to see how much even her little household eats. She's only got a cook and a maid or two."

Betsy looked suitably shocked. "You mean even after his nephew died, Mr. Francis Humphreys continued to buy groceries for his household?"

"He was a great believer in family taking care of family." The clerk shook her head for emphasis. "Leastways that's what my Flo always said about him. Flo's my half sister and she worked at Humphreys House until just before Christmas when she left to get married. Mind you, it wasn't just Mrs. Pamela he was taking care of, according to Flo, one or the other of both his family and his late wife's family was always coming around with their hand out."

"He sounds like a good man," Betsy said. "I wonder why someone would want to murder a decent person like that."

"It was probably one of his relatives." She shrugged philosophically. "No matter how much you do for some people, they want more, don't they. Flo said they were a greedy lot, always watching each other and trying to outdo one another in buttering up the poor old man. If you ask me, it must have been one of them. They all knew he was leaving them all his money. Mind you, that wasn't very smart on his part. If he'd kept his business private, he might still be alive." She stopped as the door opened and a well dressed matron stepped into the shop. "Good day, Mrs. Aldrich. I'll be right with you." She looked back at Betsy. "Anything else?"

Betsy shook her head. She knew when it was time to move on. "No. Thank you."

Pamela Bowden Humphreys made it clear she wasn't particularly happy to have two policemen in her house, but she wasn't going to refuse to speak to them.

"Please sit down." She gestured at an uncomfortable looking gray horsehair sofa as she sat down in a cozy, over-stuffed chair next to the fire. "I've an appointment with my dressmaker in an hour so you'll have to be quick."

"We'll be as brief as possible," Witherspoon assured her as he took a seat where she'd indicated. She was a short, dark-haired woman with faint lines around her blue eyes and the beginnings of jowls under her plump cheeks. She was dressed in a black wool dress with an old-fashioned high collar. "I understand you're Mr. Humphreys' niece?"

"Then you understand wrong, Inspector. My late husband was his nephew; I'm only related to him by marriage."

"Yet you live close by him," Barnes said softly. He knew he'd not much time. They'd only avoided getting saddled with Lionel by ducking out the side door when they'd spotted him hurrying up the walkway at Humphreys House. By the end of the workday, Lionel would have tracked them down and once that happened, Barnes would be officially assigned to Fulham. While he had the chance, he considered it his duty to stir the relatives up a bit. Sometimes people lost control of their tongues when you asked an unexpected question.

She turned her head and gave the constable a hard stare. "My husband bought this house before I married him. It became mine when he died. I'm hardly going to move just to get away from his relatives. Besides, Uncle Francis wasn't an ogre—we were civil to one another."

"Were you fond of him?" Witherspoon asked.

"Fond?" She repeated the word as if she'd never heard it before. "I suppose so. He's always been very decent to me."

"I understand you had lunch there yesterday as well as having tea," the inspector said.

"That's correct."

"Did Mr. Humphreys seem worried or preoccupied when you saw him at lunch?" Barnes asked.

She thought for a moment. "No more than usual. Uncle Francis was always preoccupied."

"Do you know why?" the inspector asked.

"Of course." She smiled slightly. "He was watching the clock. The timepieces at Humphreys House are very precise and he wanted to note the exact time the trains went past. That's all he ever thought about." She looked pointedly at the clock on the wall over Witherspoon's head.

"The trains?" Witherspoon repeated. "What about them?"

"You've seen his rooms. Surely you must understand." She looked at him with the sort of expression one reserves for a half-wit. "Surely you must know what I'm talking about."

"Mr. Humphreys did appear to have a fair number of train models and paintings of trains. He even had some photographs featuring trains," Witherspoon muttered.

"He was obsessed with them," Pamela snapped. "He spent almost every waking moment with his precious trains. Why do you think he built the house where it is, right on the main line of the Great Western Railway? How many other rich men have railroad tracks at the foot of their garden?"

"A large number of people are fascinated with trains," Witherspoon said defensively. He rather liked them himself. He enjoyed looking at the various engines and writing down their numbers.

"Don't be ridiculous, Inspector." She got to her feet. "This was more than a mere interest. He kept a log of the 3:09 to Bristol and wrote down the engine number every single day. He'd cut short a social engagement to make sure he saw that stupid train go past. Francis would send a telegram to the stationmaster at Paddington and the managing director of the GWR every single time the train was so much as a minute late. He's sent so many telegrams that street urchins hang about the front of the house every day and they're bitterly disappointed when the train is on time."

"Was it just that train?" Barnes asked. "Or was he equally obsessed with all of them on the line?"

"He didn't like any of them being late, but the 3:09 was

his obsession. None of us have any idea why. Uncle Francis didn't like being questioned about it."

"I'll admit it's a strange preoccupation," Witherspoon agreed.

"It wasn't just a strange preoccupation," she exclaimed. "Trains are all he cared about. He was planning on buying his own railroad. As a matter of fact, I suspect that's why he was late to tea yesterday. When we found him, the plans for the Trans Andean Railroad Company were open on his desk."

"Trans Andean?" Barnes repeated. He vaguely recalled a set of papers that had been pushed to one side. But they'd not seemed any more important than the timetable book on the dead man's desk.

"That's right." She smiled wryly. "He was planning on buying a railroad in South America."

CHAPTER 4

The rest of the household was already in the kitchen when Mrs. Jeffries returned home for their afternoon meeting. "Goodness, am I late?" she asked as she took off her bonnet and cloak and tossed them onto the coat tree.

"You're not late." Mrs. Goodge put the big brown teapot on the table. "The rest of them were a bit early."

"Then I presume we've all something interesting to report." Mrs. Jeffries took her seat at the head of the table. "I know I found out a few interesting facts."

"Why don't you go first, then," Betsy suggested as she lifted the pot and began to pour the tea into the cups.

"Thank you, I believe I will." She helped herself to a slice of buttered bread and a piece of shortbread. "I went to see Dr. Bosworth at St. Thomas' Hospital."

"Did he get a look at the postmortem report?" Smythe asked.

"No, he hasn't any connections to St. Mary's and that's where the postmortem was performed," she replied. "But even though he'd not seen the report, when I described the fatal wound he was able to give me some suggestions as to the kind of weapon the killer used."

Dr. Bosworth was one of their special friends. He often helped them with their investigations. Bosworth was something of an expert on guns, and more importantly he understood and could describe the damage a specific type of weapon could do to flesh and bone. He'd had plenty of experience in such matters as he'd spent several years practicing medicine in San Francisco, where, he assured them, there was no shortage of bullet ridden bodies. The good doctor also had some rather interesting ideas about how other features of both the crime scene and the victim could convey information if one knew how to properly analyze the situation. Thus far, no one, except for the inspector's household and one or two of his colleagues, took his notions seriously.

"Don't we already know it was a pistol of some sort?" Hatchet asked. "Surely he wasn't able to tell you the exact kind of gun it was based on nothing more than a description of the wound."

"Of course not." She laughed. "But he was able to rule out certain types of weapons. For instance, it probably wasn't anything as powerful as Luty's Peacemaker. According to the description of the wound that we got from both Constable Barnes and the inspector, a Colt .45 would have done far more damage than the small bullet hole which killed Francis Humphreys."

"Danged right it would." Luty sighed wistfully and patted the empty fur muff lying on her lap. Her Peacemaker used to always be inside, safe and sound, but the others had raised such a fuss about her carrying a gun, that she'd taken to leaving it at home. But the Colt had come in handy a time or two and she could easily lay hands on it if the need arose.

"More importantly," Mrs. Jeffries continued, "Dr. Bosworth was of the opinion that any pistol, unless fired by an expert, would have had to have been fired at much closer range than the distance from the French door to Humphreys' desk."

"So our killer knew how to shoot," Smythe murmured. "That should narrow the field just a bit. Very few people are that good with guns, especially revolvers and pistols. It takes a lot of practice to hit a target, even with a rifle." He knew from his days in Australia that simply pointing and pulling a trigger didn't mean you'd hit anything. In the bush, a body could starve to death trying to find his dinner with a shotgun; he'd almost done it a time or two.

"Agreed and that brings me to my point: One of our main tasks should be to find out which of Francis Humphreys' enemies is a good shot. As Smythe has rightly pointed out, it's not a skill that's particularly common."

"But it is common among the upper class," Betsy said earnestly. "Johnny Cooper, that lad that Wiggins met in the pub, mentioned that he accompanied Francis Humphreys to Scotland so that Humphreys could hunt."

"That's true, but he also said that Humphreys wasn't very good with either a rifle or his Enfield," Wiggins added.

"I'm aware of that," Betsy argued. "But my point is, if Humphreys went to Scotland regularly, even if it was just to drink good whisky, there's a likely chance other members of his household and most of his friends hunted as well. One of them might have been a pretty fair shot. So even though shooting isn't a skill most of us have, I'll bet there's plenty among both Humphreys' family and friends that know how to make a bullet hit the mark."

"True," Mrs. Jeffries mused. "So we can't assume that someone among his circle is the killer simply because they're a good shot. But knowing which of his enemies could shoot decently would be a help."

"It'd be more of a help if we could find one of his enemies that wasn't sittin' in the drawin' room when he was murdered," Mrs. Goodge muttered. "From what I heard today, the people most likely to have wanted the man dead were his nieces and nephews."

"What did you hear?" Mrs. Jeffries asked.

The cook shrugged. "Not much, really. But my source did say that Francis Humphreys was generous to his relations, but he didn't let them forget who controlled the money. He made them step lively and dance to his tune. I know it's not much, but I've got more sources comin' 'round tomorrow and hopefully, I'll hear a bit more about the other family members."

"I'll go next if it's all the same to everyone," Luty volunteered. She paused for a moment and then plunged straight ahead. "I found out a little about Humphreys' finances. According to my sources, he has a lot of money, most of which he inherited from his wife."

"He had none of his own?" Mrs. Jeffries asked.

"Some, but not near as much as she had." Luty grinned. "When she died, she left him everything, but only on the condition that when he died, half of the estate went to his family and half went to her nephew, Michael Collier."

"So Collier gets half of everything and Humphreys' nieces and nephews have to split the other half?" Mrs. Goodge frowned. "Hmm, that'd not make for comfortable family gatherings. I wonder if Humphreys' relatives knew about the terms of the will?"

"But Humphreys had gone to see his solicitor right before he was murdered," Wiggins reminded them. "Maybe he was changin' it all. Maybe Michael Collier wasn't gettin' as much as he thought. That'd be a good motive for murder."

"Collier was sittin' in the drawin' room when the murder was done," Mrs. Goodge said. "So he couldn't be the killer."

"But he could 'ave hired it done," Smythe suggested. "Seems to me we've already decided not to let the relatives out of the running just because they were 'avin' tea when Humphreys was shot. Any of them could 'ave hired someone to murder their uncle. It would have been easy. They could 'ave made sure a downstairs door or window was unlocked, told the killer about everyone being in the drawin' room and then the killer could 'ave snuck up the stairs, walked into Humphreys' rooms, and shot the poor man."

"But the inspector said the killer probably stood by the French doors in Humphreys' bedroom when he fired the fatal shot," Hatchet said.

"He only said that's what they thought might 'ave happened," Smythe replied. "Anyway, even if it were true, the killer could have gone into the room and walked over to the French doors before he fired the gun."

"Why would he walk twenty-five feet away from his victim?" Mrs. Goodge asked.

"I don't know." The coachman was getting frustrated. "I'm not sayin' how the killer actually did it. I'm just sayin' there's all sorts of ways an accomplice could 'ave gotten in and out of the house."

"How would he get out?" Betsy asked. "Everyone went running upstairs when they heard the shot so the killer couldn't have gotten out of the house without being seen by someone."

"You don't know that," Smythe claimed. "He could 'ave done lots of things, could 'ave hidden and waited till there was a commotion and then slipped out a window when no one was looking."

"Then why weren't there any footprints in the house?" Betsy folded her arms over her chest. "It was pouring rain—

surely someone would have noticed a set of wet footprints going from the dead man's room to a hall closet."

Smythe opened his mouth to argue further and then conceded defeat with a sigh. "Cor blimey, you're right. Someone would have seen him and no one did."

"We don't know what was or wasn't seen," Mrs. Jeffries said softly. "They've not finished interviewing the servants as yet. We'll know more when the inspector gets home tonight."

Smythe brightened considerably. "You think it's really possible the killer hid in the house until he or she could make a clean getaway?"

"It's highly doubtful, but certainly within the bounds of possibility. You do have a valid point, though. We mustn't dismiss any idea out of hand, regardless of how unreasonable it might seem." Mrs. Jeffries picked up her teacup. "But let's not speculate on what might or might not have happened just yet. We simply don't have enough details to make any assumptions at this point.

"Can I go next?" Wiggins asked. When Mrs. Jeffries nodded, he told them about his encounter with Rachel Morgan. He spoke confidently, giving them every single detail of the conversation. He told them about Rachel's fear they'd all lose their positions and about how Humphreys had gone to see both his solicitor and his banker right before the murder. He knew he wasn't forgetting anything. When Rachel Morgan had left the station café, he'd taken out his notebook and written down every word of their conversation. "When we were havin' tea at Paddington, Rachel told me the servants were all beginnin' to think he might be goin' off his head some. She said he'd always been a bit daft about trains, but they didn't get really worried until about a week ago, when the tweeny told them she heard Miss Ross and Mr. Collier arguin' over Mr. Humphreys wantin' to buy some railway in South America."

"Just because he wanted to buy a railway in a foreign country doesn't mean the man was goin' daft," Mrs. Goodge protested. "Maybe it was a jolly good investment. My sources didn't say anything about him losin' his mind."

"Neither did mine," Betsy agreed. "All I heard was that he had a houseful of relatives living with him and that he didn't scrimp on food."

"Was that all you learned?" Mrs. Jeffries reached for the teapot.

"Come to think of it, I did find out something else." She laughed self-consciously. "Francis Humphreys pays Pamela Humphreys' food bills as well as supplying her with coal. Sorry, that's the sort of detail we're not supposed to forget."

"Good heavens, is the woman destitute?" Hatchet asked.

"No, she's got a small income of her own," Betsy replied. "Apparently, Francis Humphreys began paying their grocery bills when her husband was alive, and when he passed away, he just kept on paying."

Witherspoon trudged up the steps of Upper Edmonton Gardens. He was deeply depressed. When he and Constable Barnes had parted, the constable had been cheerful and assured Witherspoon that he'd drop by every morning for a quick cup on his way to Fulham. He'd also promised to stop by occasionally in the evenings as well.

He opened the door and stepped inside. His spirits lifted a bit as he saw Mrs. Jeffries standing by the bottom of the staircase. At least everything in his world hadn't changed; there were still some comforts one could depend upon. "Good evening, Mrs. Jeffries."

"Good evening, sir." She reached out to take his hat. "How was your day?" She put the bowler on the peg.

"Not as good as some that I've had." He slipped off his overcoat and handed that to her.

"Oh dear, sir, what's happened?"

"Constable Barnes has been reassigned," he said glumly. "We got called to Yard this morning and told the news."

Alarmed, she gaped at him. She was so stunned it took a moment to find her voice. "Gracious, sir, that's terrible. Why on earth was he reassigned?"

"He's not done anything wrong," the inspector said quickly. "It's nothing like that."

"Then what was it?" She couldn't believe this was happening. It couldn't come at a worse time.

"My understanding is that the Home Office seems to think other officers could benefit from working with me and studying my methods." He tried to put as positive a face on it as possible. "But honestly, Mrs. Jeffries, my 'methods,' so to speak, are rather well known."

"Where has Constable Barnes been assigned?" She struggled to keep the panic out of her voice.

"Fulham." He sighed deeply. "But he has promised to stop by in the mornings on his way into town."

Mrs. Jeffries brought herself under control. "Well, sir, not to worry, I'm sure you'll handle the change quite readily. Shall we go into the drawing room? No doubt you could use a nice glass of sherry."

"That is an excellent idea," Witherspoon said earnestly as he followed her down the hallway. He settled himself into his favorite armchair while she fixed their drinks.

"Do you know who your new constable will be?" She handed him his glass and sat down on the settee.

"A young man named Lionel Gates." He took a quick sip. "He is related to Inspector Nivens. He's his nephew."

"Inspector Nivens," she cried. "Did he arrange for this to happen?" She wouldn't put such treachery past the man. Nivens had been trying to prove the inspector had help on his cases for a long time now. What better way than to saddle Witherspoon with one of his own relatives.

"He says not and I believe him."

"You do? But he's been trying to undermine you for years, sir," she protested.

Witherspoon smiled wearily. "He's not my favorite person, Mrs. Jeffries, but ever since our last case, he's behaved decently. He even arranged the situation so that Barnes' reassignment doesn't start until tomorrow."

She wanted to argue the point, to tell the inspector never, ever to trust Nivens, but she knew he'd not listen. Despite having solved over twenty-five murders, there was still a part of the man that was very naïve. "Constable Barnes was with you for the remainder of the day?"

"He was and he was a great help," he said. "It will be difficult not having the constable close by during the day so I can discuss the case, but at least I still have you. It does so help me to clarify my thoughts when I can talk through the details of the investigation."

"Of course, sir." She forced herself to relax. "Being called to the Yard must have interrupted your day. Were you able to continue making progress?"

"Oh yes, as soon as we'd finished with Chief Inspector Barrows, we went right back to Humphreys House to continue taking statements. His niece, Miss Imogene Ross, was very upset about his death but she was very cooperative. She lives at Humphreys House but hasn't been there very long. Apparently she had a very serious argument with Mr. Humphreys before he died." He tossed back the last of his sherry and got up. "I'm suddenly very hungry."

"Your dinner is all ready for you, sir," she said. They went into the dining room. Mrs. Jeffries took his plate off the serving tray and put it on the table in front of him. "It's one of your favorites, sir," she said as she lifted the warming lid. "Roast pork, potatoes, and sprouts."

"It looks delicious." He tucked right in.

She gave him a few moments to get a bite of food in his

stomach and then she asked, "What was the argument about, sir? The one between Miss Ross and the victim?"

"Oh that, well, it wasn't very nice. People really should be careful what they say in the heat of anger—it can often come back to haunt them. I know it did poor Miss Ross. She was terribly upset when her uncle died." He cut his meat and speared the slice onto his fork.

Witherspoon told her everything. Between bites of roast pork and brussels sprouts, he gave her all the details of his day. Her methods were subtle, but effective. As he talked, she'd shake her head in sympathy over how difficult his task had been, cluck her tongue disapprovingly at just the right moment, or sigh theatrically at his trials and tribulations.

When she went down to get his dessert, she told the others the bad news about Constable Barnes. They were as outraged and dismayed as she'd been.

"What do you mean the constable's been reassigned?" the cook cried. "Are they allowed to do that?"

"Cor blimey, that's bloomin' awful," Wiggins moaned. "What are we goin' to do without our constable?"

Betsy slapped the log-shaped suet pudding on a dessert plate and handed it to Mrs. Jeffries. "This is terrible news, Mrs. Jeffries. I didn't think this case could get any more complicated, but apparently, I was wrong. We rely on Constable Barnes to feed our inspector information that we can't give him ourselves. What are we going to do now?"

"Don't lose heart." The housekeeper put the dessert plate on the tray and picked it up. "We haven't lost him completely. The inspector said the constable has promised to stop by here every morning on his way to Fulham."

Later that evening, Mrs. Jeffries cleared up the dining room. The inspector had taken Fred for a walk, Mrs.

Goodge had already gone to her room, and Wiggins had borrowed the latest copy of *The Strand* magazine and gone upstairs. She put the dishes on the tray and took them downstairs. Betsy and Smythe were sitting at the kitchen table. The maid got to her feet and reached for the tray.

Mrs. Jeffries pulled back. "I told you I'd do the cleaning up. You and Smythe go up to the new sitting room and have some time to yourselves," she insisted. "You've both worked hard today and I know you've wedding plans to discuss." She'd also noticed the worried glances that Smythe had been giving Betsy.

"But Mrs. Jeffries, you've worked hard as well," Betsy protested.

"We all have," she agreed. "But you and Smythe need some private time together without the rest of us hearing every word. Besides, I can't sleep anyway."

"After hearing about us losing Constable Barnes, I don't think any of us will have a restful night. Can you believe that rotten Inspector Nivens?" Betsy shook her head in disgust.

"Not to worry, love." Smythe put his arm around her shoulders. "Like Mrs. Jeffries says, we'll manage."

"We certainly will," Mrs. Jeffries added. "Now you two go on upstairs."

"I'll just lock up." Smythe started for the back door. "The inspector is still out."

"Don't be silly. I'm quite capable of locking a door." She shooed them out of the kitchen. "Go on, enjoy a few moments to yourselves."

When they'd gone, Mrs. Jeffries took her time doing the cleaning up. The inspector and Fred came in and went to their respective beds. She ducked the last dish in the rinse water, put it on the rack, and hung the dishtowel on the railing to dry.

Then she took her keys out of her pocket, locked the back door, turned off the lamps, and went upstairs to make certain the front door was secured as well.

She went into the dark, quiet drawing room and sank down on the settee. She wasn't one to borrow trouble, but she had the feeling this investigation wasn't going to be an easy one. The murder was only two days old and already there were enormous difficulties: Dr. Bosworth hadn't had access to the results of the postmortem, they had very few, if any, suspects, and worst of all, they'd lost Constable Barnes.

Mrs. Jeffries prided herself on getting information out of the inspector but she'd come to rely on the good constable. He not only gave them additional information, but he often acted as a conduit to get information to the inspector. But he will be stopping by in the mornings, she reminded herself.

Yet the real problem wasn't the loss of the constable. It was the suspects. Generally, one found suspects among either people who hated the victim or people who stood to gain substantially by the victim's death. In this case, Humphreys didn't appear to have the sort of character to engender hatred. From what they'd learned thus far, he wasn't malicious or mean with people, but he was controlling. Was that enough of a character defect to make someone wish you dead? On the other hand, even if he made his family "dance to his tune," as Mrs. Goodge's source suggested, Betsy's information pointed to Humphreys being a generous man. He fed two households and took in relatives when they were unable to take care of themselves.

So what did it mean? Had he been murdered by someone who stood to gain from his death financially or by someone who hated him enough to kill him? Or perhaps it was something else altogether—perhaps the murderer felt threatened by him in some way. She got up and stared into the darkness. They might not know the identity of the killer, but it was someone who could appear at the doors of his rooms and not cause him to raise an alarm. Someone he knew. In other words, his murderer was either a close relative or a supposed friend.

And that was the problem, she thought as she moved toward the doorway to the hall. Most of his relatives and friends were sitting in his drawing room while he was being shot. Drat.

Mrs. Jeffries' spirits had improved greatly when she went downstairs for breakfast the next morning. After tossing and turning most of the night, she'd finally decided that their only course of action was to do what they always did—investigate the victim and everyone who was close to him. This method had worked for them in the past and she had no reason to believe it wouldn't be equally useful now.

Mrs. Goodge was at the kitchen table drinking a cup of tea. Samson, her mean-spirited yellow tabby cat was curled up on her lap. The animal raised its broad head and gave the housekeeper a dismissive glance. At the end of one of their previous cases, Samson had been rescued by Wiggins. His owner had been murdered, and as he was such an obnoxious animal the footman had known he'd be turned out or starved to death if he was left in his old household. So he'd brought Samson here. The cat and the cook had taken one look at each other and it had been love at first sight. Mrs. Goodge simply couldn't understand why everyone else in the household stayed as far away from the feline as possible. She thought him the sweetest creature on the face of the earth.

"Come and have a cup with me," the cook invited. "It'll be a while yet before the others come down."

But before Mrs. Jeffries could reply, they heard a knock on the back door. Samson, disturbed by the cook's startled response, leapt off her lap while Mrs. Jeffries hurried down the hallway and opened the door.

"I hope I'm not too early." Constable Barnes grinned broadly. "But I wanted to have a quick word with you and I don't want to be late to my new assignment."

"Do come in, Constable." She opened the door wider. "There's a pot of tea at the ready."

By the time they reached the kitchen, Mrs. Goodge had him a cup poured and sitting on the table. "It's nice to see you, Constable," she said as she waved him into a chair.

"Likewise." He slipped into his seat, picked up his tea, and took a drink. "Ah, that tastes good. I don't care if spring is almost here—it's still very cold in the mornings."

"And it's very good of you to stop in here on your way into town." Mrs. Jeffries sat down. "We very much appreciate it."

"I like keeping my hand in as well." He laughed.

"Go on," the cook encouraged. "What have you got for us?"

"Just a few bits of information you might not have found out from the inspector," he began. "First of all, I had a quick word with the lads that did the house-to-house and as you'd expect, none of them saw or heard anything that afternoon."

"That's to be expected," Mrs. Jeffries murmured. "It was raining so everyone was tucked up inside their houses. Even servants try to avoid going out in the wet unless they've no choice."

"I also had a look at the postmortem report," Barnes said. "I'm no medical man, but I've enough experience to know the important bits. The doctor only found one bullet in the victim, which implies he was killed instantly."

Mrs. Goodge looked confused. "Really? Why?"

"Because the murderer would have fired a second shot if the first one hadn't done the deed," Barnes explained. He took another sip of his tea, swallowed, and then seemed to hesitate.

"What is it?" Mrs. Jeffries asked. "Is there something you're not telling us?"

"It's nothing, really," he demurred. "I can't prove it and I really shouldn't say anything, it's just a feeling I've had ever since I saw the body."

"What is it?" Mrs. Goodge encouraged. "You've had too many years experience to doubt yourself, Constable."

"It was the wound in the man's skull." He grimaced. "There was something odd about it. But I can't put my finger on what it is. I don't want you to think I'm getting fanciful because I've been tossed off the case and sent to Fulham."

"We'd never think that," Mrs. Jeffries said staunchly.

"I appreciate your loyalty, Mrs. Jeffries." He laughed. "But the first rule of any good policeman is to put your faith in facts, not feelings, and the fact of the matter is that the bullet hole in the man's forehead was what killed him." He glanced at the carriage clock on the pine sideboard. "I'd best tell you the rest. You've got to make sure your lot does as much talking to Humphreys' household servants as possible."

"Of course," Mrs. Jeffries agreed. "Is there any special reason? Haven't you and the inspector already interviewed all of them?"

"No, we got called back to the Yard before I could finish and when we went back yesterday, there wasn't enough time. I suspect that if Constable Lionel Gates is anything like his uncle, he'll antagonize the servants the moment he opens his mouth." He smiled wryly. "And we both know that angry housemaids and cooks don't volunteer information. That's why I'm going to rely on all of you to suss out what you can."

"I'm flattered by your faith in us," Mrs. Jeffries said.

"But I did pick up another bit of information that the inspector didn't find out and it might be important. Another one of Humphreys' relatives had just moved in with him on the day of the murder. Joseph Leland Humphreys and his luggage had arrived that very morning."

"Why doesn't Inspector Witherspoon know this?" Mrs. Jeffries asked.

"I thought he did," Barnes replied. "I found it out from one of the maids but I didn't realize until Inspector Witherspoon and I were parting ways last evening that he didn't know about Joseph Humphreys. Just as he was walking away, he mentioned that aside from the servants the only people who lived in the victim's house were Miss Ross and Mrs. Prescott. By the time I understood what he'd said, he was already gone."

"And you think this fact might be important?" Mrs. Jeffries pressed.

"I don't know, but I do wonder why neither Mrs. Prescott nor Miss Ross mentioned that young Mr. Humphreys was now a resident."

Constable Gates kept up a stream of chatter during the hansom ride to Humphreys House. Gates had arrived at Upper Edmonton Gardens only moments after Constable Barnes had departed. Witherspoon had introduced him to Mrs. Jeffries and then they'd caught a cab on the Holland Park Road. By the time they reached their destination, the inspector's ears were ringing. Witherspoon leapt out of the cab and hurried to the walkway to the house.

Lionel paid the driver and then ran to catch up. "Shall I sit in on your interviews?" He was a few paces behind the inspector. "Or do you wish me to conduct my own interviews? As I mentioned on the drive here, I have read your preliminary reports."

Witherspoon knocked on the front door.

"If you don't mind my saying so, sir," Lionel continued, "the reports are a bit on the thin side."

Mrs. Eames opened the door. "Good day, Inspector, Constable." She waved them inside. "Mrs. Prescott and Miss Ross are both in the drawing room."

"Thank you, Mrs. Eames," the inspector said. He had been going to ask Constable Gates to continue interviewing the household staff, but he thought better of that plan. "We'll announce ourselves. I'm sure you're very busy."

She nodded and disappeared down the hallway. Witherspoon waited till she was out of earshot before turning his attention to his new constable. "My reports are intentionally brief. During the first days of an investigation, I think it's important to focus on the facts and not speculate as to what you think may or may not have happened."

"Yes, sir." Gates smiled sheepishly. "I didn't mean to speak out of turn."

"Did you bring a notebook?" Witherspoon started for the drawing room.

"Of course." Lionel patted his jacket pocket. "It's important for one to always be prepared."

"Excellent." Witherspoon stopped in front of the closed door, cocked his ear to the wood, and listened for a moment before knocking.

"Good idea, sir," Lionel whispered.

"What is?" Witherspoon had no idea what Gates was talking about. He'd merely listened at the door to ensure he wasn't barging in at an inappropriate moment. He simply wasn't up to dealing with tears or hysteria.

From inside the room, a female voice called, "Come in."

"Eavesdropping to see if any of the suspects are talking about the crime," Lionel hissed as the inspector opened the door.

"Good morning." The inspector stepped into the room. Lionel hurried in behind him.

Annabelle Prescott and Imogene Ross were sitting in front of the fireplace drinking. A trolley was next to Annabelle's chair.

"I do hope I'm not interrupting your morning tea." Witherspoon stepped farther into the room.

"Not at all, Inspector." It was Imogene Ross who replied. "And it's coffee, not tea. Would you care for a cup?"

"No thank you." He gave her a warm smile. "May I take a few moments of your time? I've a couple more questions to ask you."

"I've an appointment later this morning," Annabelle replied. "But I can spare you a few moments now. Please make yourselves comfortable."

"Thank you." Witherspoon took a chair.

As all the seats in the immediate area were taken, Lionel scurried over to a straight-backed chair near the window and sat down.

"Mrs. Prescott, when I asked you yesterday how many people lived in the household, you neglected to mention Mr. Joseph Humphreys had taken up residence." He wouldn't have known that himself if Constable Barnes hadn't mentioned it this morning at Upper Edmonton Gardens.

"I'm sorry, Inspector," Annabelle answered. "It slipped my mind. Joseph had only taken up residency in the house that very day."

"Are you saying you forgot?" Lionel Gates asked loudly. He'd been told that Witherspoon encouraged his colleagues to speak up and ask questions.

Everyone turned to look at him.

"Mrs. Prescott, this is a murder investigation," Lionel continued, totally oblivious to the startled glances and frowns all around him. "I should think you ought to weigh your answers carefully before you speak."

Annabelle Prescott raised her eyebrows. "I'll thank you to keep a civil tone in your voice when you're addressing me," she said. "Unless, of course, you feel you ought to place me under arrest for making a simple slip of the tongue."

Lionel blushed in embarrassment. "No ma'am, I won't be arresting you."

"Who are you?" she asked coldly.

"Er, I'm Constable Gates." Lionel looked down at the notebook on his lap.

"Mrs. Prescott had a very bad shock and it's quite conceivable that the matter simply slipped her mind," Witherspoon said kindly. He hadn't wanted to admonish the young man in front of everyone and luckily, Mrs. Prescott's tone of voice and demeanor had put the lad firmly in his place.

"Thank you, Inspector." She smiled gratefully. "You're right, I, along with everyone else in the household, was very shocked by Uncle Francis' death."

"It was a dreadful day for all of us, Inspector," Imogene added. "I didn't think to mention that cousin Joseph had moved in, either."

"Mr. Humphreys is your cousin?" Witherspoon reminded himself to make a chart. There were so many nieces and nephews by both blood and marriage that he couldn't keep it straight in his head.

"Yes," she replied. "He is the son of Uncle Francis' youngest brother, Yancy Osgood Humphreys. Poor Uncle Yancy is dead now, God rest his soul."

"He's also Pamela's brother-in-law," Annabelle volunteered. "Her late husband and Joseph were brothers. He was named Yancy as well, after his father."

Witherspoon knew he wouldn't remember any of this until he wrote it all down. "Is Mr. Humphreys here now?"

"We'd like to speak to him," Lionel added.

"He's in the library." Imogene rose. "Come along, I'll show you. This is such a huge house that it's easy to get lost."

"Perhaps they're not finished speaking to us." Annabelle stood up.

"I'm quite through for the moment," Witherspoon replied.

Imogene led the two policemen down the hallway to another set of doors that connected to a longer, darker corridor. "The servants' hall is just down those stairs." She pointed to a staircase at the far end. "The library is the last door before the stairs. Now, if you'll excuse me, I really must go."

· "Thank you for your assistance, ma'am." The inspector waited till she'd disappeared before he went to the library door and knocked.

It flew open and a young man stuck his head out. "Ah, Inspector Witherspoon, I've been expecting you." He opened the door wider and motioned for them to come inside.

"There are plenty of chairs about," he said as he closed the door and followed them across the huge room. "Make yourselves comfortable." He flopped down on a red loveseat, folded his arms over his chest, and stared at the inspector.

"Thank you." Witherspoon sat down in a leather chair and studied the young man. He vaguely remembered the fellow from the first time he'd been here, but truth to tell, he'd not paid that much attention to him. Even sitting down, it was obvious Joseph Humphreys was well over six feet tall and beneath his gray jacket and white shirt, his shoulders were broad and well muscled. His hair was black and his skin fair.

Humphreys gazed back at Witherspoon out of a pair of dark, deep-set brown eyes but said nothing.

Lionel eased onto an uncomfortable straight-backed chair next to the loveseat and opened his notebook.

"Mr. Humphreys, when we took your original statement, you didn't mention you'd taken up residency in your uncle's home," the inspector began.

"No one asked me that particular question," Joseph replied. "As a matter of fact, the only thing I did get asked was had I seen anyone going into or out of my uncle's rooms prior to the murder."

"No one took down your address or any other particulars?" Witherspoon pressed.

"No."

"Who took your statement?"

"A constable." Joseph looked at Lionel.

"It wasn't me," Lionel said quickly. "I wasn't even here that night."

Witherspoon grimaced. It was probably some very new officers who'd been given the task of taking the statements. "That is our error, Mr. Humphreys. Now, can you tell me what time you arrived here the day you took up residency?"

"I got here around ten o'clock that morning."

"Forgive me for being redundant—perhaps you've already been asked this question—but when you did get here, did you notice anything unusual?"

"No." He seemed surprised by the question. "But in all honesty, I wasn't paying much attention to my surroundings, either."

"Why not?" Lionel asked sharply. "I should think when one is moving to a new neighborhood, one would be very keen to learn all one could about their new surroundings."

Witherspoon gave him a quick glare, but the constable seemed not to notice.

"Well, I wasn't," Joseph said calmly. "Frankly, I couldn't care less about my surroundings. Besides, it wasn't my first time at this house. Despite our political differences, I was family and Uncle Francis had invited me here many times."

"Political differences," Lionel snapped. "What political differences? Did you fight about them? Are you one of those awful radicals?"

"I'm a member of Socialist League." Humphreys sat up straighter in his chair. "Not that it's any business of the Metropolitan Police Force."

"It most certainly is our business," Lionel argued. "You radicals are going to ruin the country. If I had my way, we'd round the whole lot of you up and—"

"Constable Gates, I'll thank you to keep your opinions to yourself," Witherspoon ordered. "This is a free country and Mr. Humphreys is entitled to whatever political affiliation he chooses as long as he doesn't break the law." Lionel gaped at him for a moment and then slumped back in his chair. The inspector looked at Joseph. "I'm sorry, sir. Now, how did you get here that day? By train?"

"I came in a four-wheeler," Joseph replied. "My uncle sent one for me. He knew all of my luggage wouldn't fit in a hansom. There were several cases and a rather large trunk."

"You'd planned on staying here for quite a while, then?"

"No, just until I was able to find another position. But I had to bring everything I owned as I had no place to store it."

"You'd made prior arrangements with your uncle about moving into this house?" Witherspoon glanced at Lionel. He was scribbling away in the notebook.

"Of course, Inspector. I didn't just show up on the man's doorstep. I'd been here the day before and discussed the arrangement with him."

"Where had you lived previously?" Lionel asked. Apparently, being admonished by a superior officer didn't dampen his enthusiasm.

"I had rooms in a house in Marylebone, on Berwick

Street." He brushed a piece of lint off the arm of his gray jacket.

Witherspoon nodded. "What is your profession, sir?"

"I'm currently between positions." He colored a bit as he spoke. "But I've had positions in insurance and in banking."

"And your reason for moving into your uncle's house?" Witherspoon pressed.

Joseph's mouth flattened into a thin, disapproving line. He looked away for a moment and then back at the inspector. "Why does anyone move into a house with an elderly relative?"

"I'd prefer you tell me rather than have me engage in speculation," Witherspoon said. He glanced at Gates again and saw that the constable was glaring at Humphreys as though he'd decided the man was guilty as sin.

"I couldn't pay my rent," Joseph admitted reluctantly. "I lost my position at the insurance company in January and I had no money. Unlike some in the family, I have to work for my living. My landlady turned me out."

"She evicted you?" Lionel asked excitedly.

"That's what being turned out usually means." Joseph stared at the constable. "She had my luggage stacked out in the hallway and had locked the doors to my rooms. If Uncle Francis hadn't taken me in, I'd have been living on the streets. I'm unemployed and I don't have a penny to my name. Add to that, I'm in debt up to my arse because it's been difficult to find work and you'll no doubt decide I'm your best suspect. Is that what you wanted to hear? Is that what you wanted to know?"

"Mr. Humphreys, what I'd really like to know is whether or not you own a gun," Witherspoon said calmly.

Joseph took a deep breath. "Yes, I do. I own a revolver. As a matter of fact, Uncle Francis was the one who gave it to me."

Witherspoon thought for a moment. "May we see the weapon?"

Joseph's dark eyebrows rose in surprise. "Why? Surely you don't think I shot my uncle. I was in the drawing room with the others when it happened."

"I understand that, sir, but it's my duty to conduct a thorough investigation. Your uncle was murdered and it would be irresponsible of me not to account for all the weapons that may have been on the premises."

"Oh, for God's sake, if you must. I'll go get the wretched thing." He got up and stalked to the door. "Wait here. It's upstairs in the wardrobe in my room."

"If it's all the same to you, sir, I'd like the constable to fetch it," Witherspoon said. "Mrs. Eames can go with him."

"Yes sir." Lionel leapt up.

Joseph stopped and glared at the inspector. He said nothing as Lionel charged past him. Then he stuck his head out the door and called, "It's in a heavy brown case on the top shelf." He turned back to Witherspoon. "I'm not the only one in this family that has a firearm. Uncle Francis didn't play favorites. He gave all the men guns." He smiled slightly. "He gave us Enfields, just like the one he bought for himself."

CHAPTER 5

—◆—

Smythe hadn't wanted to do it this way, but after two days of struggling about on his own and getting nowhere, he'd decided to put his pride to one side and do what he had to do. He pushed through the door of the Dirty Duck pub and stopped just inside, hoping his contact would be on the premises and available to see him.

The room was crowded with dock workers, day laborers, street vendors, and all manner of people who made their living off or on the river. He craned his neck over the crowd to see if Blimpey Groggins was at his usual table. He was but he wasn't alone. Two men, both of them wearing the sort of formal clothing that identified them as toffs from the financial district, or as it was better known, from the City, were with him.

Smythe would have to wait his turn. He pushed his way to the bar and squeezed into a spot where he could keep an eye on Blimpey and, more importantly, where Blimpey could see him. Knowing he had a customer waiting might make him hurry.

Blimpey Groggins had started out in life as a thief. Breaking and entering had been his specialty, but after a couple of very near misses with the long arm of the law and the realization that a stretch in one of Her Majesty's incarceration institutions wouldn't be to his liking, he'd taken a good hard look at himself and decided to change professions. His strongest suit had been his memory. Once he learned something, he never forgot it. That ability soon convinced him he could make far more money buying and selling information than he ever had as a thief. After all, as he'd once explained to Smythe, London was full of thieves, petty and otherwise, but there were very few people who could recall the owner of a building that had burned to the ground ten years ago and the insurance company that had gotten stuck paying out the damages. But Blimpey could. Insurance companies were among his best customers. But he didn't just rely on his own recollections. He actively solicited information from all over England. He had sources at the Old Bailey, the magistrate courts, the financial centers in the City, the steamship lines, all the insurance companies, and even the Ecclesiastical Courts. He also had an excellent relationship with every thief, con artist, and crook in southern England.

But Blimpey had standards. He wouldn't trade in information that caused physical harm to a woman or a child. Smythe had used him lots of times. He was both discreet and reliable.

"What'll you have?" the barman asked, jolting Smythe's attention away from Blimpey.

"A pint, please," he replied. When he looked back in the direction of the fireplace, the two men were gathering up their silk black top hats, nodding their bald heads (both of them), and heading for the door.

"Can you send my pint to Blimpey's table?" Smythe asked as he moved away from the bar.

"Meg'll bring it over," the barman replied.

Smythe pushed through the throng. "Do you 'ave a bit of time for a payin' customer?" he said as he slipped onto the stool.

"I wondered how long it would be before you showed yer homely face in here." Blimpey laughed heartily. "Must say you surprised me, it's been two days since the murder. What were you doin', trying to suss out a few bits on yer own?"

Blimpey was a short, burly man with orangish-red, thinning hair, a ruddy complexion, and a wide face. He was dressed in his usual outfit of a brown-checked suit that had seen better days and a white shirt. A long, red scarf was twined about his neck and on his head was a dirty, porkpie hat. He wasn't a poor man—he could afford the very best of everything—nor was he a miser. Smythe knew for a fact that Blimpey was a generous man, but he didn't believe in wasting good coin on something as frivolous as a suit or shirt.

"So you've heard about it, then," Smythe muttered. "And yes, you're right, I did try a bit of snoopin' on my own but all I learned was that one of the dead man's relatives 'as an attic full of mechanical bits and pieces."

"You mean Pamela Bowden Humphreys." Blimpey grinned. "Her husband liked to tinker. He used to show his little inventions at all the exhibitions, but he never made any money out of any of his gadgets. Mind you, he had enough wits about him to patent most of his contraptions."

Smythe shook his head in disbelief. "I've not even hired you yet and you already know more than I do."

Blimpey's smile faded. "What makes you think I'm workin' for you on this one?"

Smythe's jaw dropped. It had never occurred to him

that someone else would get here first. That someone else might have an interest in this case.

"Cor blimey, you should see your face." Blimpey burst out laughing. "Forgive me, Smythe, but this was priceless."

"Very funny."

"Don't be sore, you're one of my few customers that actually has a sense of humor." Blimpey broke off as the barmaid brought two pints to the table. "Thanks, luv." He waited till she'd moved out of earshot and then said, "Right, then, you're wantin' to know about Francis Humphreys?"

"Of course, even though the man didn't live in the inspector's district, he caught the case. What I need to know most of all is who might have wanted him dead."

"Usually with a rich man like that, there's lots that'd 'ave a reason for wantin' him to meet his maker," Blimpey said. "You got more names for me?"

"You mean other than Pamela Humphreys?"

Blimpey grinned. "I bet you're wonderin' how I know about her. I was tellin' the truth, her name come up in another one of my inquiries."

"What inquiry?"

"It's nothin' criminal." Blimpey waved him off. "It concerns one of the late husband's inventions. I've got a client, a confectionary maker of all things, who has just designed another device to make his sweets. He was concerned that the widow might be able to sue him. The apparatuses are very similar to one another."

"What did you tell him?" Smythe took a sip.

"That his problem was a legal matter and he'd best ask his solicitor," Blimpey replied. "Now, just to show you I've been actin' in good faith, I do know a bit about the Humphreys' matter."

"You mean you expected me to come along and hire you," Smythe corrected. Though it stung his pride that he was so predictable, he didn't take umbrage at Blimpey's comment. The man was only telling the truth. "Tell me what do you know."

He'd done business with Blimpey for so long that they didn't need to discuss rates or payment schedules. They trusted each other. Besides, Smythe had helped Blimpey court and marry his wife. That had to count for something.

"First of all, Francis Humphreys had very little money of his own," Blimpey began. "He was from one of them ancient families with lots of breeding but not many brains. His grandfather owned a lot of property in Lancashire but managed to gamble it away by the time his sons came of age."

"So there's a gamblin' streak in the family," Smythe said. "I wonder if Francis had it?"

"From what I hear, he only gambled on railroads. The fellow is mad about them. Word in the City is that before his death, Humphreys was tryin' to raise a lot of cash to buy stock in a railway in South America."

"And I take it that wouldn't 'ave been a good investment?"

Blimpey shrugged. "Who's to say what is or isn't a good investment? Besides, people in South America are just like the rest of us, they need to get from one place to another, so why wouldn't a railway be a good idea? But you're not payin' me for my ability to understand the marketplace. So what names have you got for me?"

Smythe rattled off names of everyone who'd been in the drawing room at Humphreys House. When he'd finished, he said, "These are most of his relatives and friends. They were all together when they heard the gunshot, so they've got alibis. But as they're the ones most likely to benefit from his death, we thought we'd start with them."

"You thinkin' conspiracy?" Blimpey asked.

Smythe shrugged. "Could be. Stranger things 'ave happened. It's been our experience that when someone is murdered in his own home, it's usually done by someone who was close to the victim one way or another."

"Right."

"There's another matter I need some help with." He took a deep breath. He'd thought long and hard about this course of action and finally decided it was the only choice he had. Betsy was a very private person and she wouldn't appreciate anyone nosing into her past, but if he was going to get her sister here in time, he had to act quickly.

Blimpey cocked his head to one side. "Well, 'as the cat got yer tongue. What is it?"

"Give me a second," he protested. "It's personal and I'm tryin' to think of the best way to explain what I want done. It's about Betsy."

"What about her? If she's havin' second thoughts about joinin' up with the likes of you, there's naught I can do to help you there," Blimpey said.

"It's not that." He sighed. "Blast a Spaniard, I may as well just tell ya. Look, Betsy's real private like about her life so I need to be a bit careful here."

"I'm always discreet," Blimpey retorted irritably. "Come on, spit it out. What do you want done?"

"I need you to find someone for me and it'll not be easy," he explained. "It's Betsy's sister and her husband."

"That shouldn't be difficult. They've got names, right?"

"That's not the problem," Smythe replied. "You see, Betsy thinks they might have left the country. She thinks they might have immigrated to Canada." He reached in his pocket, pulled out a slip of paper, and handed it across the table. "Here are their names and their last known address. Betsy's old address is there as well. I thought it might help."

Blimpey reached for the paper. "How long ago did they leave the country?"

"Betsy wasn't sure," Smythe replied. "She thinks it was about ten years ago. That's when she lost contact with her sister."

Blimpey put the paper down and sighed. "Look, I'll be honest with you. I'll put my best people on this, but it'll cost you a lot more than gettin' a bit of information on a few murder suspects."

"I don't care what it costs." Smythe got to his feet. "You know I've got plenty of money. You just find her sister. Betsy wants her here for the wedding in October."

"Then you better hope she's not immigrated to Australia or New Zealand." Blimpey shrugged. "You'd never get her back in time."

"I've got it, I've got it," Lionel exclaimed as he rushed back in to the library. He held up a brown case the size of a small valise. "And here's Mrs. Eames—I've brought her along to prove that I didn't do anything in Mr. Humphreys' quarters except open his wardrobe and take the case. She was with me the entire time. She can easily testify that I haven't opened it or interfered with it in any way."

Mrs. Eames, who'd come in behind Lionel, gave the constable a sour look and said, "He's telling the truth. I've been with him the whole time."

Witherspoon gave Lionel a curious look. The young man seemed very intent on making sure he couldn't be accused of tampering with evidence. He wondered why. "Please give the case to Mr. Humphreys," he said. He smiled at Mrs. Eames. "If it's convenient, ma'am, I'd like to have a word with you when we're through here."

"Certainly, Inspector," she replied as she headed for the hallway. "I'll be in the butler's pantry downstairs. Today is a busy day. The master's funeral is tomorrow and we're having a reception here afterwards." She closed the door behind her as she left.

Lionel handed the case to Joseph who whirled around and placed it on the seat of an overstuffed easy chair. He knelt down, flicked the mechanism on each side, and raised the lid. He drew back. "My God, it's empty." He turned, focusing his gaze on Witherspoon. "I swear to you, the gun was right here the last time I opened this case."

"When would that have been?" Witherspoon asked with a calmness he didn't feel. He didn't see how this case could have become more complicated, but apparently it just had. Drat.

"I checked the case just before I left my rooms in Berwick Street." He paled as he rose to his feet. "I wanted to be certain I had it. The Enfield was there. I saw it."

"Was the case unlocked?" Lionel snapped.

"I lost the key," Joseph stammered. "My God, you can't possibly think it was my gun that was used . . ."

"You lost the key." Lionel put his hands on his hips. "That's horribly irresponsible—"

"We're not making any assumptions about the murder weapon at this point," Witherspoon interrupted. He shot the constable a quelling glance and then turned his attention back to Joseph. "When you first arrived at the house, did you take the gun case upstairs to your rooms straightaway?"

"No. Uncle Francis was waiting for me. He paid the driver extra to bring the luggage inside."

"And they took it up to your rooms?"

"I suppose so," Joseph said slowly. "Everything was upstairs when I left Uncle Francis."

Lionel's mouth opened, but before he could get any words out Witherspoon silenced him with a slashing motion of his hand. "Had anyone unpacked your luggage?" he asked.

"The luggage was in the room. I unpacked the trunks and the suitcases myself."

"You didn't think to open the gun case?"

"No, I just put it on the top shelf of the wardrobe." He went back to the loveseat, sat down, and buried his face in his hands. "Dear God, I never thought anyone would even know it was there, let alone steal the damned thing."

"Now, come on, Angus, have another. I've got plenty more. My friend brought me a whole cask of the stuff." Luty gently tapped the glass decanter and smiled at Angus Fielding. He was one of her bankers and she'd asked him to visit so she could see what he knew about Francis Humphreys. She'd chosen him because he was a dreadful snob about food and drink, especially drink. He'd tell anyone who stood still for thirty seconds that his cellar held wine from every country that grew grapes and that he'd tried every beer, ale, or fermented beverage in the civilized world. Just last week she'd had to listen to him go on for hours about the "sublime taste of sake."

"I really oughtn't to," he said as he shoved his crystal glass toward her, "but honestly, I've never had anything quite like this. What did you say it was called?"

"Oh, it goes by many names," she said casually. "In the hills of Kentucky and West Virginia, they call it moonshine. It's a home brew, very strong." She'd known he wouldn't be able to resist adding this to his repertoire of tastes. A tiny voice in the back of her conscience told her she oughtn't be playing on a man's weakness, but she ignored it. At her age, she'd learned that one had to make choices when it came to morality and right now, catching a killer was more important than getting a balding, middle-aged banker a bit tipsy in the middle of the day. In all fairness, when he'd arrived, she'd also offered him tea. "Shall I pour you another?"

They were seated in Luty's drawing room. The door was closed and Luty knew they wouldn't be disturbed.

"I'll just have one more. It's . . . interesting. Besides, it's already past lunchtime and I've no important business to attend to so I suppose it couldn't hurt."

"Of course it couldn't hurt." Luty poured the clear liquid into his glass.

"How on earth did you get this into the country?" He took a swig, winced, and then smacked his lips.

"I've no idea," she replied. "My friend just showed up here at the house one day with a cask of brew under his arm." She took a delicate sip from her own glass. "I expect you're goin' to be right busy in the next few days, what with that poor Mr. Humphreys gettin' murdered. He was a client of yours, wasn't he?"

"He was." Angus cocked his head to one side and stared at her suspiciously. "But how on earth did you know that?"

"Francis told me. He was an acquaintance of mine. I happened to run into him when I was comin' out of your building. We got to chattin' and he mentioned you and he did a lot of business." The lie came easily off her lips; after all, it wasn't as if Humphreys was around to contradict her.

"I wouldn't have thought you and Humphreys had much in common. He was very eccentric, you know." He giggled, gulped the rest of his drink, and then shoved his glass toward the decanter. "Perhaps another one wouldn't do any harm."

Luty hesitated for a split second before lifting the crystal stopper and pouring him another one. She'd wanted him a bit loose, but the way he was going, he was going to be drunker than a skunk. Tarnation, maybe this wasn't such a good idea. If he was so pie-eyed he couldn't talk, that wouldn't do her any good. "How was he eccentric?"

Angus thought for a moment. "He'd no sense of humor whatsoever. His only interest in life was trains and he'd very little money of his own. I've no idea why Estelle ever married the man, but she did."

"I take it Estelle was his wife?"

"Estelle Collier." He smiled wistfully. "Wonderful woman. I admired her greatly. Like you, she was an American. Her family made a fortune in shipping and logging, oh, and railways or railroads as they call them. We were the Colliers' English bankers." He sighed. "Sad what happened to her. She passed away so suddenly."

Luty's ears tingled. "Suddenly? How did she die?"

"Pneumonia," he replied. She came down with it right after she and Francis moved into Humphreys House. One of the nieces moved in to nurse her, but she didn't get any better, and before the month was out she was dead. They'd no children. A pity, really; she'd have liked to have had children. But when you wait as late in life as those two did to marry, that's only to be expected. She was almost forty and he had to have been about the same age when they wed."

"You were friends, weren't you?" Luty said softly. Her conscience was screaming at her and she felt awful. Angus was tearing up and any second now, they'd be spilling down his cheeks.

He blinked and looked away for a brief moment. "We were good friends. My wife and I both adored Estelle. She was the kindest, sweetest person. She and Edna, my wife, used to go shopping together and she came for tea on Sunday afternoons. I think her marriage wasn't as satisfactory as she'd have liked. I once overheard her telling Edna that the only thing Francis was really passionate about was his trains. Oh well, I suppose she's in a better place now."

"I'm sure she is," Luty murmured. She was thoroughly ashamed of herself. She shouldn't have gotten him here, plied him with moonshine, and forced the poor fellow to dredge up all these painful memories.

"Of course, Estelle had the last laugh on him," Angus muttered. "He thought he'd get everything when she died. I remember how furious he got when he found out that she'd left a portion of her American railway shares to someone else."

"Huh?"

"I told you, Francis was mad about railways. My wife always said the only reason he pursued Estelle with such vigor was so he could get his hands on her railroad shares. She owned huge chunks of the Northern Pacific, the Union Pacific, and the Atchison, Topeka and Santa Fe." He laughed. "I just love that name, don't you? Apparently, so did Francis, because those were the shares he really wanted. But she left those to an old friend. Francis got the other railway shares but not the ones he coveted the most. Ah, you American women are a clever lot."

Luty's conscience shut up and she reached for the decanter of moonshine. "Who got the shares?"

Angus eagerly held out his now empty glass. "Another railway enthusiast by the name of Leo Kirkland. I think the two of them had once been very close. Edna told me that Estelle had seriously considered marrying Kirkland. But then Francis came along and swept her off her feet. I daresay, she'd have been a good deal happier with Kirkland. He loved railways, too, but he wasn't as mad about them as Francis."

"I'm sorry to interrupt you, Mrs. Eames." Witherspoon stood in the door of the butler's pantry. The housekeeper was standing at a table taking wineglasses out of a tall wooden box. "I can see that you're very busy, but if you can spare me a moment I would be most grateful." He'd gotten rid of Constable Gates by sending him off to interview the neighbors, Mr. and Mrs. Brown.

"Of course, Inspector." She motioned him in and nodded at a straight-backed chair on his side of the table. "Please sit down. If you don't mind, I'll continue with my tasks while you ask your questions."

"Thank you, ma'am." The chair groaned in protest as he sat down. "Mrs. Eames, was Mr. Humphreys planning on taking any trips? I'm asking because there was a *Bradshaw's* open on his desk when he was found."

She lifted the empty box off the table and put it on the floor. "He wasn't going anywhere, Inspector. He always had a railway guide close by. He liked reading them. Trains were his main interest in life." She turned and pulled another box off the shelf, blew the dust off the lid, and opened it up.

"I see. Uh, the French doors in his room, were they usually locked or unlocked?"

"That's hard to say." She grabbed a handful of straw, tossed it onto the floor, reached back inside, and pulled out small apertif glasses. "He spent a lot of time on the terrace with his binoculars—he liked watching the trains go past—but he usually locked the door behind him when he came inside. Yet in the past year or so, he forgot as often as he remembered. Sometimes when I'd take his tea in in the morning, I'd find the door standing wide open. It would have blown open during the night. The lock isn't very good."

"On the day of the murder, do you know if it was unlocked?" he asked.

"I've no idea." She lined the aperitif glasses into a row next to the wineglasses, reached back into the box, dug around among the straw, and pulled out a crystal bowl.

"Mr. Humphreys was in a foul mood that day. I stayed as far away from him as possible. He'd had a terrible row with Miss Ross."

"Yes, she told me about it," Witherspoon said. "Did you know that Mr. Kirkland had been invited to tea that day?"

"Yes, Mr. Humphreys told me."

"Yet you didn't say anything to Mrs. Prescott?"

She stopped and stared at him. "No, it wasn't my place to tell her who the master had invited. I thought Mr. Humphreys would have mentioned it. It never occurred to me to say anything to her. Perhaps I should have . . . Mr. Humphreys had gotten a bit forgetful lately. But honestly, he wasn't going daft or losing his mind like some would have you believe."

The girl walked as fast as a racehorse. Wiggins had been following her since he'd seen her come out the servants' entrance of the house down the road from Humphreys House. Mrs. Jeffries had been very clear at their meeting this morning that they were to do their best to learn everything they could from the Humphreys House servants. But he'd already spent half the morning waiting about for a chance to speak to one of them and none of the servants had so much as stuck a nose out. He was determined to speak to someone today so this girl would have to do. Besides, servants talked to each other so maybe she'd know something useful.

She reached the corner and turned to her left. Cor blimey, for such a tiny thing, she could sure move fast. He caught up with her as she reached Horn Lane and quickened his pace until he was alongside her. She didn't look at him but kept her gaze straight ahead.

"Excuse me, miss." He doffed his cap politely. "If I may be so bold as to ask you a question."

"I don't talk to strangers." She glared at him suspiciously for a brief moment and then turned her attention back to the road. Her face was narrow, her nose straight, her eyes blue and complexion pale. She had dark hair tucked up under her brown wool bonnet and she wore a thin brown coat that gaped open at the front. A wicker shopping basket was tucked over her arm.

He tried again. "Please, miss, I'm quite lost and if I can't find the right address and deliver this letter, my guv's goin' to sack me." He tapped the pocket of his jacket. He actually had a white envelope with him. Betsy had told him she always carried one because people were more likely to believe you weren't lying if you had something to show them.

Her footsteps slowed and she cast him a quick, uncertain glance.

"I mean you no harm, miss, and it's broad daylight," he entreated. "All I'm asking for is a few directions." Cor blimey, this was getting difficult. You'd think he was blooming Jack the Ripper instead of a decent-looking bloke wearing his best shirt and shoes. He looked respectable— he'd made sure of that before he left the house this morning.

She stopped. "Right then, where you tryin' to get to?"

"Thank you, miss. I can't afford to lose my position."

She looked him up and down, her expression frank and assessing. "From the looks of your clothes, you're not doing that badly. Those shoes must have cost you plenty. I saw a pair just like them in the window at a shop on the High Street and they're not cheap."

"They weren't cheap, but I didn't pay for 'em," Wiggins said quickly. He prided himself on his ability to think fast. "My guv gives me 'is castoffs."

She laughed harshly. "No wonder you don't want to lose your job. It'd be a cold day in Hades before my mistress gave me anything. Right then, what's the address you're lookin' for?"

"That's just it, the house doesn't have a number, only a name. But it's on Linton Road."

She rolled her eyes. "For goodness' sake, you've just come from Linton Road."

"Cor blimey, that makes me look a real idiot, doesn't it." He gave her what he hoped was an embarrassed smile. People often spoke more freely when they thought you weren't very smart. Wiggins had gotten quite good at pretending he was thick as two short planks.

"Yes," she said shortly. "And it's half a mile back there so I hope your guv isn't expecting you home anytime soon. Now there's only one house on Linton Road that has a name and not a number and that's Humphreys House down at the very end."

"That's it," he cried. "Oh, miss, you've saved my life."

"More like your job," she muttered as she started off again.

He hurried after her.

"I thought you said you were in a hurry." She regarded him warily. "So why aren't you goin' back the other way?" She pointed back the way they'd just come. "That house you're askin' about has just had a murder. The master was shot right between the eyes."

"I know, miss," he replied. "That's why I'm bein' sent around with a note. It's a letter of condolence to the household. Besides, I never said I was in a 'urry. I just said I'd lose my position if I couldn't deliver the letter. My guv's not even going to be home till later today. But I'm not followin' you, honest. And I'm certainly not a murderer. I was just hopin' you'd let me show my appreciation for your assistance by lettin' me buy you a cup of tea and perhaps a pastry. There's a respectable café just up past the church on the High Street."

She stared at him for a moment and then broke into a smile. "I know the place. It's not a cheap workers' café. It's nice."

"That's why I invited you," he said. "You've been very decent to me and I'd like to repay you. I've plenty of time."

"Actually, so do I." She giggled. "My mistress is in town bullyin' her dressmaker into gettin' her mourning clothes altered so they fit properly. She's goin' to the funeral of the man who owned the house you're lookin' to find. She won't be home till this evening. The housekeeper is gone to visit her sister—that's why I'm doing the shopping. We've run out of sugar and cocoa. Mrs. Humphreys will have a fit if there isn't cocoa for her when she gets home. Alright, then, I'll let you buy me a cup of tea. My name is Margaret Rimmer, but everyone calls me Maggie."

"I'm David Parker." He bobbed his head respectfully, took her arm, and led her in the direction of the café.

It didn't take long to reach the High Street. Her eyes widened in apprehension as he opened the café door and escorted her inside.

"It's alright," he whispered. "You just take a seat at that table by the window and I'll get the tea. Would you like a raspberry jam tart?"

"That would be lovely," she replied softly.

Wiggins went to the counter, ordered, and waited for the counterman to make up the tray. He paid and carried it to the table.

She was staring out the window but turned and gave him a smile as he put the tea and the tart on the table in front of her. He put the tray on an empty table and sat down opposite her. "It's very nice of you to come out and have tea with me," he said.

"It's a treat for me." She smiled shyly. "But I think you've guessed that already."

"Did you come straight up from the country to your position?" he asked kindly.

"I'm from a small village in Essex. I heard about the job from another girl in the village who was getting married. She worked for Mrs. Humphreys and recommended me for the position. Can't say that I like it much here in London, but there's no work in the village."

Wiggins nodded. "Is your Mrs. Humphreys nice to you?"

"She's all right." She sighed, picked up her cup, and blew gently on the surface. "But it's not like home. But I've not much choice, I need my wages."

"Most of us don't have a choice, do we? Otherwise we'd not be fetchin' and carryin' for someone else."

"But your guv sounds nice." She grinned. "Mrs. Humphreys isn't mean or anything like that. The place is warm enough and there's plenty of food. It's just that we work so hard. It's a big house and there's only me and another girl to do all the cleaning. There's a cook, of course, but she doesn't do anything but plan the meals and make the food. I'm the first one up so I can lay the fires in the kitchen for the cook. Mrs. Humphreys doesn't show her face until half past eight. Mind you, I don't think she's had such a good life, either."

"Why do you say that?"

"Minnie—that's the other girl that works there—told me that Mrs. Humphreys' late husband was some sort of inventor, but he never made any money. Sometimes I think Mrs. Humphreys is a little bitter."

"What kind of an inventor was he?" Wiggins was genuinely curious. He'd had some interesting ideas of his own for things that might be useful.

"I don't know," Maggie replied. "I mean, I've seen his contraptions lots of times, I go up to his old workroom once a week to dust, but I've not a clue what any of it might be. They're mechanical things made out of wheels and cogs and funny-colored metals. I know that he invented some sort of device that was supposed to keep the birds out of Mrs. Humphreys' garden. Minnie told me they tried to use it last summer, but it made such a horrid noise the neighbors complained."

"That's too bad. A bird scarer is right useful if you want to grow decent fruits and vegetables."

"I don't think many of his inventions worked properly because just last week I overheard Mrs. Humphreys telling Mrs. Prescott she was going to get rid of her late husband's 'silly gadgets,' as she called them, and turn his workroom into another bedroom. Mrs. Prescott was horrified by the idea. They had a big argument about it." She giggled, popped a bite of jam tart into her mouth, and then went right on talking. "Minnie and I couldn't believe our ears—they were shouting at each other like a couple of fishwives."

"Who is Mrs. Prescott?" Wiggins asked. He needed to keep up the pretense that he'd never heard of any of these people.

"Mrs. Prescott was the late Mr. Humphreys' cousin. She lives at Humphreys House. She's a widow, too."

"How long have you worked for Mrs. Humphreys?" He took a sip of his tea.

"Since last summer," Maggie answered. "I was thinkin' of movin' on, tryin' to find work closer to home, but only yesterday I overheard the mistress tellin' the cook that we might all be moving house soon."

"Would that make a difference to you?" Wiggins asked. He knew that when anyone connected with a murder case mentioned moving, it was best to pay attention. "I mean, don't you want to be closer to your village?"

"But that's just it." She smiled broadly. "Mrs. Humphreys

was tellin' Mrs. Cary that now she's to get her husband's
share of his uncle's estate, she was going to buy a house
overlooking the sea at Southend. That's not far from my
village. I'd be able to go home every week when I had my
afternoon off."

"Southend's right nice," he murmured.

"She was ever so excited about it. She went on and on,
telling Mrs. Cary that she'd always loved the ocean and
that she had friends there."

"Why didn't she move there when her mister died?"
Wiggins asked. He'd no idea if this was a useful question,
but as it had slipped out of his mouth, he couldn't take it
back.

Maggie's brow furrowed in thought. "I don't think she
could. She's got a small income of her own. I know that
because I overheard her tellin' Mrs. Cary that's why she
wasn't stuck livin' at Humphreys House like Miss Ross
and Mrs. Prescott. But I don't think she had enough to do
what she really wanted, which is to buy a big house over-
lookin' the sea." She broke off and laughed. "It's funny,
isn't it. All your life you think the rich are different, that
they're better or smarter, but once you work for 'em, you
see they're just like the rest of us."

"What do you mean?"

"I mean Mrs. Humphreys was just as petty as old Lucy,
who used to run the little shop in our village. She was a
mean-spirited person, always thinking the worst of people
and makin' fun of 'em behind their backs. Mrs. Humphreys is just like that. Mr. Francis Humphreys was right
decent to her, he helped out by payin' for the repairs to the
windows on the side of her house, furnishin' her with coal
every time he got a delivery for himself and sendin' his
gardener down to keep the hedges trimmed and turn over
the flower beds every spring. But she never appreciated it."

"I thought you said she wasn't mean?" He gazed at her in confusion.

"She weren't mean to me or Minnie or Mrs. Cary, but she didn't like her husband's relations much, I can tell you that. She told Mrs. Cary that as soon as they got the old bastard buried, she'd be putting her house up for sale and hiring an estate agent to find her a place in Southend. Good riddance to crazy rubbish, that's what she said about him."

Michael Collier lived in a gray stone four-story house on Moreton Terrace in Pimlico.

The inspector and Constable Gates waited in the drawing room while the housekeeper went to announce their arrival.

"I wonder if Michael Collier owns this house or if he's just renting it?" Lionel commented as he gazed around the room. "I've seen that wallpaper in dozens of townhouses and those paintings aren't in very good condition. He's renting the place."

"I don't see how you can possibly ascertain such a thing." Witherspoon struggled to keep the irritation out of his tone. "The wallpaper is a nice cream and blue print and the paintings seem like decent enough landscapes. Perhaps your taste isn't the same as Mr. Collier's."

Witherspoon was at his wits' end. Constable Gates simply had no idea how to behave properly during an investigation. He'd gotten rid of the fellow for a while when he'd sent him to interview the Browns, but his respite had been short lived as Mr. Brown had apparently shown the constable the door and had mentioned he'd be in touch with Gates' superiors. It had been like this all day. At every turn Constable Gates was offering an opinion, making a comment, or being so obnoxious to witnesses they clamped their mouths shut and said as little as possible. He desperately missed Constable Barnes.

Both men turned as the door opened and Michael Collier stepped into the room. "You wished to speak to me?"

Lionel stepped forward. "We most certainly do."

Witherspoon raised his hand for silence. "Mr. Collier, I'm sorry to disturb you at what must be a very distressful time, but we do have a few more questions."

Collier nodded, took a chair, and gestured for them to sit down on the couch opposite him. "Of course there are questions. Poor Uncle Francis was murdered. Ask me whatever you like."

"Do you know of anyone who wished to harm your uncle?" Witherspoon sat down on the end of the couch as far away from Gates as he could get.

"There was a feud between Mr. Kirkland and Uncle Francis, but that had gone on for years."

"We know about that." Witherspoon glanced at Gates to make sure he was taking notes. "Was there anyone else who had reason to dislike your uncle?"

Collier smiled briefly. "The Board of Governors of the Great Western Railway Company weren't fond of him. He would send them nasty telegrams when the 3:09 to Bristol was late. Apparently, that happened quite often."

"Are you accusing the governors of the GWR of murder?" Lionel asked harshly.

Witherspoon closed his eyes for a brief moment. "Constable Gates, Mr. Collier didn't expect you to take him literally."

"Thank you, Inspector." Collier's expression was more amused than offended. "I hardly think they can be considered likely suspects. If they made it a habit to murder everyone who complained about their service, half of England would be dead."

Lionel flushed and looked down at his notebook.

Witherspoon said, "What time did you arrive for tea that afternoon?"

"I was a few minutes late," he replied. "I think I got there at about five past four. I remember being surprised that Uncle Francis wasn't downstairs with the rest of the party. He's very much a stickler for punctuality."

"Were you concerned when you realized he was late?" Witherspoon asked.

"Not really." Collier hesitated. "I suppose I'd better tell you the rest of it, you're bound to find out from someone and it might as well be me."

Lionel looked up sharply. "Hear what?"

"Constable Gates, please," Witherspoon admonished him softly. "Let Mr. Collier tell us at his own pace."

"I hadn't really been invited to tea, I mean, not by Uncle Francis. I knew the rest of the family was going to be there so I asked Miss Ross if I could come as well."

"Miss Ross was your uncle's hostess?" Witherspoon clarified. "I'm sorry, I had the distinct impression that it was Mrs. Prescott who was in charge of the social functions of the household."

"She is, but I knew Mrs. Prescott would have told me to stay away if I'd asked her. So I didn't. I asked Miss Ross."

"And she invited you?" Witherspoon nodded in understanding.

"Imogene is a very sweet person. She hasn't got a greedy bone in her body. She told me to go ahead and come along."

"Why wouldn't Mrs. Prescott want you there?" Lionel asked eagerly.

"She and I have had differences of opinions about several important matters," he replied. "And I knew she definitely wouldn't want me around when the others were all present. You see, I went there that day to solicit support from Uncle Francis' side of the family. All the cousins were there. I wanted to take legal action to have Uncle Francis declared unfit to administer my late aunt's estate."

"And Mrs. Prescott would have been against such a course of action," the inspector pressed.

"Absolutely." He laughed. "The last thing that she wanted was someone competent getting control of the estate. She had Uncle Francis right where she wanted, wrapped completely around her little finger."

CHAPTER 6

—◆—

"You're the last one back," Mrs. Goodge said to Wiggins as he rushed into the kitchen with Fred bouncing around his feet.

"Sorry, I didn't mean to be late." He tossed his jacket onto the coat tree and took his seat. "But it took longer to get back than I expected."

"I take it most of you had some success today," Mrs. Jeffries said as she began to pour the tea into cups.

"I didn't find out very much," Betsy complained. "I spent hours trying to find someone from Humphreys House and didn't have any luck."

"Neither did I," Wiggins exclaimed. "I finally left and went elsewhere."

"So did I," she replied. "I went to Pimlico, to see what I could learn about Michael Collier."

"We've not heard much about that gentleman." Mrs. Jeffries helped herself to a scone. "Were your inquiries successful?"

"My luck got a bit better there. I found out from one of the shopkeepers that Collier is behind in his bills and that last quarter he let his cook and one of the maids go because he couldn't pay their wages." Betsy felt guilty. She was sure she could have found out a lot more about Michael Collier if she'd stayed in Pimlico and kept asking questions. Instead, she'd taken a hansom to the East End, to her old neighborhood in Bethnal Green. Ever since she'd told Smythe about having her sister at the wedding, she'd not been able to get the idea out of her mind. There had to be a way to find Norah and still do her fair share on this case.

"Seems to me you learned a lot," Smythe said. Under the table, he grabbed her hand and gave it a squeeze.

"I hope to find out more tomorrow," she declared. "Did you have much luck today?"

"My day wasn't too bad," Smythe volunteered. "I'm not sure I found out anything we didn't already know. But at least we know that what we've been hearin' is true. My source confirmed that Francis Humphreys was goin' to sell his late wife's railway shares to raise cash. He really was goin' to buy into that Trans Andean Railway in South America. I found out a few bits and pieces about Pamela Humphreys as well." He continued with his report, but when he got to the part about her late husband being an inventor, Wiggins interrupted.

"I found out the same thing," he exclaimed. "But the fellow never made any money out of his contraptions."

"I'd not be too sure of that," Smythe countered. "Maybe he didn't make any money out of his gadgets, but accordin' to my source, his widow might be able to turn one of them into cash. Yancy Humphreys patented some device that is very similar to an invention a confectionary manufacturer is trying to patent. My source heard the two devices are so similar that she might be able to sue over the issue."

"Does the widow know she might have a case against the confectionary company?" Mrs. Jeffries asked.

Smythe shrugged. "I don't think so. My source said the manufacturer was advised to seek legal advice on the matter."

"Maybe that's why Francis Humphreys was murdered," Luty muttered. "Maybe someone was trying to get their paws on his nephew's inventions."

"If that were the case, madam, the killer should have murdered the widow, not the uncle," Hatchet pointed out.

"Not necessarily," she argued. "You don't know that the widow is the legal owner of them gadgets. Maybe Yancy Humphreys left them to his uncle, not his widow."

"That's not true," Wiggins interjected. "It's Mrs. Yancy Humphreys who got stuck with all his contraptions. She had a real row with Mrs. Prescott over 'em. Oh, sorry, Smythe, I didn't mean to speak out of turn. Finish what you were sayin'."

"I'm through." Smythe reached for a slice of buttered bread.

"If it's all the same to everyone," Mrs. Goodge said, "I'd like to go next." She waited for a moment, and when no one objected she continued. "I sent an old colleague of mine that works in Bristol a note asking about Miss Ross and I received her reply today. Lucky for us, there was quite a bit of gossip about the matter."

Wiggins helped himself to a scone. "Didn't Miss Ross tell the inspector she'd lost her position because the mistress of the house wanted to give her job to someone else?"

"She was lyin'," the cook said flatly. "My source has it on good authority she was let go because she was accused of thievery. Apparently, several pieces of jewelry and some silver had gone missin'. Supposedly, a pair of diamond earrings belongin' to the mistress of the household was found in Miss Ross' room."

"That doesn't mean she stole them," Betsy said defensively. She'd once been unjustly accused. "It wouldn't be the first time the mistress of a household has gotten jealous of a younger, prettier woman and done something vicious to ruin her reputation."

"That's exactly what I thought," the cook replied. "When you've spent as many years in service as I have, you learn that the servants are usually the last people in a household that do the thievin'. Most servants are too worried about losin' their positions to risk stealing. It's almost always a family member or a family friend that's doin' the deed."

"Did the family call the police?" Mrs. Jeffries asked. To some extent she agreed with the cook, but it certainly wasn't entirely unknown for a servant to pilfer or steal.

"They did not." Mrs. Goodge smiled smugly. "And the only reason they didn't want the police involved was because they didn't want a lot of questions bein' asked. If they really thought Miss Ross had stolen diamond earrings, they'd have had her arrested."

"But if Miss Ross was an innocent victim, why didn't she tell our inspector the truth?" Mrs. Jeffries asked.

"She might have been embarrassed," Betsy ventured. "Even if you're innocent, it's hard to admit that your employers fired you for something like that. Especially if you can't prove you didn't do it."

"She was frightened," Hatchet added. "There'd just been a murder in the house. If Miss Ross had told the truth, she might have feared she'd become the main suspect in her uncle's murder."

"But she was sitting in the drawing room with a dozen other people when he was killed," Wiggins reminded them. "So she couldn't have done it."

"She could if it was a conspiracy," Smythe said.

"But we've no evidence that it is," Mrs. Jeffries interjected quickly. "And we all know the dangers of too much speculation too early in the case." She didn't want them getting wedded to an idea and then going out and looking for the evidence to support what they already believed. "We must gather as much information as possible before we start making any assumptions. Now, who is next?"

"I'll go," Luty responded eagerly. "I had a little chat with a feller named Angus Fielding today. I got right lucky—not only was he Francis Humphreys' banker, but he was also a good friend of Humphreys' late wife, Estelle." Without mentioning that she'd loosened Fielding's tongue with liquor, she repeated everything he'd told her. "Francis Humphreys loved trains more than anything in the world," she concluded as she leaned back in her chair.

"Including his own wife," Hatchet said softly.

Luty grinned broadly. "But she had the last laugh on him." She repeated Angus' words. "He didn't get those railroad shares he really wanted. Leo Kirkland got the Atchison, Topeka and Santa Fe stock."

"She may have outsmarted him there, but she ended up giving his relatives almost as much as she left her own flesh and blood," Mrs. Goodge muttered. "Michael Collier only gets half an estate and the Humphreys' nieces and nephews get to divvy up the other half. That doesn't seem fair. Francis Humphreys didn't bring very much to the marriage."

"This is gettin' right confusin'." Wiggins frowned. "I think the inspector needs to speak to Humphreys' solicitor and find out exactly how Mrs. Humphreys' will was done up. Seems to me the whole thing is right strange."

Mrs. Jeffries regarded him curiously. "Why do you say that?" Wiggins was no fool. Francis Humphreys' estate was complicated but no more so than any of their other cases.

"Because I found out a bit about Mrs. Yancy Humphreys and she's gettin' her husband's share of Humphreys' estate. Now, seems to me that if Yancy Humphreys was dead and in the ground before his uncle died, wouldn't his share of the estate go to the other blood relations, not the widow?"

"That's generally what most families do," the housekeeper agreed. "But people have the right to will their property where they choose."

"Do you know for a fact that Pamela Humphreys is inheriting her late husband's share?" Hatchet asked. "Could your informant have been mistaken?"

"Maggie says that Mrs. Pamela Humphreys is happier than a pig in swill that Francis Humphreys is dead because now she can sell her house and move to Southend. She seemed pretty certain about what she was sayin'," Wiggins replied. "Pamela Humphreys inheritin' when she's not even blood just doesn't seem right," he concluded.

"No, it doesn't," the housekeeper agreed. "But I'm sure we'll find out the truth soon enough. It's standard procedure for the inspector to find out the terms of the will." But she made a mental note to put that particular flea in the inspector's ear, just in case he forgot.

"Seems like Pamela Humphreys is movin' pretty fast," Smythe muttered. "What's the 'urry? She's got to know her actions will set tongues waggin'."

"She probably doesn't care," Mrs. Goodge replied. "Sounds like she's sick to death of the Humphreys clan."

"You're right about that," Wiggins continued. "She had a right old row with Mrs. Prescott a week or so before the murder." He told them the rest of what he'd learned from the maid.

When he'd finished, Luty asked, "What's a bird scarer? Is it like a scarecrow?"

"It has the same function as a scarecrow," Hatchet explained, "but it works differently. Some of the more common ones are statues of hawks or cats, usually with colored glass for eyes so they'll catch the light and scare the birds off. Less common are the wheel-shaped ones with multiple spokes. Each arm of the wheel has a lightweight rattle on the end. They can make a goodly racket, but they aren't very efficient. They don't work unless there's a decent wind blowing."

"I've got it," Wiggins announced. "I think that Mrs. Prescott is in cahoots with the confectionary manufacturer. Why else would she make such a fuss about a bunch of old contraptions. Accordin' to Maggie, they've been sittin' up in his workroom for ages gatherin' dust and no one has cared about them."

The inspector arrived home earlier than usual that evening. Luckily, Luty and Hatchet had just gone and the household was going about their usual chores.

"You look very tired, sir," Mrs. Jeffries said as she took his hat.

"I am. It's been a very difficult day." He sighed deeply and then snatched back the bowler she'd just hung up. "I'm going to take Fred for a walk. We could both use some fresh air and exercise. How long will it be before dinner?"

"Mrs. Goodge has made a lovely lamb stew," she replied. "It's in the warming oven so you can eat whenever you like."

"Excellent." He grinned like a schoolboy and dashed toward the back stairs. "Fred, Fred, come on old fellow, let's go walkies," he cried as he charged down to the kitchen.

Drat, Mrs. Jeffries thought. She'd hoped he might want a sherry before dinner. He was always just a tad more talkative over a glass of Harveys. As it turned out, when he came back he did want his sherry and insisted Mrs. Jeffries have one as well.

"Is the case progressing favorably, sir?" she asked as she handed him his glass. She sat down on the settee.

"Not as well as I'd like," Witherspoon admitted. "It's very difficult working with a new person. I don't wish to cast aspersions at Constable Gates—I'm sure he's doing the best he can—but he's very aggressive. It's most disconcerting. Mind you, I did have a bit of a respite this afternoon, I sent the lad off to interview the neighbors, Mr. and Mrs. Brown. Of all the guests that were there that day, they seemed to have no reason whatsoever for wanting Mr. Humphreys dead." He grinned mischievously. "Then at the end of the day, after we'd interviewed Michael Collier, I sent him to see Joseph Humphreys' landlady in Marylebone. I told him we really needed to confirm his assertion that he was turned out of his lodging because he couldn't pay his rent."

"Very clever of you, sir." She took a quick sip from her glass. "I suppose you'll be speaking to the victim's solicitor soon?"

"I've an appointment to see him tomorrow," he replied. "I should have spoken to him earlier, but honestly, it's taken a long time just getting statements from all the people who were in the house. As I told you, we spoke to Michael Collier today and he had plenty to say."

"Really, sir?"

"Oh yes, apparently, he'd not been invited to tea that day by Mr. Humphreys. He'd asked Miss Ross if he could come along." He told her about his interview with Collier.

When he'd finished, Mrs. Jeffries laughed softly. "I agree with you, sir," she said. "I don't see the Board of Directors of the Great Western Railway as murderers."

"Neither did Mr. Collier." Witherspoon smiled. "I don't quite know what to make of all this. Collier admitted he went to the house that afternoon to speak to the other relatives in order to gain their support to have their uncle declared incompetent. But I don't see how he could possibly have thought he was going to be successful in such an endeavor. Francis Humphreys was eccentric, but so far I've seen no evidence he was incompetent."

"But what about wanting to sell his late wife's shares and invest in that railway in South America," she pointed out. "That could be considered a very risky venture."

"But lots of people take risks with their money. That merely makes them foolish, not incapable." He downed the rest of his sherry. "Of course the oddest part was his assertion that Annabelle Prescott hadn't wanted him there in the first place because she controlled her uncle. None of the other witnesses we've spoken to have even so much as hinted at something like that."

"Perhaps the others were being discreet," she suggested. "Or perhaps they didn't see it that way. I believe the funeral is tomorrow morning, isn't it?"

"Yes, that's correct."

"Well, as soon as the poor man's been laid to rest, perhaps it would be a good idea to have another word with the servants." She broke off and forced a laugh. "Oh silly me, that's exactly what you were planning to do, isn't it?"

He blinked in surprise. "That's my idea precisely. Mind you, I intend to speak to the relatives again as well. As I always say, once the dearly departed is in the ground, people are often less sentimental about them."

"Of course sir," she answered. He'd never said such a thing in his life, but she knew he had strong doubts about his own abilities as a detective. She and the rest of the household had gotten in the habit of bolstering his confidence whenever possible.

"I was able to have a word with Mrs. Prescott and Miss Ross today as well," he said. "They both confirmed that they'd merely forgotten to mention Mr. Joseph Humphreys had moved into the house. And then, of course, there's the matter of the guns."

"Guns?"

"Yes, apparently Francis Humphreys had given the young men in the family Enfield revolvers," he replied. "Goodness, all of a sudden, I'm very hungry."

"I'll bring the stew right up, sir." She got to her feet and hurried to the door.

She went to the kitchen, got his dinner, and was back upstairs in short order. She kept up a quiet but steady barrage of questions as she served him and waited patiently as he chewed before pressing for an answer. He'd told her about the disappearance of Joseph Humphreys' revolver and had moved on to Michael Collier when they were interrupted by a loud knock on the front door.

"Were you expecting anyone, sir?" Mrs. Jeffries half rose as she heard a murmur of voices in the front hall. A moment later, they heard footsteps.

Witherspoon stared at the open doorway with a puzzled expression. "No."

Betsy appeared. "Constable Gates is here to see you, sir," she announced. Gates was right on her heels.

"Gracious, Constable," Witherspoon exclaimed. "Has there been progress on the case? Has someone confessed?"

Lionel dodged around Betsy. "No sir, I just thought you'd like to hear my report firsthand." His gaze fastened onto Witherspoon's dinner plate and his eyes brightened.

"What report?" Witherspoon asked.

"From Mr. Joseph Humphreys' landlady," he said, still watching the inspector's food.

"You didn't need to come all the way over here to give me an update. That could have waited until tomorrow." Witherspoon's voice trailed off as he saw Gates staring at the lamb stew.

Mrs. Jeffries looked at the inspector's face and silently prayed that for once in his life he wouldn't be kind or polite.

"Would you care for some supper, Constable?" the inspector asked. He glanced at the housekeeper. "There's plenty, isn't there?"

"Of course, sir," she replied tightly. She wanted to kill Lionel Gates. The fool was ruining her chances to find out about Collier's gun.

"I don't want to be any trouble, sir," Lionel said quickly. "But it does look ever so tasty."

"Take a seat, lad," Witherspoon said kindly.

Mrs. Jeffries wanted to scream in frustration but instead she smiled politely. "I'll just nip downstairs and get another plate."

When she reached the kitchen, the others looked at her expectantly. Betsy had told them that Gates had shown up at the front door.

"I need another plate. The inspector is feeding the little sod," she muttered darkly.

"He's the manners of a pig," the cook snapped. "It was bad enough that he got Constable Barnes exiled to Fulham, now we've got to feed the pup dinner as well."

"We've no choice." Mrs. Jeffries went to the sideboard and took down what she needed. Betsy handed her a serviette and the cutlery and then she rushed to the back stairs. Everyone knew she didn't care if Gates got his dinner, but she was concerned she'd miss something important if she didn't get back quickly.

"Shall I serve, sir?" she asked as she came back into the dining room. She paused long enough to put down the cutlery and the serviette next to the unwelcome guest.

"Thank you, Mrs. Jeffries." Witherspoon nodded graciously.

She lifted the silver warming lid off the stew, ladled the

smallest amount she dared onto Gates' plate, and shoved it in front of him. "Will there be anything else, sir?" she asked.

"No, that'll be all," the inspector replied.

Mrs. Jeffries left the dining room, closed the door behind her, and then stomped down the hallway, making sure the occupants inside the room could hear her footsteps. Then, of course, she tiptoed back and put her ear up against the wood.

From inside, all she heard was the soft murmur of voices and the clank of silver against china. Drat, she thought. Gates was more interested in stuffing food into his mouth than in telling the inspector anything useful. After a few moments, she heard Lionel say, "Mr. Joseph Humphreys' landlady wasn't very forthcoming. I had to get very stern with her."

"What do you mean, 'stern,'" Witherspoon demanded. "You didn't bully the woman, did you?"

Mrs. Jeffries smiled.

"Of course not," Lionel stammered. "I merely pointed out that this was a criminal investigation and it was her duty to answer my questions. There was no bullying, Inspector. I was stern but very polite."

Mrs. Jeffries snorted silently. She didn't believe him for a moment. He was just like his odious uncle, an overbearing little man who had an exaggerated sense of both his abilities and his importance to the world.

"Did the landlady confirm Mr. Humphreys' account?" Witherspoon asked.

"Indeed, sir. On the day of the murder, Mr. Joseph Humphreys and his belongings were picked up by a four-wheeler. But what Mr. Joseph Humphreys neglected to mention was that his uncle paid off his back rent. I think it significant that Joseph Humphreys didn't tell us that particular fact, don't you, sir?"

Mrs. Jeffries strained to hear, but she couldn't quite catch the inspector's answer.

Mrs. Jeffries stared out the window of her room toward the gaslight across the road. This was one of the most frustrating cases they'd ever had and every day, something else seemed to go wrong. By the time Constable Gates had finally finished eating it was so late the inspector had gone right up to his room as soon as the man had left the house. She'd not had a chance to find out any additional details of his day.

She took a deep breath, sat down in the chair, and focused her gaze on the pale light of the lamp. The room was dark and she was comfortably dressed in her nightclothes and a heavy, wool dressing gown. She wanted to give her mind a chance to wander freely over the bits and pieces they'd learned thus far. She was under no illusions that she'd form any workable theories or come to any useful conclusions, but in the past she'd found that relaxing and thinking of nothing often pointed her in the right directions. Her vision blurred gently as she kept her gaze on the feeble glow of the streetlamp. Francis Humphreys loved trains more than anything, including, it seemed, his entire family. Yet he believed in fulfilling his obligations to his relatives, even to the point of keeping a roof over some of their heads and putting food on their tables. But he made them dance to his tune. She blinked and the lamp came back into sharp focus. She wondered how much those that depended on him resented the dependence. Annabelle Prescott acted as his hostess and according to Michael Collier had her uncle under her thumb. But none of the servants or the other family members had said anything of the sort.

Imogene Ross appeared to value her independence, so much so that she was willing to risk losing the allowance

Francis Humphreys doled out each quarter. She wondered how far Miss Ross might be prepared to go to stay self-sufficient? Imogene was the youngest of the cousins and according to Witherspoon she was attractive. She'd worked for her own living for years. Perhaps she'd met someone who wanted to help her keep her freedom without having to be at the beck and call of an elderly relative. Someone who'd be willing to kill for her. After all, she'd had a screaming row with her uncle earlier that day—perhaps that had been the straw that broke the camel's back. She had left to go into town at approximately the same time as Joseph Humphreys had arrived. An unlocked gun case, an angry woman with a friend from her past. How easy would it have been to nip into Joseph's room, steal the gun, meet her accomplice, and arrange for a door or window to be unlocked?

Mrs. Jeffries caught herself. Good gracious, she was doing exactly what she'd told the others they mustn't do. Finding a theory to fit the few facts they had thus far. She shook her head, stood up, and took off her robe. There was absolutely no evidence that Imogene Ross had anything to do with her uncle's murder. Nevertheless, as she climbed into bed, a small voice in the back of her mind reminded her that of all the family, Miss Ross did have both motive and opportunity to set the events of the day in motion.

"I didn't think that Constable Gates was ever goin' to leave last night," Wiggins complained as he took his spot at the table. "Cor blimey, he was in the dining room till almost half past eight. He must have talked the inspector's ear off."

"Humph." Mrs. Goodge snorted delicately. "He certainly made himself at home when it came to eating. There wasn't so much as a spoonful of stew left when Mrs. Jeffries brought the tray downstairs and I know the inspector never overindulges."

Mrs. Jeffries poured herself a cup of tea. "He did give the inspector some information. He verified Joseph Humphreys' account of his movements that day."

"And it took him the better part of the evening to do it," the cook shot back. "There's seven of us at our meetings and it never takes us that long to tell what's what. I think the man was just takin' advantage of the situation so he could make a pig of himself."

"One can hardly blame him for that." Hatchet grinned broadly. "Your food is always superb. You are a wonderful cook."

"Why thank you, Hatchet." Mrs. Goodge beamed proudly. "But I still think the man is a menace. Still, enough of my carping. Let's let Mrs. Jeffries tell us everything she found out from the inspector before Constable Gates arrived and ruined everyone's evening."

Mrs. Jeffries repeated what she'd heard from Witherspoon. She took her time, making sure she mentioned every detail. She had just finished her recitation when she was interrupted by a loud knock on the back door. "Perhaps that's Constable Barnes," she said as Wiggins got up and sped down the hallway.

"It better be the constable. I can't talk to my sources with you lot sittin' here," the cook said.

"Cor blimey, you're a sight for sore eyes." Wiggins' voice rose in excitement. "The others will be ever so pleased to see you. Come on inside, we're just having our morning meeting."

They heard a soft murmur in reply and a moment later, the footman burst into the kitchen. He was followed by a smiling woman of late middle age. She was slender, blonde, blue eyed, and wore a pearl gray dress with black lace around the collar and cuffs. "Look who I found," he said cheerfully. "It's Lady Cannonberry."

Lady Cannonberry, or Ruth, as she was known to the

household, lived at the other end of the communal garden. She and the inspector were very "special" friends, but their relationship kept getting interrupted by her late husband's relatives. They were old, lonely, and prone to every ailment under the sun. They constantly demanded Ruth come and nurse them through one imaginary illness after another. "I'm so sorry to barge in like this," Ruth said. "But I didn't want to miss the morning meeting."

"Don't apologize," Mrs. Jeffries scolded. "You know you're always welcome, regardless of the time. Do sit down and have tea. You haven't missed much; we've only just started."

"How did you know we had a case?" Hatchet asked.

She laughed and slipped into the empty spot next to Wiggins. "The news of the Humphreys' murder is in all the papers. I was sure Gerald was going to head the investigation because they always seem to stick him with the wicked ones. So I came back last night."

Ruth Cannonberry was the widow of a peer of the realm. But she'd been raised the daughter of a country vicar and had taken the admonition to love her neighbor quite seriously. She possessed a strong social conscience, an affinity for radical politics—especially when it came to giving women the vote—and a serious dislike of the British class system. She was the one who insisted that everyone in the Witherspoon household call her by her Christian name, except, of course, in front of the inspector. Ruth was very sensitive to the feelings of others and she knew the staff would be uncomfortable addressing her in such a manner in front of their employer. She had helped them on a number of the inspector's cases and, like the others, made sure that "dear Gerald" was completely in the dark about the extent of her or their assistance.

"What about your aunt Maude," Wiggins asked. "Did she get better then?"

"There wasn't anything wrong with the woman in the first place," Ruth retorted. "She was simply bored and out of sorts. I told her she'd feel much better about life if she spent her time helping others rather than lying about in a daybed worrying about her health. She didn't appreciate my advice and she's annoyed with me for leaving so quickly. But I wanted to get back so I could help."

"That's very good of you, Ruth," Mrs. Jeffries said. "As soon as the others have gone, I'll give you a complete report on what we know so far."

"That would be wonderful, but I've not much time this morning," Ruth answered. "That's why I was adamant about getting here before you all left. I can help with the case."

"Gracious, you're full of surprises," Mrs. Jeffries said.

"You're all wondering how I could possibly have anything useful to contribute when I've no idea who your suspects might be," she began. "But Aunt Maude knew Francis Humphreys. He was at Eton with her brother and often came to the house to visit. She's not seen him in many years but she was very upset when she found out he'd been murdered."

"Murder is upsettin', especially when it's someone you know," Smythe said softly. "Did she know anythin' about who might want to kill 'im?"

"Unfortunately, no. She kept insisting he had no enemies. I told her he must have had at least one as someone had shot the poor man." Ruth shook her head. "She did ask me to go to his funeral on her behalf."

"But it's this morning." Mrs. Jeffries glanced at the clock. "It's already half past eight."

"The funeral isn't until ten thirty." Ruth took a sip from

her cup. "And I'm already dressed so I've plenty of time. Which brings me for my reason for getting here so early: Is there anyone I ought to keep my eye on?" She looked around expectantly. "You know, one of your suspects. Someone you think might have done it."

No one said anything for a long moment. Then Luty laughed. "We're a sorry bunch, ain't we. You're goin' to have to keep your eyes on everyone and keep your ears open, too," she said to Ruth. "So far, we ain't got any idea who might've done the deed."

"Oh dear." Ruth looked very disappointed.

"Even worse, we're beginnin' to think this murder might've been a conspiracy," Wiggins added cheerfully. "And you know 'ow 'ard conspiracies is to solve. Cor blimey, remember the last one? It took forever before Mrs. Jeffries sussed it all out."

The offices of Roberts, Richter & Spinney, Solicitors, was located on the second floor of a commercial building on the Strand. Witherspoon stepped into the room and then stopped, blinking in surprise. There were four clerks' desks, but only one of them was occupied. The room reeked of neglect. The books on the shelves along the walls were dusty; boxes, files, and papers were stacked on the three unoccupied desktops and the two windows facing the street looked as if they hadn't been cleaned in years.

A middle-aged man wearing a pair of spectacles rose to his feet as they entered. "Good day, I'm Mr. Roberts' clerk. He instructed me to take you right in to him when you arrived. His office is over here." He gestured for them to follow and then hurried to a door on the left side of the room. He knocked once and stuck his head inside. "The police are here," he announced.

"Thank you," Witherspoon said as he stepped past the man and into the office.

"Come in, come in." A tall, white-haired man with a huge mustache, bony face, and watery gray eyes waved them forward. "Your man can take the chair by the door. You come sit here." He pointed to a spot just in front of his desk.

"Does he want me to sit here?" Lionel glanced at the uncomfortable-looking straight-backed wooden chair. "But there's a perfectly decent seat right next to yours."

"We're in his office, Constable, and we'll sit where we're told," Witherspoon retorted quietly. He started toward the elderly man. "Good day, sir. I'm Inspector Gerald Witherspoon and this is—"

"I know who you are." The man grinned and pointed to the constable. "And I don't care who he is."

"Well, really," Lionel muttered as he flopped down.

"I'm Eldon Roberts." He rose up and extended his hand to the inspector. "Have a seat and I'll tell you what I know about poor old Francis."

Witherspoon shook hands, took off his bowler, and sat down in the chair opposite the solicitor. "Thank you, sir, we'd appreciate any help you can give us."

"I've no idea whether my information will be useful or not—that's for you to say," he told them. "But I am all ready for you." He flipped open a folder that was on his desk. "I'm the last of them, you see. Just me and Gideon. He's my clerk. The others are all dead, and now that Francis is gone, I expect as soon as the estate is settled, I'll be gone as well."

"You're shutting your firm, sir?" Witherspoon asked politely. That explained the air of neglect and the empty desks.

Roberts laughed. "Humphreys was our last client. I would have retired, but his shenanigans were just enough to keep Gideon and I coming into the office a few days a week." He reached into his desk and pulled out a silver flask.

"Gideon," he suddenly shouted at the top of his lungs. "Bring us a couple of glasses and this time, blow the ruddy dust off of them."

Alarmed, Witherspoon started and then sank back onto his seat. "There's no need for a glass for me, sir. I'm on duty. Though your offer of hospitality is much appreciated."

"Hum . . . really? You don't want a nip? It's bloody good whisky." He shrugged. "Gideon," he screamed again. "Don't bother with the glasses." He saluted the inspector with his flask. "I'll just drink straight out of this. Now, what would you like to know about poor old Francis?"

Witherspoon took a deep, calming breath. "Who inherits the estate?"

Roberts tipped back the flask and took a drink before he replied. "That's a very interesting question. You see, it's all rather complex."

The inspector's heart sank. Why were his cases always so complicated? Why couldn't it have been just a straightforward will and testament? But he knew it wasn't going to be, he knew that as surely as he knew his own name. "Complex in what way?"

"To begin with, most of the estate didn't belong to Francis Humphreys. It belonged to his late wife." He took another quick nip. "The only thing he actually owned was some land, and considering that, I'm quite proud of the concessions we did manage to get out of those American lawyers of hers."

From behind him, he heard Constable Gates clear his throat. "I'm a bit confused, if Mr. Humphreys had no money, what was his source of income? How did he live? That house is nice and modern, but it must cost a fortune to maintain."

"It does." Roberts yawned. "But Francis Humphreys was a rich man; he could well afford to maintain it properly. Estelle Collier Humphreys was a wealthy American heiress. When she married Francis, her family insisted on certain terms before they would give their blessing to the union. Mainly, that her estate was to be entailed with certain terms and conditions, as it were. Because she brought far more assets to the marriage, her family wanted to ensure that in the event there was no offspring and let's face it, when you and your husband are both in your forties when you marry, there's a fair chance there won't be any offspring, that upon Francis' death, at least half of the estate was to pass to her heirs."

"But that's madness," Lionel cried. "A woman's money ought to go to her husband."

"It did," Roberts snapped. "Francis had full control of the estate while he was alive, but when he died half of it was to go to her heirs. Namely, one Mr. Michael Collier. He's the son of Estelle Collier's older brother and her only living relative. Her lawyers were good, but we were pretty smart ourselves." He smiled proudly. "Remember, Francis brought very little to the table. He's lived a damned good life on her money all these years."

"So he had complete control of the estate?" Witherspoon wanted to be sure he understood properly. "He could buy and sell her assets and invest them as he saw fit?"

"He could," Roberts confirmed.

"And that includes buying a railway in South America?" Lionel asked loudly.

"He could do what he liked as long as a court didn't declare him unfit to see to his own affairs." Roberts took another nip from the flask. "We also made sure he got ownership of the house as long as he was alive. That was only fair. As I said, Francis had some money of his own, he'd already bought the land in Acton, and when the house was built he induced her to add a codicil to her will giving him ownership outright in the event of her death."

"Who gets it now that he's dead?" Constable Gates asked. He had to raise his voice to make himself heard.

"His niece, Annabelle Prescott." Roberts chuckled. "He added a codicil to his will when she moved in leaving her the house outright. He wanted to ensure she always had a home. The rest of the estate is split down the middle. His wife's heirs get half and his heirs get half."

"And if his heirs are deceased?" Witherspoon continued. He was thinking about the gossip he'd heard about Pamela Bowden Humphreys moving house to Southend.

Roberts laughed again and took another swig. "You're thinking of Yancy Humphreys' widow? That was a mistake on our part. I suspect if the rest of the Humphreys clan realizes we made such an error in how those clauses were worded, they will sue us. Originally, the language was put into the will to protect the rights of any children the Humphreys side managed to produce, but, unfortunately, we made a bit of a mistake in the precise phrasing of that particular paragraph and Yancy's shares will pass to his widow. That family is exceedingly unlucky when it comes to offspring. So Mrs. Yancy Humphreys is going to get a real windfall."

"Was there anything else odd about the estate?" Witherspoon asked.

"When Estelle Humphreys died, she left some of her railway shares to an old friend. Francis was furious. He wanted them for himself and wanted to have that part of the will declared invalid." Roberts laughed again. "I told him that if he tried that, he risked having the entire will invalidated and he'd lose it all. It wasn't worth losing thousands of pounds just for a few shares of the Atchison, Topeka and Santa Fe Railroad. For God's sake, man, I told him, if you want the ruddy railway shares, buy some of your own. For once, the fool actually listened to me. Besides, he'd no grounds for legal action. Estelle Collier Humphreys was of sound mind when that will was done."

"Who got the shares?" Witherspoon asked.

"An old friend of hers, a man by the name of Leo Kirkland. He was delighted to receive the legacy."

"Did the heirs know about the terms of the will?" The inspector thought that a very good question.

"Of course. Francis told them. He was a peculiar man, but he had a real sense of family. He took in his niece when her husband died suddenly and left her penniless, and from what I understand he's taken in more of his relatives. He made no secret of the fact that they'd all be getting quite a lot of money when he died." He sobered and shook his head. "I told him he ought to keep his own counsel on such matters. It never comes to any good when you raise people's expectations."

Witherspoon came to attention. "You were afraid someone was going to kill him?"

Roberts thought for a moment before answering. "I don't know that I expected anyone to try and kill him. But I wasn't surprised when I heard he'd been shot. When you've done as many wills as I have, when you've seen family after family torn apart by greed and arrogance, by a sense of entitlement that they're 'owed' something by an elderly relative, then nothing really surprises you when it actually happens. Mind you, I don't think anyone would have done it if it hadn't been for this latest idea of his."

"And what was that?" Witherspoon already knew the answer, but he wanted to see how widespread the rumor about Humphreys' intentions had become.

"Francis was going to sell off all of his American railway stock and use the money to invest in a Trans Andean line in South America."

"And you think it wouldn't be successful?" Witherspoon asked.

"Oh no, I've a feeling that a project such as this could be very lucrative." Roberts smiled ruefully. "But then, I'm an intelligent man. People everywhere need transportation and getting in at the beginning of a new enterprise has made a number of fortunes. Unfortunately for Francis, most of his relatives are complete fools, and one of those fools actually managed to figure out a way to murder the poor devil."

CHAPTER 7

———

"Alright, alright, give a body a bit of time. I'm coming as fast as I can," Mrs. Goodge yelled as she hurried down the hallway. The trouble with everyone being out on the hunt meant that she had to answer the ruddy door herself. Normally, she'd never complain, but her rheumatism was acting up and her knee hurt something fierce.

She flung open the door and her jaw dropped in surprise. "Gracious, it's you," she said to the tall, gray-haired woman who stood there.

Mollie Dubay, housekeeper to Lord Augustus Fremont, smiled tentatively. "Hello, Mrs. Goodge. How are you?"

"I'm well, thank you," Mrs. Goodge stammered. Oh drat, she thought, what am I going to do now? Her cousin Hilda's boy, Owen, was due here any time and she'd planned on seeing what she could get out of him. The lad worked as a footman in Mayfair and was one of the nosiest people on the face of the earth—in other words, a perfect source. She stared at her unwelcome guest for a brief moment and saw that despite Mollie's brave smile, her face was pale and there was a hint of fear in her deep-set blue eyes.

It wouldn't hurt to invite the woman in for a quick cup of tea. She'd no idea what Mollie might want; they'd not seen or spoken to one another in years. She could always get rid of her when Owen arrived. "Do come in, Mollie."

"Thank you." Mollie stepped past her into the house. "I'm glad to find you still here and I do apologize for just dropping in unannounced. I don't generally indulge in that sort of common behavior."

"Your manners have always been excellent," Mrs. Goodge agreed as she fell into step behind her. "But announced or not, you're always welcome here."

Mollie hesitated at the entrance to the kitchen, her gaze locked on Fred who'd gotten up from his rug and was now wagging his tail in welcome.

"Just ignore the dog." Mrs. Goodge shoved her gently across the threshold. "He'll not hurt you. Go over to the table and take a seat." Fred settled back down to his nap.

Mollie stared at the table as she pulled off her gloves. A plate of damson tarts and two place settings complete with serviettes were already laid out. "Oh dear, I'm interrupting," she cried. "I'm intruding, I'd better leave."

"Don't be silly," the cook retorted. She'd heard the tremor in Mollie's voice. "You must stay and have tea."

"But you've got company coming," Mollie protested feebly.

Mrs. Goodge turned and put the kettle on the cooker. "It's only my cousin Hilda's boy comin' for a visit. You sit down and make yourself comfortable. I can see you've got trouble. Your eyes are red and you look pale." Maybe Owen would be late, she thought hopefully, then immediately felt guilty as she heard Mollie sniffle. But drat, Owen might know something. Mollie was a gossip herself, but she worked for a household of much higher status than Francis Humphreys and his ilk.

Mrs. Goodge heard the chair creak as Mollie sat down. "I've been sacked," she said, her voice barely above a whisper.

"Sacked?" She whirled around and saw Mollie staring off into space, her face a mask of misery.

"I've lost my job." Mollie looked at her, her expression confused. "I can hardly believe it. It's been a terrible shock."

"Lord Fremont let you go?" Mrs. Goodge demanded. "But why? You're a wonderful housekeeper. You work hard. You've been there for ages."

"He said I was getting too old." Mollie's lower lip trembled. "He said he needed a younger person to do the job. God, when I think of all the years I've given that ungrateful family, it's not fair. Where am I to go? What am I to do?"

Mrs. Goodge regarded her sympathetically. She knew exactly how Mollie felt, having once been in the exact same position. "Don't you have family you can go to?" The kettle boiled and she picked up a tea towel, grabbed the handle, and poured the boiling water into the waiting pot.

"Family?" Mollie snorted. "How many of us in service ever had the chance to have a family? Things were different when we were young. Back then, if you were caught with a young man, you'd lose your position. You remember how it was. It's not like today. We had no freedom. We had to do what we were told and then look what happens, you spend your life serving others and when you get old and gray, they toss you out into the streets."

"I remember what it was like," Mrs. Goodge agreed. "But when I asked if you had family you could go to, I meant a brother or a sister, someone like that." She glanced at the clock, hoping that Owen wouldn't show up now.

Mollie would be so humiliated if anyone else saw her like this.

"If we so much as even looked at a young man, we'd get reprimanded." Mollie continued her tirade. "Remember the time that Oswald Simmons—he was the first undergardener at Lord Fremont's country house—brought me a bouquet of wildflowers? Remember what happened? I got sent back to town two weeks early and he lost his position. My God, the way we were treated was terrible, absolutely terrible."

"It's changed quite a bit in recent years," the cook murmured. She poured a big mug of tea, added sugar and milk, then took it and placed it on the table in front of Mollie. "Here, drink this. I've put extra sugar in it and it'll do you good."

"Thank you." Mollie pulled a handkerchief out of her sleeve as tears spilled down her cheeks. She dabbed at her eyes. "Oh Lord, Mrs. Goodge. I didn't mean to come here, when Lady Fremont told me the news this morning, I just left the house and started walking. I'm so sorry. I've no right to come barging in on you, but when I found myself on this street, I remembered you were so kind to me the time I was here before. You made me a seedcake and even opened a bottle of Harveys."

Mrs. Goodge could barely recall the time she'd invited Mollie to tea, but she did remember she'd only extended the invitation to get information for one of the inspector's earlier cases. Regardless of Owen's impending visit and the other sources she was expecting today, she couldn't shove poor Mollie out the door, not now. That wouldn't be right. "The Lord must have sent you here for a reason," the cook said firmly. "Now drink up while we think what to do."

Luckily, Owen didn't appear and for the next half hour, the two women discussed the situation. Mollie had a substantial bit of money saved, had always wanted to live by the sea, and wasn't opposed to buying a small house and taking in lodgers. "So if you've money and already had an idea about what you wanted to do when you left service, why were you so upset when you were let go?" Mrs. Goodge asked. "After all, let's face it Mollie, neither of us is young anymore."

"It was being sacked that bothered me." Mollie pursed her lips. "Do you know how humiliating it was to be called into the morning room and told your services are no longer needed? How dare they? I know I've bragged about working for Lord and Lady Fremont, but the truth is, he's a nasty old lech, she's a tyrant, and their children are blithering half-wits, especially the oldest son."

"Then why did you stay?" Mrs. Goodge wasn't in the least surprised by these revelations. She'd had enough experiences with the upper classes herself to know their characters were no better or worse than anyone else.

"I was used to the place." Mollie shrugged. "I suppose I was afraid that if I'd gone anywhere else, it might have been even worse."

"I understand what you mean. You never really know about a house until you're working there, and by then, if you've made a mistake, you're stuck until you can find somewhere else."

"I was thinking of giving notice this summer, anyway. With a small house and a lodger or two, I could make ends meet well enough. At my age, getting sacked isn't the end of the world. It's not as if I had any pressing plans for the future." Mollie smiled suddenly. "You always did have an uncommon amount of good sense. I'm glad I found myself here—you were just what I needed."

Mrs. Goodge inclined her head in acknowledgment of the compliment and pushed the tray of damson tarts toward her guest. "Would you like another one?"

"Lovely, thank you." She helped herself. "Goodness, Mrs. Goodge, you've been so very helpful to me. I feel so much better now. I wish there was something I could do for you."

"I don't suppose you know anything about Francis Humphreys?"

"Who?" Mollie asked.

"Francis Humphreys, the man who was murdered a couple of days ago. My inspector has got the case and I'm always listenin' for any little morsels of gossip I can pass on to him," she explained. She was wasting her breath. Acton and Mayfair were worlds apart.

"You mean Estelle Collier Humphreys' husband." Mollie nodded eagerly. "But I know all sorts of things about that family. They had a huge flat just around the corner from the Fremonts'. At least they did until the husband drug her off to the outskirts of town." She paused and cocked her head to one side. "Why goodness, I do believe the husband's name was Francis. Funny, I read about the murder in the paper, but I didn't put two and two together and recall it was Estelle Collier's husband that had been shot."

Mrs. Goodge couldn't believe her luck. "They lived around the corner?" she prompted. She knew it didn't take much to get Mollie's tongue moving.

"Oh yes. They used to have the most wonderful parties." Mollie grinned. "It used to annoy Lord Fremont. But I expect his nose was out of joint because he was never invited. He kept referring to her as 'that upstart American woman.' Estelle Collier was an heiress, you know."

Mrs. Goodge nodded eagerly as dozens of questions raced around her head. "When did the Humphreys move to Acton?"

Mollie's long face creased in a frown. "I'm not sure; I think it was a few years before Mrs. Humphreys passed away. She died of pneumonia, you know, and there was some awful talk about the circumstances. Even though they'd moved house, we heard about it in Mayfair."

"What kind of talk?" Mrs. Goodge leaned forward.

"Supposedly, when she became ill, she was expected to recover." Mollie dropped her voice dramatically. "From what I understand, her husband became ill as well so he sent for one of their nieces to come and nurse them both. But he recovered, and she was thought to have been on the mend as well when all of a sudden she took a turn for the worse and died."

Confused, Mrs. Goodge frowned. "But why would that cause talk? Pneumonia is a dreadful disease. Lots of people die from it."

Mollie smiled slowly. "Yes, but it killed poor Mrs. Humphreys right after she told her husband that some money had gone missing. She was insisting he bring the police in to investigate. The next day, she was dead."

"How on earth did that story get out? I mean, did someone else in the household overhear this conversation?" Mrs. Goodge wanted to make sure this story wasn't the product of an overactive imagination.

"Yes indeed," Mollie declared. "Her maid heard the whole thing. Mind you, as soon as the poor woman was buried, the girl was let go. Mr. Humphreys said that now the mistress was gone, the household didn't need a lady's maid and the niece had scampered off somewhere, so she didn't need one, either."

"Do you happen to recall what the niece's name was?" Mrs. Goodge asked.

Mollie thought for a moment. "No, I don't think I ever heard it said. Still, it doesn't seem right that a young maid should lose her position simply because the mistress of the house dies. Lucky for the girl, the Chalmers household needed a scullery maid. Mind you, I'm sure that was a bit of comedown for the girl, but sometimes we all take positions that are beneath our training. Still, Francis Humphreys should have kept her on as a housemaid. I expect that's one of the reasons the story got spread about so quickly. People ought to be careful when they sack the help. We've got ears, you know, and there's lots we could say about a household if we've a mind to." She snorted angrily. "Believe me, I'll not hold my tongue if anyone asks about the Fremont household. There's plenty I can say about that miserable family."

"I'm so delighted you could come on such short notice." Ruth poured a cup of tea from the silver pot. "It's been ages since we've seen one another." She silently congratulated herself on having the foresight before she went to Humphreys' funeral to send Marisol Pulman, one of London's most notorious gossips, an invitation to tea. She'd learned absolutely nothing at the funeral, and when she'd introduced herself to the family she'd not been invited back to the house for the reception.

Marisol laughed softly. She was a short, fat woman with sparse reddish hair pulled back in a twist on the nape of her neck. Her face was as round as a full moon and her eyes were a lovely cornflower blue. Her ample figure was swathed in a teal blue day dress with blue and gray checkered overskirt. She wore a sapphire ring the size of a lima bean on one hand and a square-cut emerald on the other. "I had nothing to do this afternoon," she admitted as she reached for an éclair. "I was glad to get your note. Are you still keeping company with that police detective?"

They were seated in the small morning room. A fire was blazing in the hearth and on the table were sandwiches, éclairs, sliced bread, and pots of jam.

"We're still very good friends," Ruth said. One of the reasons Marisol wasn't particularly well liked was that she said whatever happened to pop into her head. Discretion wasn't one of her strong suits. "As a matter of fact, I was wondering if you knew anything about Francis Humphreys. I was at the poor man's funeral this morning."

"He's the one that was just murdered."

"Yes."

Marisol picked up a fork and sliced into her pastry. "Why do you ask? Did your detective get that case?"

"It is his case," Ruth hedged. "But I'm not asking because of him. I'm simply curious. As I said, Mr. Humphreys was a friend of Aunt Maude's and she asked me to go to represent the Cannonberry family, but I didn't know him." Even if it got back to Gerald that she'd been asking questions, it would sound like gossip, not investigating. "You always know so much about people."

"Are you implying I'm a gossip?" Marisol demanded.

Ruth was ready for that. She laughed. "Don't be absurd. Of course you're no gossip. But you are one of the most intelligent and observant people I've ever met. But if I've offended you, please forgive me."

"You haven't really offended me." Marisol grinned ruefully. "And I am a gossip. I can't help it, I'm just so curious about people. I know it's wrong and that I ought to mind my own business, but that's so boring."

"We're all interested in other people." Ruth gave her tea a stir. "There's no harm in that. You're not malicious. I've never heard you spread gossip that wasn't already out and about."

Marisol gave her a grateful smile. "It's good of you to say so, but we both know it's probably not true. Anyway, as for Francis Humphreys, I don't know too much about him. But I know a lot about his niece and nephews and they're the ones that are set to inherit all that money."

"Gracious, really?" She waited patiently while Marisol forked a delicate bite of éclair into her mouth.

"Yes indeed. One of his nieces, Annabelle Prescott, was the talk of the town a few years back. She was getting ready to leave her husband, but then he conveniently died."

"You mean she was going to divorce him?" Ruth asked.

"That's the gossip that was going around at the time." Marisol picked up her teacup. "Her husband, Hollis Prescott, was from one of those rich old families with lots of breeding but no money or brains. He and Annabelle married after a very short courtship. Supposedly, one of her servants heard her screaming at him that he'd married her under false pretenses." She took a quick sip.

"What kind of false pretenses?"

"He pretended he had money."

"I take it the reality of her life turned out quite differently," Ruth commented. "If Hollis Prescott had no income, how did he support them?"

"He did what many people of that class do in those circumstances," Marisol replied. "He sold off everything valuable the family owned—paintings, sculptures, rugs, jewelry. Everything the Prescott family had ended up on the auction block. It caused quite an uproar among his relatives. They were absolutely furious."

"I don't understand." Ruth frowned. "It was his property to sell, wasn't it?"

"It was. Hollis was the eldest and had inherited the family estate, or what was left of it. I think by that time it consisted of a rundown manor house outside Chingford and a small home in Chelsea. What caused the resentment was that the other men in the family had proper positions."

"They worked for their living?" Ruth clarified.

"That's right." Marisol grinned broadly. "And they didn't appreciate Hollis selling off every valuable heirloom he could lay his hands on. He'd been trained as a banker, you know. When he died, he left Annabelle penniless and both the properties went to his brother, not to his widow."

"But surely his family felt some responsibility for the woman," Ruth protested.

"Not at all." Marisol's smile faded. "They didn't like her and they asked her to vacate the premises within a month of his funeral."

"That's dreadful." Ruth could feel herself getting angry. "What kind of a world is this? Society won't allow women to be educated properly so they can work to support themselves and if they lose their spouse, they often get tossed out into the streets without so much as a by-your-leave."

"True enough," Marisol concurred. "But don't waste too many tears on Mrs. Prescott. She received an excellent education. She was taught alongside her cousin Yancy Humphreys, and the two of them were privately educated by a series of expensive tutors."

"She and Yancy Humphreys were cousins?"

"That's right, the poor boy was a sickly child and the family thought he'd learn better if his cousin was in the schoolroom with him. Her parents certainly didn't object. They couldn't afford to properly educate her," Marisol explained. "Apparently she was quite a brilliant woman. Supposedly she excelled at mathematics and wanted to study engineering, but of course no university would ever give her a place."

"I'll bet he got one though, didn't he?" Ruth muttered.

"I'm sure he did. Anyway, what good would going to university have done someone like her?" Marisol speculated. "She married."

"There were no children?" Ruth asked.

"No," Marisol replied. "Odd, isn't it? Neither she nor her cousin and his wife had children. I guess that family just wasn't very lucky." She suddenly clamped her mouth shut and a red flush crept up her round cheeks.

Ruth stared at her. "What on earth is wrong?" she asked.

"Uh, well, perhaps I shouldn't have said anything, perhaps I'm being indelicate," Marisol sputtered.

Ruth suddenly understood. "Oh, Marisol, you haven't been in the least indelicate. Though it is good of you to be concerned about my feelings, I assure you, I'm not unduly sensitive about never having been blessed with a child. It happens more often than one would think. I loved Lord Cannonberry very much, but the truth is I'm quite satisfied with the way my life has turned out."

Marisol closed her eyes briefly and sagged in relief. "Thank goodness. I do like you and you're one of the few women I know that actually seem to like me as well. I would hate to lose you as a friend."

Ruth said nothing for a long moment. Marisol Pulman, for all her wealth and position, was a very lonely woman and Ruth was suddenly deeply ashamed of herself. The only time she ever sent her an invitation was when she needed information for one of Gerald's cases. "You haven't offended me in the least. As a matter of fact, I wanted to ask you if you were interested in the cause of women's suffrage."

"You mean women voting?" Marisol frowned in confusion. "I don't know. I've never thought about such a thing."

"If you ever do decide you're interested in the subject, please let me know. I'd love to take you to one of our meetings. I belong to the National Union for Women's Suffrage and we could use an intelligent and observant woman such as you."

Betsy hoped the girl would get tired soon and find a place to sit down. She'd followed the young maid from Humphreys House and they were now all the way to Ealing Broadway. The girl finally slowed her pace and stopped to gaze in the window of a tea shop. This was her chance. She walked up beside her quarry. "Is this your afternoon out?" she asked cheerfully.

The girl turned and stared at her. Her hair was tucked under a brown wool cap, but curly, honey-colored tendrils had escaped and framed her pretty face. Her eyes were brown, her mouth a well-defined shape, a sprinkling of faint freckles appeared across her nose. She wore a three-quarter-length gray jacket over her dress, and a pair of sturdy black shoes peeked out beneath her hem. "What makes you think I'm a domestic?"

Betsy shrugged. "Well, seeing as you're wearing a pale lavender dress under your jacket, which is what I wear and I'm a maid, I was hoping you were in service as well. It gets lonely having my few hours away from my work on my own. But if I've made a mistake, miss, then I beg your pardon." She started to walk away. She'd not expected the lass to be so sensitive.

"Wait, I'm a tweeny," the girl cried. "And it is my afternoon out. I'm sorry, I didn't mean to be rude. My name is Agnes. Agnes Wilder."

"I'm Mary Higgins," she lied. "Are you thirsty? We could go in that tea shop. Would you like that?" She forced a laugh. "As I said, I'm sick of my own company and the household I work in has nothing but old people. I'm dying for a bit of chatter with someone near my own age."

Agnes hesitated. "I'd love to, but I really oughtn't. I send most of my wages home and I'm savin' to buy a bolt of nice cotton for a new dress."

"It's my treat." Betsy took her arm. "I'm lucky, I can spend my wages on myself. Come along, then. Let's go inside."

"Are you sure?" Agnes protested halfheartedly but let herself be led through the door.

The tea shop was busy, but Betsy spied two women just getting up from a table on the far side of the counter. She gave Agnes a gentle shove in that direction. "Get us that table while I get the tea. Would you like a bun as well?"

"That would be lovely," she replied.

Betsy gave the girl behind the counter their order and then surveyed the establishment while she waited. It wasn't exactly a workingman's café, but it wasn't posh, either. The dozen or so tables were filled with clerks, office workers, typewriter girls, and nicely dressed housewives, and at the table closest to the door were two postal workers with their canvas bags draped over the back of the chair. Agnes sat alone, looking around uncomfortably. Betsy understood how she probably felt. She was scared and excited at the same time. She'd bet her next quarter's wages that the girl hadn't been in London long and that this was the first time she'd set foot in a café.

"Here you are." The counter girl placed two cups of hot tea on the counter. "The lad will bring your buns over. He'll be right behind you."

"Thank you." Betsy handed her the money, got her change, and then made her way carefully across the crowded room. She set the cups down and then nodded her thanks at the boy who'd followed with their pastry. "Go ahead and help yourself," she told Agnes as soon as he'd put the plates down.

"This is very nice of you." Agnes smiled shyly. "I've never been in a place like this before. Even when I first come down to London, I only had a cup of tea at the train station. My cousin Bobby was with me then. He came all the way up to Castle Donington to fetch me when I got my position. He's a waterman on the Thames."

"Your cousin sounds very nice," she murmured. "How long have you been working in the area?"

"Two months. I can't say that I like it much." Agnes picked up her bun and took a small bite.

"Does the mistress work you hard, then?" Betsy took a slow sip of her tea.

"Oh, it's not that," Agnes protested. "I'm used to hard work. It's the loneliness I don't much like."

"Aren't there other young girls in your household?"

"There are," she replied. "But the only one who was my friend just got sacked this morning and now she's gone away. The others are older. I mean, there's a housekeeper, a cook, and scullery girl, but she's the cook's niece so she thinks she's too good to spend much time with someone like me. My friend Rachel was the upstairs maid and, well, I do the downstairs most of the time."

"I thought you said you were the tweeny." Betsy unloosed the ties of her bonnet.

"That was what they told me when I was hired," she explained. "But once I got there, I ended up doin' the downstairs as well. I'm just hopin' that with the state the household is in now that I don't get stuck takin' care of everything."

"I hope not, too." Betsy smiled. "What's wrong at the household?"

Agnes looked down at the tabletop. "My master was murdered."

Betsy gasped. She was getting to be a very good actress. "Gracious, that's awful. Have you had the police around?"

"Oh yes, they are there all the time," Agnes replied. "It's not too bad. The man in charge is very nice, but he's got a right nasty constable with him. None of us much like the bloke so we don't tell him anything."

"But don't you want whoever killed your master to be caught?" Betsy asked. She had to be careful here; she didn't want to say the wrong thing. "I mean, not telling the police what you know, that's not very good, is it?"

Agnes shrugged. "I suppose not, but that Constable Gates is so rude. He talks to you like you were a half-witted animal and that's not right."

"I agree," Betsy said gently. "It must be awful for you, being so far away from home and having a terrible thing like a murder happen in your household."

"And my friend gettin' the sack," Agnes added eagerly. "That's the worst of it. Now I've got no one to talk to at all and poor Rachel hadn't done anything wrong."

"Why did she get let go?" Betsy nibbled at her bun. "Surely they gave a reason for sacking the poor girl."

"Not really. Mrs. Eames just came into our room early this morning and told her that she'd be paid through the end of the quarter but that she was to pack her things and go. The household didn't need her."

"That's all that she said?" Betsy frowned thoughtfully. She knew that the order to fire a housemaid hadn't come from the housekeeper.

"That's all." Agnes shook her head in disbelief. "Rachel started cryin' and askin' why but Mrs. Eames just told her not to make a fuss and to get her case packed. Mind you, once she stopped cryin' she went downstairs and cornered Mrs. Prescott, demanding to know what she'd done."

"Is Mrs. Prescott the lady of the house?"

"She runs the house, but she's not the owner." Agnes paused. "Wait a minute, I tell a lie. Now that Mr. Humphreys is dead, I guess she is the owner. Leastways that's what I heard her tellin' the others. Anyway, she told Rachel that she'd not been doin' her work properly and she was tired of warnin' her."

"Rachel had been warned?"

Agnes nodded reluctantly. "Mrs. Eames kept tellin' her that with Miss Ross and Mrs. Prescott in the household, one of them was bound to notice she didn't do a very good job. Truth to tell, Rachel was a bit lazy. She didn't like the smell of that furniture polish so half the time she didn't use it and she was always sweepin' the dirt under the chairs or the rugs."

Betsy hid her disappointment as best she could. Now that more of the story was coming out, it sounded very much like a lazy maid finally getting sacked. It wasn't surprising that it should happen now. People under stress were less likely to be tolerant of little things like a dusty mantel or a streaked mirror than they were when life was going smoothly. "I hope your friend finds another position."

"She'll be alright," Agnes said. "She's got family in the area so she'll not starve. When she was packin' her case to go she told me that her aunt works at a pub just off Ealing Broadway. She was goin' there to see if she could get taken on to help out until she can find another position."

Betsy nodded sympathetically. "So this Mrs. Prescott, is she your mistress now?"

"That's what I overheard her tellin' Miss Ross and Mr. Humphreys."

"I thought you said that Mr. Humphreys was murdered," Betsy interrupted. It was important to pretend she knew nothing of the household or its occupants.

"Mr. Francis Humphreys was the one who was killed," Agnes explained patiently. She took another sip of tea. "Mr. Joseph Humphreys is his nephew. He moved into the house the day of the murder."

"And who is Miss Ross?"

"She's another relative," Agnes said. "Mr. Humphreys took her in when she lost her position as a governess. She's well educated is Miss Ross. I like her, she's very kind. But she's got secrets of her own."

"That sounds interesting." Betsy smiled eagerly. "What kind of secrets?"

Agnes laughed. "Most likely I'm just bein' fanciful, but twice I saw her slippin' out the side door and both times, she was carryin' a stack of letters."

"What is so odd about that?" Betsy asked. "Maybe she has a lot of friends and likes to correspond with them."

"Then how come she was sneakin' about?" Agnes asked. "That's why I noticed it so special-like. Miss Ross would come down to the foot of the stairs and take a good look around to make sure no one in the household was close by before she slipped out. She'd always come back about ten minutes later and she'd stick her head inside to make sure no one was about before she slipped back inside and dashed up the back stairs."

"How come she didn't see you?" Betsy asked. She took care to keep her voice friendly as she spoke. It wouldn't do to ruffle Agnes' feathers by implying the maid had been deliberately spying.

"She didn't see me because I was on the landing just above her. I can look down between the railings at the back hall. I like to sit there when I'm foldin' the kitchen linens. It's quiet and there's no one about. She weren't lookin' in my direction. She didn't care if a servant saw her comin' and goin', she just wanted to make sure there wasn't someone from the family in that part of the house."

"Perhaps you ought to tell the nice policeman what you've seen," Betsy suggested. "And all the other things you've overheard. You know, like Mrs. Prescott telling the family the house is hers now."

"I suppose I ought to do that," Agnes mused, her expression thoughtful. "Mr. Joseph Humphreys seems like a nice man. Mind you, I'm not sure how long he's goin' to be stayin' now that she's the owner. I don't think she likes him much. But then again, I heard him tellin' her not to be so sure she was gettin' anything at all." She paused and took another sip of her tea. Then she leaned forward. "He told her that they'd not had the will read yet, but when it was she might be in for a surprise."

"What 'ave you got for me?" Smythe asked as he slipped onto the wooden stool opposite Blimpey Groggins.

"Not as much as you'd like, I'm sure." Blimpey grinned. "But enough to show you've not wasted your lolly. Do you want a pint?"

"Not today," he replied. "I've got to get back soon."

"Right, then I'll get to it. I found out that Mr. Michael Collier had already gone to a solicitor to discuss the particulars of how to go about gettin' someone declared incompetent and by 'someone,' he meant his uncle Francis."

"So if he was plannin' on takin' him to court and havin' him declared unfit, he'd have no reason to kill the old man," Smythe murmured.

"Don't be too sure of that," Blimpey warned. "I ain't told you what the solicitor told your Mr. Collier. He told him that proving incompetence is a lot harder than it might appear. Apparently, the old men running our court system don't look kindly on those that come into their courtrooms moanin' about how dear old Uncle Francis wants to spend the family fortune investin' in South American railways. Judges need a lot of evidence before they'll take away a man's right to spend his money as he sees fit and despite what the Humphreys' nieces and nephews thought, the estate belonged to Francis."

"And maybe Collier didn't want to take the risk he'd lose in court," Smythe added. "In which case, 'avin' his uncle conveniently die solved his problem for him." He looked at Blimpey speculatively. "How come you know what was said inside a solicitor's office?"

"Don't be daft, man." Blimpey laughed. "It's my job to know these sorts of things. Unfortunately, I've not heard much else except for a bit about Joseph Humphreys. Right around the time he was askin' his uncle to take him in and put a roof over his head, he went down to one of them pubs in the East End where the radicals congregate and he was braggin' to anyone who'd listen that the 'days of the autocrat' were numbered and that soon there'd be good money in the hands of the workers." He made a face. "What nonsense. Seems to me that the minute the worker gets a bit of lolly in his hands he's no better than the toffs that got it now."

"I wonder if Joseph meant his uncle when he made that remark," Smythe said.

"It's hard to say." Blimpey sighed. "My sources tell me that Joseph was well liked by the others in the pub, though he wasn't much of a drinker and usually just nursed a pint for the entire evening. But that night, he came in and got well and truly snoggered. His mates were openly speculating about where he got the money for the gin. He usually gave all his spare coin to the Socialist League."

"Sounds like he was tryin' to drown his sorrows," Smythe mused. "Or maybe he just lucked into a bit of money and decided to enjoy himself. What pub was it?"

"The Sun and Moon. It's on Leman Street just off the Whitechapel High Street."

"You got anything else?"

"Nah, but I've got my lads out and about," Blimpey replied. "Now as to that other matter, much as it pains me to say it, I'm not 'avin' much luck."

"What do you mean? Blast a Spaniard, Blimpey, it's important for me to find Betsy's sister."

"I know it's important and I'm doin' my best for you," Blimpey said patiently. "But you've given me very little to go on. I've got my lads askin' about her old neighborhood and checkin' as many shipping lines as will let us 'ave a gander at their passenger manifests, but so far, they've turned up nothin'."

"Then keep on lookin'."

Blimpey leaned forward, his expression serious. "Look, this is goin' to cost you a fortune, Smythe. Shippin' clerks are decently paid and we're 'avin' to bribe the ones that'll take a bit of lolly on the side to get a look at their records."

"I don't care what it costs," he snapped. "I can afford it. You of all people ought to know that. If payin' out the bribes is eatin' into your cash, I can pay now—"

Blimpey interrupted. "You don't need to do that. I've got plenty of operatin' capital. But you're one of my best clients and a friend so it was only fair that I warned you that the bill was startin' to mount up."

"I know you'd not cheat me," Smythe stated.

"Fair enough, then, we'll keep at it. But I warn you, there's a good chance that even I can't find 'em. It's like Norah and Leo Hanrahan have disappeared off the face of the earth. Are you sure yer Betsy doesn't have some idea of which country they went to or the exact year they left?"

"I've told you everything she knows." He sighed and closed his eyes. With all his money, he couldn't give the woman he loved the one thing she really wanted. Her sister at her wedding. "Blimpey, you've got to find her. I don't care how much it costs or how many clerks you need to bribe. We've more than seven months before the wedding, which should give you enough time."

"I'll do my best." He raised his palm in a gesture of calm. "But like I told you before, this sort of thing might better be done by one of them fancy private inquiry agencies—"

"I don't want a private inquiry agency," Smythe interrupted. "This is personal and private. I could only give it to someone like you, someone I trust. I know it won't be easy, but I know you can do it."

"And if I do find her and she's not the sister your lass remembers, what then?" Blimpey asked. He was no fool. He knew that Smythe would do anything to protect Betsy's feelings.

"Then I'll cross her palms with silver until she becomes exactly what my Betsy remembers."

Mrs. Jeffries pulled her cloak tighter against the cold March wind. She'd come out to the garden to have a think. She hoped that this afternoon's meeting would give her a few more facts to work with. So far, the investigation didn't appear to be progressing very well at all. She had no idea if the suspects were really suspects, the motive for the murder might not be at all what she thought, and to top it off, she wasn't seeing, sensing, or feeling any sort of pattern for this crime. If anything, the more facts she learned, the less anything made sense. Her own inner voice, as it were, seemed to have completely deserted her and her confidence was disappearing with each passing day. What was worse, she knew the others were counting on her. And she was terrified that this time, she'd fail them.

She bent down, picked up a fallen branch that had tumbled onto the gravel path, and tossed it onto the side. She slowed her steps and took long deep breaths, hoping the abundance of oxygen in her lungs would help her brain to function more efficiently. But alas, by the time she reached the end of the path and started back, she was still as much in a fog as she'd been earlier.

What if this was a conspiracy, she thought. What then? How could they prove it? Conspiracies were dreadfully difficult to solve unless one were very lucky or one found a great deal of physical evidence linking the killer to the crime. But so far, they had no physical evidence whatsoever; the police hadn't even found the weapon. Well, of course they hadn't, she thought irritably. The killer must have taken it with him. Mrs. Jeffries stopped as a glimmer of idea nudged the back of her mind, but it faded before she could grab the wretched thing and make sense of it. She continued walking, letting her thoughts drift where they would.

The Humphreys family seemed a very unlucky clan; they were childless, tended to die young or become widowed, lost their livelihoods, and got turned out of their accommodations. Lucky for them, they had a rich uncle who was predisposed to support the whole lot of them, even if he was difficult to live with. But how hard was it for the ones who resided in Humphreys House? Was the man such an ogre that one of his dependent relatives conspired with someone to dispatch him before his time? Was that what this murder was all about; had someone simply gotten fed up with dancing to Francis Humphreys' tune? She sighed in annoyance. Even letting her mind wander freely didn't appear to help much.

But she wasn't going to give up so easily. She slowed her steps and took another deep breath. What about the relatives from the country? She stopped and gazed off into the distance. The Elliots had come all the way up from Dorset and paid for a hotel room. Had they gone to all that trouble just to have tea with Francis Humphreys? She made a mental note to ask the inspector a few more questions about them.

"Yoo hoo, Hepzibah, wait for me. I'm just coming." Ruth's voice jarred her out of her thoughts. She turned and saw her friend running toward her, her cloak streaming behind her as she hurried down the path.

"Hello," Mrs. Jeffries said. "I was just out taking a walk. It must be almost time for our meeting."

"I saw you from my window," Ruth replied breathlessly. "I've got some very interesting information to report."

"Excellent." She took Ruth's arm. "I do hope your report will shed some light on this dreadful crime, because frankly, I can't make heads nor tails of anything thus far."

Ruth patted her hand reassuringly. "Don't be silly, Hepzibah. You always say that and you always, always end up with the right answer."

"I'm very flattered by everyone's confidence in my abilities." Mrs. Jeffries gave a self-deprecating laugh. "But one of these days, I'm bound to fail. No one is perfect all the time."

"But you've always managed to solve the crime." Ruth smiled confidently.

"We've always caught the killer," Mrs. Jeffries replied. "But there have been times in the past when I've been wrong about some rather pertinent details. Oftentimes as naught, my conclusions are a bit off the mark and it's only been luck that has led the inspector to arrive on the scene, as it were, at the best possible moment to arrest the guilty party." There was one killer that they hadn't caught, but as her accomplice had been convicted of the crime, she supposed that counted as "catching the killer."

"Nonsense, even on those cases where you were a tad 'off the mark,' as you put it, your analysis of each and every situation was always right. Now stop doubting yourself. We've all got tremendous faith in you. You'll not fail the cause of justice."

CHAPTER 8

—◆—

Leo Kirkland smiled sardonically at the two policemen. "I was wondering when I'd get a visit from the police." He glanced at his butler. "That will be all, Perry. You may go now. If the gentlemen and I need anything, I'll ring the bell." The man nodded and withdrew, closing the heavy double doors silently.

"We already have your statement, Mr. Kirkland," Witherspoon said. "But there are a few more questions we'd like to ask you. I'm forgetting my manners, though. I'm Inspector—"

"Gerald Witherspoon," Kirkland interrupted. "I know who you are, sir. Please make yourselves comfortable and I'll answer any and all of your questions." He waved them toward an emerald green velvet sleigh-back sofa, waited till they were comfortably seated, and then settled himself down in the armchair opposite them.

They knew little of Leo Kirkland, save that he'd been visiting the victim on the day of the murder so the inspector was trying to get some measure of the man by surreptitiously examining his home. When he and Gates had climbed down from the hansom that had brought them here, he'd noticed the house was a large, four-story brown brick with a white-painted edifice and a separate side entrance for the servants. Witherspoon glanced around the drawing room, noting the furniture was of excellent quality with no tears or faded spots on the upholstery. Side tables draped with brightly colored fringed shawls were placed strategically around the room, drawing the viewer's gaze to the fine porcelain figurines, snuff boxes, and ceramics artfully arranged on each one. The walls were painted a pale beige and cream and green striped curtains hung at the windows. Next to where they sat was a fireplace with a pink marble façade and mantel. Above that was a huge mirror in an ornate gold frame.

"This room was decorated by my late wife," Kirkland said softly.

Witherspoon started, unaware his perusal had been so obvious. "Your home is very beautiful, Mr. Kirkland."

Kirkland looked amused. "Unfortunately, my Katherine has passed away. We didn't have many years together so I've left everything just as it was when she was alive. But I'm sure you didn't come here to discuss home decorating with me. How may I help you?"

"We need to ask you questions," Lionel said harshly. He was perched at the end of the couch with his notebook and pencil at the ready. He did not look happy. Witherspoon was certain the lad hadn't gotten over having to sit by the door at the solicitor's office.

"There's no need for rudeness, Constable," Witherspoon chided. "Mr. Kirkland has been most gracious. I'll ask the questions. You can take notes."

Lionel gasped, caught himself, and muttered, "Yes sir."

The inspector turned his attention back to Kirkland.

"How long have you been acquainted with Mr. Francis Humphreys?"

"A very long time," Kirkland replied. "We're both train enthusiasts and we met twenty years ago at my club."

"Which one is that, sir?" Witherspoon glanced at Gates to make sure he was taking notes and saw that he was writing away in his little brown book.

"The Hayden on Salisbury Street," he said. "I forget precisely how it happened, but one day we both realized we loved trains. It was Francis' only real passion."

"Had you been invited to have tea with Mr. Humphreys on the afternoon that he was murdered?" Witherspoon asked. He couldn't recall, but he had the distinct impression that Kirkland had been a very unwelcome guest.

"As a matter of fact, I was." Kirkland smiled wryly. "I know what you've heard, Inspector. Francis and I were at odds over a certain matter and when I arrived at the house that day, it was obvious that my appearance was a surprise to the rest of the family, but I assure you, I was an invited guest." He reached inside his coat pocket, pulled out an envelope, and handed it to the inspector. "See for yourself."

Witherspoon pulled out the note page, opened it, and read the contents.

> *Leo,*
> *This nonsense has gone on long enough, come along this afternoon for tea. When the others leave, you and I can settle our differences like gentlemen. We've known one another too long to let another year pass without speaking to one another.*
> *I'll expect you at four o'clock sharp.*
> *Francis*

Witherspoon hesitated for a moment and then handed the paper back to Kirkland. He'd no reason to take the note into evidence. Thus far, the man wasn't a suspect. "Thank you, sir. We appreciate your cooperation. Now, can you tell me the nature of your disagreement with Mr. Humphreys?"

Kirkland pursed his lips. "Is that necessary, Inspector? I assure you, it's nothing to do with why he was murdered. It was a small matter and I'd prefer to keep it private."

Lionel cleared his throat and opened his mouth, as though he wanted to speak, but Witherspoon gave him a quick frown and the constable sank back into his seat.

Witherspoon knew what the lad was going to say, and though the inspector regretted having to delve into personal matters, especially with a gentleman of Mr. Kirkland's generation, it had to be said. "Mr. Kirkland, I'm very sorry, but this is a murder investigation and I'm afraid respecting the privacy of the deceased is out of the question. We need to know everything."

"I was afraid of that." Kirkland smiled wearily. "It's not a very pretty story, Inspector. As I told you, Francis and I had known each other for a very long time. Fifteen years ago, I met an American woman named Estelle Collier. We'd been introduced at a ball by a mutual acquaintance who felt we'd have much in common. I loved railways and her family had a substantial interest in every major railway in North America. But that wasn't why I fell in love with her. I've plenty of money of my own. At that time in my life, I was well into my forties and had assumed I'd be a bachelor for the rest of my days." He broke off and shrugged. "I'm sure you can guess the rest. I made the mistake of introducing her to my good friend, Francis. Then I was unexpectedly called back to the family estate in Northumberland because my father was very ill. He died a few weeks after I arrived home."

"I'm very sorry, sir," Witherspoon murmured.

"He was an old man and he had a long, good life," Kirkland replied. "But I digress. It took several months to sort his affairs and by the time I arrived back in London, Estelle and Francis were engaged."

"Did Mr. Humphreys know of your feelings toward the lady?" Witherspoon asked. It didn't seem likely that someone would wait fifteen years to seek revenge upon a romantic rival, but the inspector had once had a case where a man waited more than thirty years to get back at the people who'd wronged him.

"He did." Kirkland crossed his arms over his chest. "I'd told Francis of my intentions toward Estelle before I left for the north. He knew full well I was going to ask her to be my wife. Of course I was furious when I found out and Francis and I had words. I won't bore you with the details, but suffice to say, afterwards, we were no longer friends. I spoke to him only one other time before he died."

"And that was the day he was murdered?" Witherspoon pressed.

He shook his head. "I didn't actually speak to him that day. The last time we exchanged words to one another was just after Estelle died, when her will was read. Her solicitor asked me to come to the reading as I was one of the beneficiaries. She left me a number of shares in the Atchison, Topeka and Santa Fe Railroad." He chuckled. "Francis was furious. He made a dreadful scene. He accused me of unduly influencing his wife. I told him I'd not seen her in years and that I'd happily take the shares. It would give me something to remember her by."

"He didn't offer to buy them from you?" Lionel asked politely.

Witherspoon gave the constable an approving glance. Perhaps the lad was finally learning that one got far more cooperation if one was courteous and civil.

"He did, but I was furious myself and I refused to sell." Kirkland sighed. "You see, I knew how badly he wanted those shares. My Katie told me I was being foolish and that no good could come of repaying evil for evil, that the shares meant nothing to me and everything to him so I ought to let him have the wretched things. But I didn't listen."

"Do you have any idea why she left the shares to you?" Witherspoon asked curiously.

He uncrossed his arms and stared off into the distance for a few moments. "I think she wanted to hurt him. You see, I had seen Estelle after her marriage to Francis. It was about a year after their wedding, and we ran into one another at a ball. Francis wasn't with her; he'd gone hunting in Scotland. We sat down and had supper together. She was much too loyal to tell me straight out that she'd made a dreadful mistake, but it was obvious from her manner that she wasn't happy."

"You weren't angry at her for trifling with you? She up and married someone else when she should have waited for you," Lionel blurted. "Oh, sorry, sir, I didn't mean that quite the way it sounded."

"She hadn't trifled with me," Kirkland shot back. "She'd no idea I'd been in love with her and like the arrogant fool I was, I'd not bothered to tell her how I felt. But that's not the point. By then, I was no longer in love with her, but she'd hurt my pride and I was less than kind that night. She wanted us to be friends, but I told her I was engaged and my fiancée was very particular about our social acquaintances. It was a lie; of course my Katie would have been the first to extend the hand of friendship to a lonely woman like Estelle. Years later, when Estelle died and left me the shares, I felt guilty that I'd let her down when she needed my friendship the most. She left me those shares because she didn't want Francis to have them so keeping them was the only way I knew to make up for what I'd done. So I refused to sell them to him. Then a few days ago, he sent me the note asking me to come to tea."

"Why did he invite you?" Witherspoon asked. That was the real question.

"Was it to get you to sell the railway shares?" Lionel asked eagerly.

"When my wife died last year, I sold the wretched things and gave every penny of the money to the Battersea Orphan's Home." Kirkland straightened up. "I don't think he invited me for any reason other than he wanted to try to mend our friendship. We were once very close. Not only did we both love trains, but we spent a lot of time together as well. We used to go shooting out in the country. He'd bring his nieces and nephews out to my country house in Kent, and we'd load everyone into a hay wagon and head into the fields to shoot. It was great fun. I think he was simply getting old and lonely. But then again"—he sighed heavily and slumped back against the cushions—"aren't we all?"

Mrs. Jeffries slipped into her chair and plastered a serene smile on her face. There was an air of excitement around the table this afternoon and that, of course, meant that everyone had learned something. She only wished she could say the same for herself. "Who would like to go first?"

"Well, mine will likely be the shortest," Luty said. "I had a word with an acquaintance of mine that runs the Exhibition Hall at the Crystal Palace."

"Crystal Palace?" Hatchet stared at her incredulously.

"Now just hold your horses and your tongue," Luty warned. "I know it don't seem like an exhibition hall has anything to do with our case, but if you'll think for a minute—"

"I see what you mean," Wiggins interrupted. "You went there to find out if anyone knew Yancy Humphreys. He used to show off his gadgets in some of them exhibitions."

Luty nodded in satisfaction. "That's right, and it turned

out it was good that I went there. Archie did know Humphreys, well, he didn't know him personally, but he remembers the man. Seems Yancy Humphreys exhibited a bunch of his contraptions in the hall a few years back. He was tryin' to drum up some interest in his inventions. Archie said a couple of them were pretty interesting. One of them was a mechanical device that used a clockwork spring of some sort so that every hour or so it . . . uh . . . well, it did something . . ." She broke off, frowning in confusion. "Nells bells, I can't recall all the fancy words Archie used, but the heart of the matter is that from the way Archie described it, the contraption was the kind of invention a confectionary manufacturer might have seen and copied. Archie said it was designed so the timing mechanism could be changed from seconds to minutes to hours and that bits on it could be changed to suit whatever purpose was needed. Archie said that Humphreys claimed the thing had lots of uses. I got to thinkin' that if you're makin' candy, you cook it for so long, then you add your other ingredients, and then you pour it out right quick and set it to harden."

"I see what you're sayin'." Mrs. Goodge nodded enthusiastically. "Of course, imagine if you could have a machine that did all your mixin' and addin' for you."

Luty nodded. "So I asked Archie and he had a look at the old records and there were three confectionary representatives registered when Yancy was showin' off his gadgets. I just thought it was mighty suspicious that right when Francis Humphreys was murdered, Smythe finds out that there's someone worried about whether Pamela Bowden Humphreys might be able to sue for patent infringement."

"But she wasn't the one that was murdered," Hatchet reminded her.

Luty rolled her eyes. "I know that. But that don't mean the two events aren't connected."

"You're absolutely right, Luty." Mrs. Jeffries intervened quickly. "At this point in the investigation, we don't want to ignore any information. As you say, we've no idea what might or might not turn out to be useful."

Luty smiled triumphantly. "Thank you. That's all I've got."

"I'll go next," Ruth volunteered. She waited a fraction of a second and when no one objected, she plunged straight into her report. "I didn't have much luck at Francis Humphreys' funeral this morning. Truth to tell, I didn't even get invited back to the house for the reception."

"You didn't hear anything?" Mrs. Goodge asked. "That's a pity."

"Not unless you count eavesdropping on two women as I left the church, but all they were talking about was the seating arrangements for the service. Apparently, one of the women thought it unseemly that Michael Collier, a single man, was sitting right next to Imogene Ross, a single woman." Ruth giggled. "But as the church was packed full of people, I don't expect that anyone, even the family, had much choice in the seating arrangements. But even though I had no luck at the service, I'd invited my friend Marisol Pulman around for tea this afternoon and she was a veritable fountain of knowledge." Ruth told them everything she'd learned. She didn't embellish or form any opinions. She simply repeated as much of the conversation as she could recall. When she'd finished, she sat back in her chair, picked up her cup, and took a sip of tea.

"That's sad, isn't it," Betsy commented. "Annabelle Prescott married and then felt she'd been cheated." She looked at Smythe. "Stupid woman, she ought to have taken the time to get to know her man."

"What's the old adage? 'Marry in haste, repent at leisure,'" Mrs. Goodge muttered. "I always thought that was a stupid saying. I've seen a number of miserable marriages where both parties had known each other for years. Seems to me that sometimes you never get to know people very well. Take what happened this morning, for instance. You could have knocked me over with a feather when I opened that back door and saw Mollie Dubay standin' there. Oh, sorry, Lady . . . Ruth . . . were you through with your report?"

"Yes, thank you."

"Then why don't you tell us about your day," Mrs. Jeffries suggested. It was obvious the cook was dying to go next.

"If you insist. Well, as I was sayin', I opened the back door and instead of it bein' the source I was expectin', there was Mollie Dubay. She worked in Lord Fremont's house or rather she did until this morning, but she got sacked—"

"There's a lot of that going about these days," Betsy interrupted. "Agnes' friend just got sacked from Humphreys House."

"Who got sacked?" Wiggins demanded. "What's 'er name?"

"Can I finish my report?" the cook cried.

"Sorry." Betsy smiled apologetically and glanced at Wiggins. She mouthed "Rachel" as Mrs. Goodge continued speaking.

"As I was sayin', it was a bit of a shock finding Mollie on my doorstep, but luckily, it turned out she did know something about our case." Mrs. Goodge told them what she'd heard from her unwelcome guest. She gave them all the facts, but out of loyalty to her friend, she said nothing about Mollie's emotional state. An old woman's humiliation and tears wasn't anyone else's business. "I think we ought to send someone to the Chalmers household in case Estelle Collier's maid is still there," she concluded. "It would be good to know the name of the niece that was nursing her when she took a turn for the worse."

"Especially as the poor woman died just when she was insisting the police are notified about the missing money," Ruth added. "Not that I'm saying the niece is guilty—the two events happening at the same time could be a coincidence."

"But who could we possibly send on such an errand?" Mrs. Jeffries murmured. Her fingers drummed lightly against her teacup as she considered the problem.

"And the maid might not even still be there," Betsy pointed out. "If she was a properly trained ladies' maid and could do hair and knew how to take care of a wardrobe, she'd have not stayed long in a household as a scullery girl."

"Agreed, but Mrs. Goodge is right. It's important we find out who nursed Estelle Collier," Mrs. Jeffries said. "Even if the maid is no longer at the Chalmers household, they'll have some idea where she went. As to who to send there, I think we ought to send Luty."

"Madam doesn't even know the Chalmerses," Hatchet objected.

"Oh, that don't make any difference." Luty chuckled. "I'll git into that house and have myself a nice, long chat with someone. Just leave it to me. I'll find out everything we need to know."

"Be careful of your boasts, madam. You've no idea who these people are or if they even still reside in the neighborhood. If they do, they're quite likely to show you the door," Hatchet replied irritably.

"You worry too much. What do you say we take a little bet on whether or not I can git in there and find out the girl's whereabouts," Luty retorted.

"We all have complete faith in your abilities," Mrs. Jeffries interjected quickly. "So there's no need for wagers. Just do your utmost to find out our information by tomorrow's meeting. Can you do that for us?"

"You'll know the niece's name by tomorrow night," Luty promised.

"Excellent." Mrs. Jeffries turned to Betsy. "Why don't you go next?"

Betsy, who'd just taken a sip of tea, swallowed and put down her cup. "I tried talking to some of the shopkeepers in Michael Collier's neighborhood, but no one seemed to know much about him, so I went to Acton and got very lucky. Just as I arrived, a young maid came out the servants' entrance so I followed her." She grinned. "And my luck got even better. I ended up having tea with Agnes Wilder, one of the few maids that is still left at the Humphreys home."

"So it *was* Rachel that got the sack?" Wiggins shook his head sadly.

"That's right, but according to Agnes, she was very lazy and had been warned about her work," Betsy replied. "So I'm not sure it's got anything to do with the murder. But let me tell you the rest." She told them everything Agnes had told her. "So it seems Mrs. Prescott is definitely playing the lady of the manor," she finished.

"I'm more interested in why Imogene Ross is sneaking in and out the side entrance," Hatchet mused. "Surely it wasn't just to mail a few letters?"

"It'd be more than a few if she was actively lookin' for a new position," Mrs. Goodge said. "So that would explain the stack of correspondence Agnes saw her carryin' out of the house. Believe me, when you're lookin' for work, you send inquiries to every prospect you see in the advertisements."

"Mrs. Prescott appears to be certain she now owns the house," Mrs. Jeffries muttered. "But does she?"

"If the inspector went to see the solicitor today, he ought to be able to give us that information when he gets home." Smythe stared at the clock on the pine sideboard. "And if we don't get on with this meetin', he's goin' to arrive and catch us sittin' here. If Betsy's finished, I'd like to say my bit now."

"Go on then." Betsy grinned. "I'm done."

Smythe told them what he'd learned from Blimpey Groggins.

"Cor blimey," Wiggins cried when he'd finished his report. "This case is so ruddy complicated it's goin' to take Mrs. Jeffries a month of Sundays to suss it all out. Collier goin' to a solicitor, Joseph Humphreys drinkin' like there's no tomorrow, poor Rachel gettin' sacked for no reason—"

"But there was a reason," Betsy protested. "The girl was lazy."

"Maybe so, but she was sacked on the day of Humphreys' funeral," Wiggins pointed out. "Seems to me if they was 'avin' a funeral reception at the 'ouse, they'd need all the servants to work and if you were goin' to sack someone, you'd wait until the poor man was decently in the ground. Accordin' to your Agnes, Rachel was fired that morning, before the funeral!"

"Wiggins is right." Mrs. Jeffries looked at the footman. "That is odd. Do you think you can find Rachel?"

"According to Agnes, she was going to a pub somewhere on Ealing Broadway," Betsy supplied helpfully. "There couldn't be too many of them."

"But what should I ask her?" Wiggins looked confused. "I mean, I think it's right important we talk to her, but now that I think about it, I'm not sure what it is we're wantin' to find out?"

Mrs. Jeffries wasn't sure, either. "I don't know, but I suspect that Rachel might have seen or heard something on the day of the murder."

"So you think Annabelle Prescott is the killer?" Luty asked eagerly. "She's the one that gave the instruction to sack the girl."

Mrs. Jeffries shook her head. "We don't know that. Furthermore, I think it equally important that Smythe go to the Sun and Moon pub and if possible, find out why Joseph Humphreys was uncharacteristically drinking himself into a stupor."

The meeting broke up only minutes before Inspector Witherspoon arrived home. "Good evening, sir," Mrs. Jeffries said as she reached for his bowler. "Did you have a good day?"

"It was productive, I think." He frowned as he unbuttoned his coat. "But then again, one is never sure." His fingers stopped over a buttonhole. He took a deep breath, sniffing the air. "Ah, Mrs. Jeffries, what is that heavenly smell?"

"Roast chicken, sir. Mrs. Goodge has also done potatoes with an onion and parsley sauce, sprouts, and an apricot fool for dessert," she replied. "It's ready to eat whenever you are, sir."

"I'm not in a hurry." He resumed his task. "We can eat later. I think I'd like a nice glass of sherry. I take it you will join me?"

"Of course, sir." She took his overcoat and hung it on the peg. She'd been hoping he'd want a sherry. "Go on into the drawing room, sir."

A few moments later, he was ensconced in his favorite chair and she was handing him a glass of Harveys. "Thank you, Mrs. Jeffries." He reached for his sherry and took a quick drink. "This is precisely what I needed. It's been a very busy day and I must say, Constable Gates isn't the most useful fellow to have along when one is investigating a murder."

"Really, sir?" Mrs. Jeffries ducked her head to hide a smile. "Perhaps he's just inexperienced."

"That's what I thought," he replied, taking another sip and this time, almost draining the glass. "He did fairly well for most of the day, especially after Humphreys' solicitor put him firmly in his place, and I thought the rascal had learned his lesson. Bullying people simply does not work; honestly, you'd think these young pups had never heard of the admonition to do unto others as you would have done unto you."

Mrs. Jeffries was a bit alarmed. The inspector generally didn't quote scripture when he was on a case. "I beg your pardon, sir."

He sighed. "It's one of my secrets, Mrs. Jeffries, and not something I'd normally share with anyone, but I trust you." He drained the glass completely and held it out to her for a refill. "May I have another, please?"

"Of course, sir." She took the glass and got to her feet. But she was very confused. Gracious, this case was already muddled enough, Barnes was gone, Gates was a nuisance, the inspector was quoting the Bible, and now he wanted another drink. She went to the cupboard and poured another sherry. She took a deep breath and got hold of herself. Getting upset before she heard what the inspector had to say was foolish. "You were saying, sir," she reminded him. She handed him his glass and took her seat.

"I was saying that it's one of my secrets," he said. "It's how I get people to talk to me. Let's be honest, Mrs. Jeffries. Most people, especially those who would be considered the criminal element, don't generally like policemen. But I've found that if I treat everyone, including suspects, as I would wish to be treated, then I get very good results." He leaned forward, his expression earnest. "It's one of my 'methods,' as it were, but not one I've shared with anyone other than yourself."

Mrs. Jeffries stared at him. In a bizarre sort of way, it made perfect sense. No one appreciated being bullied or patronized or dismissed. "I'm flattered you trust me with your secret, sir. I promise I'll not tell anyone. I take it Constable Gates was unable to live up to your standards?"

"He did his best, I suppose," Witherspoon murmured. He took another sip. "But he's still very much a bully. Constable Barnes could be quite firm, but he only resorted to that particular tactic when people refused to cooperate. But as I said, the Humphreys' solicitor put young Lionel firmly in his place." He giggled. "He made him sit by the door."

"Really, sir?"

"Oh yes, but all in all, the solicitor was very cooperative. He didn't hold anything back." Witherspoon went on to tell her everything Eldon Roberts had shared with him. "After that, we went along and had a brief word with Mr. Robert Eddington. He'd just come back from the funeral. I didn't think it proper to question the family on the day they were burying their uncle."

"Of course not, sir," she responded. "Mr. Eddington was in the house on the afternoon of the murder, wasn't he?"

"He was one of the guests," Witherspoon replied. "But I'm afraid he could tell us very little."

"How unfortunate." She took a sip from her glass.

"All he said was that there was a loud boom and everyone rushed upstairs," Witherspoon muttered. "Of course we already knew that."

"What relationship did Mr. Eddington have with Francis Humphreys?"

"They were both train enthusiasts," Witherspoon explained. "They've known one another for years. Mr. Eddington did say he was rather surprised by the invitation to tea, though. Apparently, he'd not spent much time with Humphreys in the last year or so."

Somewhere deep inside, the bare bones of an idea nudged Mrs. Jeffries' brain, but it scampered away before she could grasp the thing and make it tell her anything useful. Drat. "Were they estranged?" she asked. "Was there discord between them?"

"Not according to Mr. Eddington," Witherspoon said. He tossed back the last of his sherry. "He said they'd simply become interested in different aspects of the railway. But I'm not sure that's quite true as he was going on about those people who like 'broad gauge' as opposed to those who favored 'narrow gauge.' I'm quite an enthusiast myself, Mrs. Jeffries, but all I ever wish to do is look at the engines as they come through a railway station. But apparently, there are many who are very interested in every detail. Apparently, Eddington and Francis Humphreys were on opposing sides of the gauge issue, odd as it may seem."

"Do you seriously consider Mr. Eddington a suspect?"

He smiled wearily. "Not really. He had nothing to gain by Humphreys' death, despite their disagreement over the best gauge for a railway."

"What about the Elliots, sir?" she asked. She remembered from her walk in the garden that she was going to bring them up. "When are you going to interview them? After all, sir, as you said, they came a long ways just to have tea with Francis Humphreys." He'd said no such thing, but his memory was such that she was fairly safe in making the assertion.

"I said that?" he asked, raising his eyebrows in surprise. "Well, yes, of course, that's a very valid point. I haven't spoken to them as yet, but I'll be sure to bring it up tomorrow."

"Will they be here, sir? Or will they be going back to Dorset now that the funeral service is over?" she asked innocently. "Oh yes, of course they'll stay. They'll want to hear the will read."

"Quite right." He nodded in agreement. "And I shall interview them tomorrow." He was annoyed with himself and, if truth be told, with Constable Gates. He'd completely forgotten about the Elliots and if he'd been working with Constable Barnes, Barnes would have reminded him. "I do miss our Constable Barnes."

"As do I, sir," she murmured before she caught herself. "Did you learn anything else today?"

"Not really." He got to his feet. "As I've said, the family had been to the funeral and it didn't seem appropriate to bother any of them today. But now that the poor man is decently buried, I'll be having another interview with everyone."

Constable Barnes was at their back door well before breakfast the next morning. Mrs. Jeffries, who'd not slept more than a few hours, was already up and about the kitchen when she heard his soft knock in the wee hours of the morning.

"Good morning, Constable," she said softly as she ushered him in the back door.

"Sorry to be here so early," he replied with an embarrassed grin. "I saw your light and I wanted to have a quick word with you."

"Come on in and have a cup of tea," she invited. "And you're always welcome, you know that."

They went into the kitchen. Mrs. Jeffries motioned him into a chair while she poured him a cup of tea. "Drink this, Constable, it's cold outside." She passed him a mug.

"Ta, Mrs. Jeffries," he thanked her, taking a swig of the warm, sweet brew. "I'm sorry I haven't been by in the evenings, but we've had a series of burglaries in the Fulham area and that's kept me busy. I've been doing a bit of investigating on the Humphreys case as well. The past couple of nights I've not been free until well past ten and by then it's really too late to come barging in on the inspector's household."

"Gracious, Constable, then what on earth are you doing here so very early in the morning? You should have stayed abed and gotten some rest."

He shook his head. "I don't need as much sleep as I used to, Mrs. Jeffries. I'm fine. Is the inspector all right?"

"He misses you very much," she replied. "But he's coping. Constable Gates is a bit of a trial, I'm afraid."

Barnes chuckled. "Hearing that makes me feel good, though I am sorry the inspector is having a difficult time of it. Nonetheless, I did stop in for a reason. I've not spent every waking moment playing at burglars."

She grinned. "Do tell."

"I managed to get over to the Records Room at the Yard, and as I had a few hours to myself, I went through the alphabetical files."

"What were you looking for?" She lifted her cup to her lips and took a sip of the hot liquid.

"I had the list of names of the people who were at the house the afternoon Humphreys was murdered," he replied. "I know none of them could have done it, but I wanted to see if any of them had any known criminal associates."

"You keep records of such things?" she asked. She was genuinely curious and a little apprehensive.

"We try to," he answered. "Mind you, it's a bit haphazard. But ever since those Ripper murders, the force has done its best to be more efficient and well organized about illegal activities and the people involved in them."

"They appear to have done an admirable job," she murmured. "Yet keeping records about ordinary citizens is also a bit—"

"Disturbing." He finished the sentence for her. "Most policemen would agree with you wholeheartedly, Mrs. Jeffries. Let me assure you, the only people in the files are those that have either been witnesses to a crime, in which case they're noted as witnesses, or criminals who have been arrested."

"And if they are acquitted?" she queried.

"The records show that as well," he said.

"Of course, Constable. Please forgive me, I've no right to waste your precious time in this sort of ridiculous debate. What did you find out?"

"As you'd suppose," Barnes began, "the guests having tea in Humphreys House the afternoon he was murdered aren't the sort of people one would find in the criminal files. But one of them was." He paused for a brief moment. "Ten years ago, Michael Collier was arrested."

"On what charge?"

"Assault," Barnes replied. "Allegedly, Collier got into an argument with one of his neighbors from the flat next door to his home. The disagreement got heated and fists started to fly. Another neighbor tried to pull them apart, but by then Collier had supposedly lost his temper and punched the poor fellow who was trying to separate them. One of the women watching the fight ran to the corner and summoned the beat constable."

"Who, then, arrested Michael Collier?" she asked.

"Both men were arrested," Barnes replied. "The other man, a fellow named Artemis Jones, was charged with disturbing the peace. Jones paid a small fine and was let go. But Collier was charged with assault, a much more serious crime."

"Who started the altercation?" she asked.

"According to the testimony of the witnesses," Barnes said, "Jones was clearly at fault, but the reason Collier was had up on the more serious charge was because once the fight started, he beat Jones mercilessly. He went so far as to kick him when he was lying on the ground begging for

Collier to stop. That's why the neighbor jumped in and tried to pull Collier back. He told the arresting officer that he was afraid Collier was going to kill Jones."

Mrs. Jeffries thought for a moment. "Was Collier sent to prison?"

"He did three months in Wormwood Scrubs. Lucky for him, Jones recovered from his injuries and even testified in court that he'd been the one to start the fight." Barnes smiled cynically. "There was a note in the report from the arresting officer. He went by the Joneses' flat right after the trial was over. Jones and his missus seemed to have come up a bit in the world. They were moving from the flat into their own little terraced house in Brixton. Now considering Jones was an unemployed bricklayer at the time, it makes you wonder where he got the money to buy his own home, doesn't it?"

"You think Collier paid him off for his testimony in order to get a lighter sentence?" Mrs. Jeffries wrapped her hands around the outside of her mug to warm her fingers; the kitchen was still very chilly.

"The arresting officer thought someone had been spreading a bit of money about, because he had a chat with the other neighbors. One of them told him that just before the trial started a well-dressed man and woman were seen going into the Joneses' flat. The neighbor remembered the incident distinctly because she overheard the woman talking and she had an American accent." Barnes stared at her for a moment, hoping she'd come to the same conclusion he'd reached.

"So Estelle Collier Humphreys and her husband bought the Jones family a house to get her nephew a lighter sentence," Mrs. Jeffries said. "Is that what you're thinking?"

Barnes nodded. "She'd plenty of money. Why wouldn't she spend it to help her only living relative? The officer concluded his report by saying he didn't think there was enough evidence to do anything about the bribery so he had to let it go."

"Mores the pity." Mrs. Jeffries shook her head in disgust. "At least Collier served some time in prison, even if it was a very light sentence."

"And that's the other reason I came to see you." Barnes cocked his head to one side. "He served time in prison, Mrs. Jeffries, and the Scrubs holds all kinds—pickpockets, thugs, burglars, and killers."

It took a moment before she understood what he was telling her. "You think Collier met someone in prison who'd be willing to commit murder."

"For the right price, oh yes." He snorted faintly. "And it wouldn't even cost that much. We know Collier couldn't have done the deed himself—he was sitting in a roomful of people when his uncle was murdered—but he had access to the house, and he could have easily left a door or window open for an accomplice."

"And he'd not been invited to tea that day," she mused. "He asked Imogene Ross for an invitation."

"If Collier is the killer, he needed to be at the house to get his accomplice inside."

"Collier claimed he went there to drum up support from the other cousins to have their uncle declared incompetent to manage his own affairs," she said. "But he'd already been to a solicitor and been told that he'd probably lose if he went to court. Today the inspector found out the exact terms of Humphreys' will. He confirmed that except for the house, which goes to Annabelle Prescott, the rest of the estate is to be divided in half."

"Don't tell me, let me guess." Barnes put his cup down. "Michael Collier is getting one half all for himself and the relatives are having to share their half? Right?"

CHAPTER 9

"What I'd like to know is how he knew to come to the back door," Betsy whispered to Wiggins. They were standing at the entrance to the back hallway, staring at Lionel Gates as he made himself at home in the kitchen. He was sitting at the table shoving Mrs. Goodge's hot cross buns into his mouth as fast as possible.

The footman bit his lip and looked down at his shoes. "It's my fault," he replied softly. "Yesterday I accidentally mentioned that Constable Barnes always used the back door when he came to fetch the inspector."

"I ought to box your ears for that," the cook muttered as she came up behind them. She'd gone to the dry larder to fetch more supplies. "That rascal is eatin' all the buns I made for my sources," she hissed. "Go and find Mrs. Jeffries. She's got to get him out of here before I do something we'll all regret."

"I say, Mrs. Goodge." Lionel twisted in his chair and grinned at them. "This is jolly excellent pastry."

Just then, Mrs. Jeffries came down the back stairs. She took one look at the cook's thunderous expression and rushed over to the table. "You'd best come upstairs now, Constable," she ordered in a tone that brooked no argument. "The inspector is almost ready to leave." That was a lie—Witherspoon had just started to eat his breakfast—but she knew if she didn't get Gates out of the kitchen and away from those buns, Mrs. Goodge was likely to do the man grievous bodily harm.

"Right away, Mrs. Jeffries." Lionel jumped up, grabbed another bun, and followed the housekeeper to the back stairs.

"Grrr," the cook growled as she raced across the floor, snatched up the plate of pastry, and went back toward the dry larder. "I'm hiding these in case that uncouth rascal comes back down. I've got to have something to feed my sources."

"And I've got to get goin' if I'm to find Rachel. It's not fair that we didn't have time to have a proper meetin' this mornin'," Wiggins complained. "I'd like to have found out a bit more so I'd know what I ought to ask her."

"Just find out as much as you can about everyone's movements in the 'ouse on the days leadin' up to the murder," Smythe suggested as he slipped on his overcoat.

"And it's your fault we didn't have a proper meeting." Betsy glared at the footman. "How could we with Constable Gates barging into the kitchen like he owned the place. If you'd kept quiet, we could have stuck him in the drawing room while we had our meeting."

"I didn't mean to tell 'im," Wiggins cried. "It just slipped out. But at least I managed to head off the others before they got here. You've got to give me credit for that. Now Gates can't go tattlin' to the inspector that Luty, Hatchet, and Lady Cannonberry was sittin' around the kitchen table talkin' about his case."

When Lionel had knocked on the back door, Wiggins had had the foresight to slip out and keep the others away from the house. But Lionel's intrusion into their private place had put everyone in the household in a bad mood, and Wiggins knew it was his fault. He patted his coat pocket, making sure his gloves were still inside. "I'm off, then," he said. "I'll do my best with Rachel."

"See that you do," Betsy retorted as she put on her hat. She was the most annoyed. Mrs. Jeffries had only given them the bare bones of what she'd learned from the inspector at dinner last night and hadn't even begun to tell what she'd heard from Constable Barnes before they'd been interrupted.

"Now don't be too hard on the lad." Smythe draped her jacket over her shoulders. "He just 'ad a slip of the tongue. It could 'appen to anyone."

Betsy glanced at the footman as she put her arm into the coat sleeve. His shoulders slumped, his lips were turned down, and he looked miserable. She knew he hated it when he thought anyone in the household was angry at him. They were family.

"Oh, Wiggins, I'm sorry. I shouldn't have been so nasty," she apologized. "I know you didn't mean to get us stuck with Gates."

He smiled in relief. "I'll mind what I say in the future; leastways, I'll try to. Where are you goin' today?"

Betsy glanced at Smythe and saw he was watching her. So of course she smiled innocently at the two men and lied. "I thought I'd have another go at Michael Collier's neighborhood. If I don't find out anything useful there, I thought I'd see if I could find out anything more about Imogene Ross." She did plan on going back to Collier's neighborhood but only because she had to pass through Pimlico to get to the East End. She was determined to find out if anyone from their old neighborhood might know her sister's whereabouts She knew her fiancé wouldn't approve of her going to Tredway Street on her own. Sometimes Smythe forgot that she'd grown up in that neighborhood and could take care of herself. Nevertheless, she'd found it easier to simply keep the truth to herself. "And where are you off to?" she asked her beloved.

"To the Sun and Moon," he replied. He patted his chest, checking for the wad of pound notes he carried in his inside coat pocket. "I want to see if anyone knows why Joseph Humphreys was drinkin' himself into a stupor. Afterwards, I'm goin' to see one of my sources."

Betsy nodded, glad that she'd asked his plans. It wasn't likely that she'd run into her fiancé. The East End was a big place. Nevertheless, she'd keep a sharp eye out just to make sure their paths didn't cross.

"Be back on time for our meeting," Mrs. Jeffries said to them as she hurried into the kitchen. "I've a feeling we'll have lots to discuss." She had a few plans of her own today.

Luty stood in the small portico of number 6 Deering Place, Mayfair, and reached for the huge brass door knocker. It had taken her less than five minutes to find the address of the Edwin Chalmers household and she'd not wasted any time getting here this morning. She was bound and determined to find out what she needed to know by their meeting this afternoon.

"Are you sure this is a good idea?" Julie, her maid, whispered. Julie was standing right behind her. Luty had brought her along to prop up the tale she was going to spin.

"It'll be fine." Luty banged the knocker. "Quit worryin' and just do what I told you. Leave the talkin' to me."

Julie bit her lip nervously. "I don't think this is right." She wasn't in the least frightened of arguing with her mistress. Luty Belle Crookshank expected her staff to be respectful but never to be afraid to air their opinions. "Mr. Hatchet will be very upset if he knows that you're using something he accidentally overheard about Miss Betsy's family . . ."

"You let me worry about him," Luty hissed as the door opened. She plastered a smile on her lips as an elderly butler appeared and stared at her out of a pair of watery, cold gray eyes. "Yes?" he said coolly.

"Good afternoon," she said brightly. "Is this the Edwin Chalmers household?"

His gaze flicked over her slight frame and onto the young woman standing behind her. Then he looked past her to the road where her carriage and driver waited. Luty grinned to herself as she saw the butler's eyes widen as he saw her carriage. The coach was perfect, the silver studs on the bridles and reins were brightly polished and the doors waxed to a high gloss. On top sat a driver dressed in full livery of silver and forest green. Keeping this kind of rig in London cost the earth and that's precisely why Luty had forced poor Ned into the uniform he'd only worn one other time in his life, made him hitch up all four horses, and spend the early hours of the morning with polish and wax. She wanted to make sure she got in the front door of the Chalmers house and she'd dressed herself, Julie, and the carriage to achieve that end.

"Yes ma'am," the butler replied, forcing his gaze back to her. "How may I help you?"

"Sorry to just arrive unannounced." Luty grinned. "But if Mr. or Mrs. Chalmers is available, I'd like to speak to them on a matter of life and death. If it makes any difference, I'm a friend of Lord Barraclough." She was counting on her American accent and the name-dropping to get her in the front door and into the drawing room. The English were merciless about uncouth behavior from other Englishmen but amazingly tolerant of eccentricities from outsiders. It was as if they expected foreigners to have no manners.

The butler hesitated, flicked another glance at Luty's sable muff, and opened the door wider. "Please come inside and I'll see if Mrs. Chalmers is at home."

"Thank you. Here's my calling card." Luty handed it to him. The card was on heavy cream-colored paper and her name and address were written in an elegant black script.

She and Julie stood in the foyer and as soon as the butler was out of earshot, Luty said, "I told you we could do it. Now, when we're talkin' to Mrs. Chalmers, you just do what I told you. Dab at your eyes and see if you can squeeze out a tear or two."

"But I can't make myself cry," Julie protested.

"Use that hankie I had the cook rub with onions," she ordered. "That's why I had you bring it along. It wasn't because the thing smells pretty."

"I've tried that and it doesn't work," Julie retorted. "It just makes my nose itch something fierce and I don't think this is right. If Mr. Hatchet knows that you're usin' Miss Betsy's story—"

"I told you, let me worry about that," Luty hissed. Guilt speared through her, but she shoved it to the back of her mind. This was a murder and she had to use what weapons came to hand. Besides, if all went as planned, Betsy would never know what she'd done. But the tale was too good to pass up, and well, it wasn't her fault that Hatchet had inadvertently heard Betsy and Smythe talking. She'd told him how she'd not seen her sister in years and how she'd give anything to have some of her family at the wedding. Hatchet had shared this information with Luty in confidence, swearing her never to repeat it. But it wasn't like she was spreading the story about for the sake of gossip. She was simply borrowing it for the sake of justice. Betsy would understand that.

She whirled about as she heard the butler coming.

"If you'll come this way, please." He led them to a set of doors at the far end of the hall, knocked lightly, and then stepped inside. "Mrs. Crookshank, ma'am," he announced. He stood to one side as they stepped into the room.

A short, plump woman sat at a secretary. She smiled and rose to her feet. "Thank you, Riggs. That will be all," she said to her servant before turning her attention to her visitors. "Good morning, I'm Margery Chalmers. I understand you'd like to speak with me."

"That's right, ma'am, and I do appreciate you seein' us," Luty replied. "It's a rather personal matter concernin' this young woman here"—she nodded at Julie—"and I'm hopin' you can help us."

Margery Chalmers regarded her thoughtfully for a long moment. "I've heard about you, Mrs. Crookshank. You're an American, aren't you. But where are my manners. Please sit down." She indicated a floral print loveseat and took the chair next to it for herself.

"Thank you." Luty sat where she'd been told, glanced at Julie, and noted that the girl had the onion-soaked hanky in her hand. Good. "Now, as I was sayin', I've come on a rather delicate matter."

"Please, tell me how I can be of help," Margery Chalmers replied. She sounded amused.

Luty looked up sharply. But despite the woman's tone, she stared back at her guilelessly. "This young lady here is Julie Brown. She's not seen her sister in almost ten years. Last we heard, her sister was working as a ladies' maid to a woman who lived near here, a Mrs. Humphreys."

"There was a Humphreys family that lived in a flat around the corner from here," Margery answered. "But they left a long time ago."

"We know that," Luty said. "This is why we're here. You see, Julie is getting married in October and she'd dearly love for her sister to be at the wedding. Trouble is, her sister has more or less disappeared. The last Julie knew of her, she was working as a ladies' maid for Mrs. Humphreys but that poor woman up and died. Then Julie's family heard that she'd been hired here, as a scullery maid."

"That's true. We employed her."

Julie sniffed loudly and dabbed at her eyes. "I'd dearly love to see my sister," she said. She tried her best to make her voice tremble.

"I'm sure you would. May I ask why you've waited so long to come looking for her? It's been a number of years since Mrs. Humphreys passed away."

Luty was ready for that question. "Poor Julie was taken to Australia by her father. She's only recently come back to England. Her father passed away last winter." Luty paused expectantly, waiting for Mrs. Chalmers to tell her where the maid had gone when she'd left here. But instead of speaking, Margery Chalmers got to her feet, walked to the door, and rang the bellpull. It opened immediately and the butler stuck his head inside. "Please go and fetch Mrs. Blake," she instructed him. "Tell her to come quickly, I think her long-lost sister is here."

Luty's heart sank to her toes. She'd been sure the girl would have moved on. All she'd wanted from the Chalmers woman was a name, dang it. She'd never have used this story if she'd thought there was any possibility the maid still worked here. Nells bells, she'd seriously miscalculated. But Betsy had said a trained ladies' maid wouldn't stay working in the kitchen. She heard Julie moan faintly.

Luty summoned up a smile and looked at her hostess. "Uh, you know, come to think of it, I might have made a mistake."

"I'm quite sure you have," Mrs. Chalmers said. "Mrs. Crookshank, why don't we dispense with this charade right now and save us all a great deal of embarrassment. Why have you come here today?"

"I told you this wouldn't work," Julie whispered.

"Well, fiddlesticks, I didn't think she'd still be here," Luty replied without thinking. "All I wanted was the name of Estelle Humphreys' maid." Luty had played enough poker to know when a bluff was going south. She took a deep, calming breath to give herself a few moments to tell the truth without actually telling the truth.

But before she could come up with anything useful, the drawing room door opened and a woman in a black housekeeper dress stepped into the room. She was tall with dark hair, a dignified woman who looked to be in her midthirties. She stared at Luty and Julie for a moment and then looked at Margery Chalmers. "Riggs said you wished to see me, ma'am. Something about a long-lost sister?" She sounded very confused. "I didn't quite understand the message. I don't have a sister and I've never seen either of these two women before in my entire life."

"But you were Estelle Collier Humphreys' maid?" Luty blurted. She was determined to find out something useful from this fiasco.

"I was," the housekeeper answered. "But I don't see that that is any of your concern."

"Of course it is," Luty replied. "And if you've got an ounce of justice in your soul, it'll be your concern as well."

Smythe stopped across the road from the Sun and Moon pub and examined it closely. The one-story brick building was old, sagged slightly in the center, and had a sheen of dirt on it that had probably been there since the Stuarts had sat on the throne. He crossed the road and then hesitated before going inside. He wasn't very sure of himself when it came to finding things out on his own. That was one of the problems with being rich: Though you could hire work done that you used to do for yourself, when you found yourself in a spot where you *had* to do the work yourself, you were just that bit uncertain of your own abilities. But then he remembered the slip of paper in his pocket and he grinned at his own foolishness. Being able to hire work done did have its advantages.

On his way here, he'd stopped in to see Blimpey and found out that Blimpey's people had located a ship's manifest with the Hanrahans listed as passengers. They'd sailed third-class on the *Golden Chance* bound for Halifax. Blimpey had advised Smythe that as his resources didn't stretch all the way to Nova Scotia, at this point, it would be best to hire a private inquiry agent to continue the search. Blimpey knew just the firm to handle such a personal, private matter as well. Smythe had agreed that was the best course of action and now it was only a matter of time before Betsy's sister and her family were located. Smythe couldn't wait to see the look on her face when she walked down the aisle of the church on her wedding day and saw her family sitting in the first pew. It would be the best gift any groom could give his bride and truth to tell, he was right pleased with his own cleverness. He laughed, grabbed the door handle, and stepped into the pub. Any man who could find his fiancée's long-lost relatives could suss out a little information on his own.

The Three Swans Inn had once been a coaching stop. The coming of the railways had almost ended its business, but by changing its rates and advertising, the inn had managed to stay in business by catering to traveling salesmen, middle-class families, and the occasional tourist from the United States who couldn't afford one of the big London hotels.

Inspector Witherspoon sat across from the Elliots in one of the overstuffed chairs in the small, dimly lighted lobby. Constable Gates, who had to keep ducking to avoid being smacked by the fronds of an oversized fern from the table behind him, sat on a straight-backed chair next to Jeremiah and Grace Elliot.

"I don't know what we can tell you," Mr. Elliot muttered. "We saw nothing out of the ordinary. Then we heard the shot." He was a small, balding man with a reddish complexion and a bulbous nose. His wife sat next to him. She was middle aged, slightly plump, and wearing a navy blue traveling outfit. A blue umbrella and black traveling bag were at her feet.

"I understand you and Mrs. Elliot live in Dorset," Witherspoon said.

"That's correct," Mr. Elliot replied. "We came up to have tea with cousin Francis."

"You came all the way from Dorset just for tea?" Lionel asked. He jerked to one side as the frond tickled his neck.

"We had other business to attend to as well," Mr. Elliot explained. "When Francis heard we were coming up to town, he asked us to come for tea."

"What kind of business?" Lionel turned and slapped at the fern.

Mr. Elliot glanced at Witherspoon before replying. "I don't believe that's any of your business."

"This is a murder investigation," Lionel began.

"I take it your reasons for coming to London had nothing to do with your cousin," Witherspoon interrupted. "Is that correct?"

"That is correct, sir." Mr. Elliot glared at Lionel.

"Then we'll not trouble you about it again, Mr. Elliot," the inspector said. "What time did you arrive at your cousin's home that day?"

"Just before four o'clock."

"Did you notice anyone hanging about the place or

anything else that struck you as odd?" Witherspoon shifted slightly in his chair.

"No, it was as it always was," he said. "Except, of course, there were rather more people in the house than there had been the last time we visited. Two more of Francis' relatives had taken up residency."

"I see." Witherspoon literally couldn't think of what to ask next. He glanced at the traveling bag. "Are you going back to Dorset today?"

"We're taking the two o'clock train," Mrs. Elliot answered. "We want to go home. We'd not have stayed so long except we wanted to go to Francis' service."

"Aren't you going to stay for the reading of the will?" Lionel asked.

"Why would we?" Mrs. Elliot studied him in silence for a moment. "We're not Francis' heirs. Despite what anyone in his family may have told you, we didn't expect to receive anything from him. For goodness' sake, he was only a distant cousin."

Lionel had the good grace to blush. "Sorry, ma'am, I didn't mean to offend, but it is our job to find out who murdered Francis Humphreys. Sometimes we have to ask uncomfortable questions in the course of our investigation."

"Then you ought to try asking his nieces and nephews your questions," she told him. "Though what you'll get from any of them is anybody's guess. Honestly, we'd not been in the drawing room five minutes before Mrs. Yancy Humphreys started whispering to Miss Imogene that Mrs. Prescott was up to her old tricks." She pursed her lips in disgust. "Once Pamela starts carping on a subject, she won't stop. Jeremiah and I pretended we wanted to have a look at the garden. It gave us an excuse to get up and go to the window. You know, make it less obvious we were changing our seats. I didn't want to spend the whole afternoon listening to Pamela Humphreys complain."

"What was Mrs. Humphreys complaining about?" the inspector asked.

She shrugged. "I'm not certain. I tried not to listen."

"Pamela said that Annabelle Prescott was borrowing Yancy's gadgets without permission again," Mr. Elliot said. He grinned at his wife. "I'm not as high minded as you are, dearest. I like a bit of gossip every now and again."

Grace Elliot tried to look disapproving, but then she broke into laughter. "Oh, alright, you've caught me. I did hear what she was saying. I just wanted to pretend I hadn't. Eavesdropping seems such a common habit."

"Did you hear anything else?" Witherspoon asked.

"Only that Pamela said she was going to have the lock to the side door changed to keep Annabelle from helping herself," Mrs. Elliot replied. "It was an old issue, Inspector. Annabelle, er, Mrs. Prescott and Yancy grew up together. She was devastated when he died and she bitterly resented the fact that Pamela ended up with her late husband's inventions."

"Mrs. Prescott wanted them for herself?" Lionel turned and slapped at the frond again.

Mrs. Elliot looked at her husband, who gave the briefest of nods, before she replied. "I don't think Annabelle wanted anything for herself, but she bitterly resented the fact that Pamela had nothing but contempt for her own husband and that contempt was reflected in the way she treated his life's work. Pamela always said the only reason she hadn't gotten rid of Yancy's gadgets, as she called them, was because she was afraid it would upset Francis. But now that he's dead and gone, she'll probably toss the whole lot of them out with the rubbish."

Mrs. Jeffries sat across from Tommy Parker and noted with satisfaction that he wasn't in the least intimidated by

his surroundings. Considering that young Tommy wore a
brown shirt with a frayed collar, black trousers with
patches on both knees, a gray jacket with half the buttons
missing, and a green flat cap so old that the crown was
threadbare in spots, the young lad's poise was admirable.
Tommy stared at her for a moment and then turned his attention to the waiter. His twelve-year-old eyes widened as
the waiter put a plate of pastries down next to a pot of tea.
"Would you like me to pour, madam?" he asked Mrs. Jeffries.

"No thank you, I can manage," she replied. He inclined
his head, cast a quick, disapproving glance at Tommy, and
left.

Tommy caught the waiter's disgruntled expression and
kept his gaze squarely on the server's back as he went back
toward the kitchen. A man in a formal black frock coat,
most likely the manager, waved the waiter over. Across the
crowded café, Mrs. Jeffries watched them whispering together, the manager's gaze flicking to Tommy every few
seconds. She hoped the manager wasn't going to ask them
to leave. It would be awkward to make a scene, but make a
scene she would. The boy was her guest.

"They aren't used to seein' the likes of me in here."
Tommy grinned. "It's nice. I've never been inside here as a
customer before."

Mrs. Jeffries turned her attention back to her companion and wondered what the boy was thinking. He'd been
surprised when she'd walked up to him at Ealing station
and asked if he knew anyone who'd recently been taking
messages to the telegraph office for Francis Humphreys.

When she'd left Upper Edmonton Gardens, she'd not
meant to seek the boy out. Her only thought had been to
have a look at Humphreys House. She'd hoped seeing where
the murder had taken place might help. But as she'd gotten
off the train, she'd seen the street urchins hawking their

talents. They'd shouted at passing travelers, offering to carry cases, take messages, or even shine shoes, and she'd remembered what Pamela Humphreys had said to the inspector. There were always lads hanging about in front of Humphreys House when the 3:09 to Bristol went past.

"You've been in here for other reasons." She reached for the pot and poured the tea.

"I've carried parcels and cases in for ladies and gents," he told her proudly. "But I've never had a proper sit-down."

She put the cup in front of him. "Help yourself to a pastry."

"Thank ya, ma'am." He grabbed his fork, speared an apricot tart, and slapped it onto his plate. He glanced at her apprehensively before he took a bite.

"How often did you take messages to the telegraph office for Mr. Humphreys?" She helped herself to a slice of seedcake.

"Every time the ruddy train was late," he said around a mouthful of tart. "It was usually two or three times a week. Hope they catch the blighter that done him in. Took away a right good customer of mine."

"Were you there last Tuesday?"

"You mean the day he was killed." He shoved another bite into his mouth, chewed, and swallowed. "Course I was, but the ruddy train was on time, mores the pity. Came screaming down the line blowin' that bloomin' whistle long enough and loud enough to wake the dead. I knew right then I was out of luck and there'd be no telegram sent. So I come on back here to wait for the 3:25." He put the rest of the tart in his mouth.

"When you were there, did you see anyone on the property?" she asked. "Anyone who oughtn't to have been there?"

"Nah, I didn't see anyone exceptin' the family and servants. Miss Ross waved at me from the front window and a maid come out and polished the brass knocker, but that's all I saw." He looked at the pastry plate.

"Have another," Mrs. Jeffries ordered softly. She picked up her fork and took a bite of her cake. It wasn't as good as Mrs. Goodge's, but it was nice nonetheless. They ate in companionable silence for a few minutes.

"This is the second patch I've lost in this neighborhood," Tommy muttered. "I think I'm goin' to have to be movin' on."

"Patch?" she asked curiously.

"A patch is the area that's yours to work, you know, where your customers live," he explained. "I had another just down the road, but then Mr. Yancy Humphreys died, so that ended."

"Mr. Yancy Humphreys sent you with messages to the telegraph office as well?" she asked.

"Oh no, it was his neighbors sending me to fetch the police when he was out in his garden playin' about with his bird scarer." Tommy laughed. "Poor Mr. Yancy was had up for disturbin' the peace half a dozen times that summer and every time, I'd earn a sixpence for goin' to fetch the constable. But Mr. Yancy didn't care. I overheard him telling the police that he was testin' the contraption and that the thingies it fired weren't dangerous. Mind you, I don't rightly blame them for makin' a fuss—it boomed louder than thunder and scared the horses. Then Mr. Francis Humphreys started sendin' me to the telegraph office." He broke off and sighed deeply. "But now that he's gone, I'm goin' to have to find a new patch. Even a clever lad like me can't get milk out of a cow that's gone dry."

Mrs. Goodge shook her head and closed the back door. The butcher's boy, her only source so far today, had absolutely nothing useful to say. He'd not even heard of the murder! She stalked into the kitchen. As she came through the door, she spotted Fred under the table licking the floor. "Well, bother and blast," she muttered. "Betsy cleaned that floor this morning and now someone's gone and spilled something." She bent down to see how bad it was and spotted a little brown notebook next to the table leg. Fred, who'd finished eating whatever had been spilled, tried to lick her face. "Not now, boy," she said and gently pushed him aside. Unoffended, the dog ambled off to lie down on his rug.

She took a deep breath and eased her considerable bulk a bit lower, reached out her arm, and grabbed the notebook. She stood up and flipped it open. When she saw the name written on the inside flap, she laughed, pulled up a chair, and sat down to have a read. She had no qualms whatsoever about finding out what young Lionel Gates had been up to recently. If he'd not been stuffing her buns in his mouth this morning like a greedy little pig, he'd probably not have lost his notebook.

Betsy knew she was late for their afternoon meeting, but she couldn't bring herself to move any faster down the path through the communal garden. When the Witherspoon house came into view, she stopped completely. What was she going to do? One part of her desperately wanted to talk to Smythe and ask for his advice, but she didn't want to tell him where she'd been. She'd gone to Bethnal Green, to the road just up from Tredway Street, this time in search of Leo Hanrahan's family. She'd hoped one of his relatives might still live there. But Leo's family had disappeared as completely as her own had and none of his old neighbors had any idea where any of them had gone.

She ought to have left then, but she'd foolishly gone into the corner shop, the one that had refused to give her family credit when the baby was dying and her mother was out of work. Betsy closed her eyes as a wave of remembered humiliation swept over her. She'd stood there on Tredway Street, staring in through the tiny grease-stained window, and had seen Mrs. Muir behind the counter. My God, who would have expected the cow would still be alive after all these years. She'd forced herself to cross that old crone's threshold and go into that dark, miserable shop.

She sighed in disgust. She was acting like a ninny. She had no reason to be afraid. Besides, she told herself as she started toward the back door, Mrs. Muir was always a nasty person, she was probably making the whole thing up just because it had annoyed her to see Betsy wearing nice clothes and carrying a purse with coin in it. But still, it had bothered her when Mrs. Muir had told her she'd no idea where Norah and Leo had gone but that a well-dressed man had been in the shop only the day before asking after Betsy. Would Betsy care to leave her address and Mrs. Muir would be sure to send her a note if she heard anything about Norah and Leo's whereabouts? She assured Betsy she'd ask around the neighborhood on her behalf. Betsy hadn't fallen for the ploy, of course. She knew good and well the witch was going to sell her address to whoever had been inquiring after her. That's what was so frightening. Betsy couldn't think why anyone would be asking questions about her. She needed to talk to Smythe. She wasn't frightened of his reaction—she knew he'd never hurt her—but she knew he wasn't going to be happy when he heard what she'd done.

By now, Betsy had reached the back door. She pulled it open and started down the hallway, shedding her jacket and bonnet as she walked. "I'm so sorry to be late," she apologized as she came into the kitchen. "But the traffic was terrible."

"We've only just sat down," Mrs. Jeffries said. "So you're in good time."

Everyone was already sitting at the table with tea poured

and plates loaded with food in front of them. Betsy slipped into her seat next to Smythe. He grinned at her, grabbed her hand, and gave it a welcoming squeeze.

"Before we begin, I've got somethin' I'd like to show everyone." Mrs. Goodge giggled as she held up the little brown notebook. "You'll never guess what this is."

"It looks like Constable Barnes' notebook," Wiggins guessed.

"Nope." The cook laughed. "This one belongs to Lionel Gates. I found it on the floor under the table. It must have fallen out of his pocket when he was makin' a pig of himself on my buns."

"Have you read it?" Mrs. Jeffries asked.

"Of course, and guess what—there's information in here we've not gotten from the inspector," she declared. "Seems to me that young Constable Gates is sneaking about behind the inspector's back, interviewin' suspects and takin' statements that he'd not shared with our inspector."

"What things?" Luty asked.

"This sort." The cook flipped open the book and began to read. " 'Interview with Della Robertson, scullery maid at Yancy Humphreys' residence. Miss Robertson asserts that she saw and heard nothing untoward on the day Mr. Francis H. was murdered.' " Mrs. Goodge looked up. "I'm assuming that Mr. Francis H. is Francis Humphreys." She continued reading. " 'The only thing odd about the day was she saw Miss Imogene Ross coming out of the servants' entrance of Humphreys House when she (the maid) went out to take the linens down from the clothesline. I asked the girl if she'd seen anything unusual in the days prior to the murder and she asserted that she'd seen Mrs. Prescott going in the side door of Mr. Yancy Humphreys' home and coming out ten minutes later carrying a covered object that the girl was unable to identify. She also claims she saw Mr. Joseph Humphreys standing outside of Humphreys House two days before the murder.'" Mrs. Goodge looked at them over the top of her glasses. "We've not heard any of this, and if you ask me, the inspector's probably not heard it, either. Gates is sneaking' about behind our inspector's back, trying to solve the case on his own and snatchin' all the credit for himself."

"That does seem a definite possibility," Mrs. Jeffries agreed. "May I read it?"

"Of course." The cook handed her the notebook. "And then we've got to decide what to do about it."

"Let's have our meetin' first," Luty suggested. "It's gettin' late and we don't want to be interrupted before we even begin, like this mornin'."

"Good idea," Mrs. Jeffries agreed. "Why don't you go first."

"Yes, madam, do tell us if you've achieved your objective and found out the name of Estelle Collier Humphreys' maid?" Hatchet asked innocently.

Luty was ready for him. She'd die before she'd tell them everything that had happened today and she'd made darned sure that Julie was going to keep on her own counsel on the matter as well. "I have," she replied with a smirk. "The maid's name is Beatrice Blake. She's a housekeeper now and she recalls quite clearly the name of the niece takin' care of Estelle Collier Humphreys." Luty paused. "Imogene Ross. The girl was between positions and came to help her uncle take care of his ailing wife. But before any of you jump to any conclusions, Beatrice said all the other nieces and nephews were in and out of her room and that when Mrs. Humphreys died, no one thought it was anything other than nature takin' its course. The woman was right sick."

"Well, madam, you have indeed done precisely what you claimed you could do." Hatchet gave her a sour smile.

"I, on the other hand, have found out nothing except that the cook at Humphreys House was annoyed that so many guests had arrived for tea. She'd only been expecting six and consequently had to prepare more food when both Mr. Collier and the Browns unexpectedly arrived."

"Seems to me you found out something." Luty smiled graciously. "Not as much as me, but something."

"I should like to go next," Mrs. Jeffries said quickly. "As you all know, Constable Barnes came along early this morning, but we were interrupted by Constable Gates before I could tell you what he said." She relayed what she'd learned about Michael Collier.

"Cor blimey, he could 'ave hired it done," Smythe murmured when she'd finished. "There's plenty in the Scrubs that'd be happy to do a dirty deed for a bit of cash."

"But just because he did time in the Scrubs doesn't mean he hired someone to murder his uncle," Hatchet said. "Considering what we've learned about his financial situation, where would he get the money to pay an assassin?"

"Maybe he borrowed it," Ruth suggested. "Though I must admit, asking for a loan so you could purchase a murder for hire does seem a bit far-fetched."

"I'm not accusing Collier of being our killer," Mrs. Jeffries said, "but thus far, he's the only one with a motive, an alibi, and access to individuals who might be willing to kill for a price. We can speculate for hours, but until we've more facts we must continue moving forward. I've also found out a few other interesting pieces of information." She told them about her meeting with Tommy Parker. "It was actually quite amusing," she concluded with a laugh. "It was apparent the café manager was most upset about young Tommy's presence as a customer; however, he didn't quite have the nerve to chuck us both out the door. Now, who would like to go next?"

"I'll have a go," Smythe said. "Mine won't take too

long. I talked to a few people at the Sun and Moon pub. According to them, Joseph Humphreys drank himself into a stupor the night before he moved into his uncle's house because he was ashamed."

"Ashamed of what?" Luty asked, her expression incredulous. "Bein' unemployed? Nells bells, losin' your job ain't no reason to hang your head like a whipped dog. Mr. Crookshank lost more jobs than most people have had hot dinners before we struck it rich in the silver mines of Colorado."

Smythe laughed. "Oh, he wasn't ashamed because he'd lost his position. He was ashamed because he wasn't a good enough socialist. His friends told me he spent the whole evening moaning about how if he was a true socialist he'd live on the streets instead of moving in with the true enemy of the working class."

"You mean his uncle," Wiggins cried. "Cor blimey, he's not a grateful sort of feller, is he?"

"Gratitude certainly doesn't appear to be one of young Mr. Humphreys' strongest characteristics," Mrs. Jeffries murmured. "And his gun was missing."

"Even so, he was still in the drawing room with the others when his uncle was murdered," Hatchet pointed out. "So unless he conspired with one of his radical friends, I don't see how he could have committed the murder."

Something tugged at the back of Mrs. Jeffries' mind, but it was gone before she could grab the idea and make any sense of it.

"I think them radicals like to talk and march," Mrs. Goodge declared. "I've never heard of any of them killin' people." She'd die before she'd ever admit it, but she had a grudging admiration for those who challenged authority and tried to change the world. Sometimes she wondered what her life would have been like if she'd been less willing to accept the given order and more willing to make a fuss and assert her rights. Oh well, better late than never, she told herself. She'd changed and if someone like her could change, there was hope for the whole world.

"If Smythe is finished, I'll go next," Wiggins volunteered. He waited for a moment and then went on speaking. "Findin' Rachel was dead easy, the 'ard part was gettin' her alone for a moment so we could talk a bit. But I managed. According to 'er, nothing unusual happened on the day Mr. Humphreys died exceptin' the bits we already know."

"You mean Miss Ross' argument with her uncle," Ruth said.

"That's right. Other than that, Rachel insists it was a day like any other. Miss Ross had the row with her uncle and then slipped in and out the servants' entrance, Mr. Joseph arrived and left all the cases in the front 'all for Rachel to lug upstairs, Mrs. Prescott carried some old stuff up to the attic, and Mr. Kirkland and Michael Collier showed up unexpectedly for tea. She said that's all that happened. 'Oh, I tell a lie,' Rachel said. She heard Mrs. Eames complainin' to the cook that Mrs. Prescott had invited Mr. Eddington and the Browns from next door to tea. Like Hatchet said, the cook was right upset as because all them extra mouths meant she had to make a whole tray of extra sandwiches."

Mrs. Jeffries sighed. "I'd so hoped that Rachel getting the sack meant something useful, but obviously the girl was fired because she was lazy."

The clock struck the hour and Mrs. Goodge said, "It's getting late. We've got to decide what we're going to do about Constable Gates' notebook? Should we give it to the inspector and let him know about the young rascal sneakin' about behind his back?"

"I think we ought to keep it," Wiggins said. "You never know when it might come in 'andy. We can always use it as an excuse to go find the inspector, you know, if we need him to go somewhere or do something right quick. I'm not explainin' this very well—"

"Sure you are," Luty interrupted. "We all know what you mean. I agree, we ought to hang on to it."

"So do I," Hatchet added.

Mrs. Jeffries glanced around the table. The others were shaking their heads in agreement as well. "Then we're decided." She smiled. "We'll keep it for the time being. Perhaps it may come in useful in another way as well; it might help to keep young Constable Gates in check if he goes too far behind our inspector's back."

CHAPTER 10

———

Witherspoon leaned back in his chair and took a sip of the sherry Mrs. Jeffries had just handed him. "I don't think I shall ever get this case solved," he complained. "I've interviewed at least twice every possible person who had anything to do with the victim, and I've found out nothing that brings me any closer to catching the murderer."

She was determined to make sure the inspector knew about Michael Collier's imprisonment in Wormwood Scrubs, but before she could decide on the best way to state the matter, he continued speaking. "This morning I thought my luck might have changed for the better. When I reported in to the station, there was a file on Michael Collier lying on the desk. I think Constable Barnes must have sent it over. That's the sort of background work he'd think to do."

Bless you, Constable Barnes, she thought silently. "A file on Michael Collier. Was it something useful, sir?"

"At first I thought so." He took another sip. "Collier did

a stretch in prison for assault. Naturally, it seemed to me that associating with the criminals one would find at Wormwood Scrubs could be just the break I needed in this case." He broke off and sighed. "But when I asked Mr. Collier about the matter, he readily admitted what he'd done and offered me a list of the people he'd associated with while incarcerated. He had the list written up and ready for me when I went to see him today. He claimed he knew we'd find out about his imprisonment and wanted to prove he had nothing to hide."

"Gracious, sir, do you think he was being sincere or simply trying to put the best light on the incident?" she asked.

"He was trying to make himself look as good as possible." The inspector nodded his head at Mrs. Jeffries' question. "And I can't say that I blame the man. The truth of the matter is, the moment I heard he'd been in prison, my mind immediately cast him in the role of possible murderer. But that's not fair. We've no evidence against him whatsoever."

"What did Constable Gates think of Mr. Collier's actions?"

The inspector grinned. "He wasn't with me, and frankly I haven't shared that interview with him."

"But I thought Constable Gates was supposed to be helping you today? He came along this morning to fetch you."

"He had to go haring off on an errand of his own," Witherspoon replied. "I think he lost his notebook and didn't want me to find out, but it was so obvious something was amiss. One minute he was checking his pockets and the next he was muttering some nonsense about verifying witness statements and running for the door. But I didn't mind, it gave me an opportunity to interview Collier on my own. Unfortunately, though, Constable Gates caught up with me at the Three Swans Inn when I went to speak to Mr. and Mrs. Elliot.

"Had Constable Gates found his notebook?" she asked.

"I don't think so," Witherspoon said. "He was using a new one when we were interviewing the Elliots. I could tell because when he pulled it out of his pocket and opened it, he started writing on the first page. If he'd been using his old one, he'd have started taking notes halfway through the book."

Mrs. Jeffries stared at him in surprise. Noticing a detail like that was the mark of a first-rate detective. Perhaps she and the others were taking a bit too much credit for themselves. Perhaps they weren't helping him quite as much as they'd thought. She shoved that uncomfortable notion aside and inquired, "Were Mr. and Mrs. Elliot very helpful to you, sir?"

"They told the same story as everyone else who'd been in the drawing room when Humphreys was shot," he said. "But I've more or less eliminated them as suspects. They had no reason to want Francis Humphreys dead. There was no animosity between them and they claimed he was only a distant cousin. They weren't expecting to inherit anything from him." He told her about the rest of the interview and broke into a laugh when he got to the part about Pamela Humphreys complaining about Annabelle Prescott. "I don't think the two women are overly fond of one another," he concluded.

"That happens in all families." She took a sip of sherry. She wondered if they'd been wise to keep the fact they'd found Gates' notebook a secret.

"Just as I was leaving, Mrs. Elliot also mentioned that she thinks Imogene Ross has, oh dear, how did she put it? Ah yes, she said, 'that young Imogene had set her cap for Michael Collier.' Not that I think that has anything to do with the murder."

Mrs. Jeffries was suddenly fully alert. "Did she say why?"

"Why what?" Witherspoon drained his glass and got to his feet.

She took a slow, calming breath as a dozen different notions flew through her mind. "Why she thought Miss Ross had set her cap for Mr. Collier?"

Witherspoon yawned. "I didn't think to ask. The interview became a bit uncomfortable. Mr. Elliot seemed to find his wife's assertion very amusing and he laughed. Then he told her she was the loveliest, most romantic woman in the world, grabbed her hand, and began to kiss her fingers. Constable Gates and I decided we'd best go."

She forced herself to smile even though she wanted to box his ears. Honestly, sometimes men couldn't see what was right under their noses. Imogene Ross and Michael Collier as a couple made perfect sense. They weren't related by blood to one another and if they were attracted to each other, they could marry. And if he inherited half of Francis Humphreys' estate and she inherited a portion from her side of the family, she'd never need to worry about losing a position again. "I quite understand, sir."

"I think I'll pop over and have a quick word with Lady Cannonberry before I have my supper," he announced. "She's going to some sort of charity function this evening, but she told me she didn't need to leave until half past seven so if I hurry along, we can spend a few minutes together."

The house was quiet as a tomb, the shades properly drawn and the doors securely locked. It was half past eleven and everyone, save Mrs. Jeffries, was in bed. But she knew she wouldn't be able to sleep and so she'd not even bothered to go upstairs with the others. Instead, she sat at the kitchen table with a tin of polish and the good silver service that Witherspoon had used only twice in all the years she'd been his housekeeper. Sometimes, repetitive tasks got her mind moving in the right direction. She hoped that would happen tonight, because once the initial excitement of hearing about Imogene Ross and Michael Collier wore off, she'd realized she hadn't any idea of what to do next.

She grabbed the polishing rag and swirled it around in the open tin, picked up a fork, and slathered the polish from one end to the other. She knew that at their morning meeting the others would be expecting her to give them directions or tell them what they ought to do next. She took the rag, and using long, quick strokes, she buffed the fork. But she'd no idea what to do next. Absolutely none.

She polished the fork until it gleamed in the soft light of her lamp, put it back in the niche in the velvet-lined box, and pulled out a spoon. As she polished and buffed, she let her mind drift. She didn't try to direct her thoughts; she simply let them come and go as they would. Imogene Ross was the one nursing her aunt, Michael Collier had been in prison, and Joseph Humphreys' gun was missing, she mused. She held the spoon up to the light, making sure she'd not missed any spots. *"Mrs. Eames told me to go about my business and take the coal box down to Mrs. Humphreys."* She put the spoon back and took out the knife. *"She had Uncle Francis right where she wanted, wrapped completely around her little finger."*

She went still, staring off into the distance as the bits and pieces swirled through her mind. Then she shook herself, popped the unpolished knife back in the box, slapped the top on the tin of polish, and got up. Even a boring task like this wasn't helping her come up with anything useful, so she might as well go to bed.

Mrs. Jeffries put the cleaning supplies and the silver

back in their proper places, picked up the lamp, and went upstairs to her room. As she climbed into her bed, she told herself that tomorrow was another day and they might find the one clue they needed to catch this killer. But she wasn't sure she believed it.

She pulled the bedclothes up to her chin and stared through the darkness at the ceiling. She'd always known that one day there would be a murderer whom they didn't catch. It wouldn't matter if the killer was clever or lucky. The only thing that would matter was that he or she wasn't caught. Depressed, she sighed and rolled onto her side, squeezed her eyes shut, and hoped that sleep would come soon.

Hours later, Mrs. Jeffries started awake. *"He was so angry with me, he didn't even reply when I knocked at his door."* She sat bolt upright in bed, shoved the covers to one side, and leapt out. My gracious, how could she have been so stupid? The answer was staring her in the face the whole time. She laughed out loud and whirled about in a circle, giggling like a giddy schoolgirl.

For once, she'd figured it out in plenty of time: Innocent people weren't being arrested, the guilty weren't rushing off to the continent, and no one was in danger of being murdered. She had plenty of time to come up with an idea that would bring the inspector around to seeing what had been right under their noses from the very beginning.

"How come you're so cheerful all of a sudden?" Mrs. Goodge asked. She put the tea down on the table.

"I had a very good night's sleep," Mrs. Jeffries replied calmly. She glanced around the table and saw all of them staring at her with speculative expressions on their faces. She'd thought she'd done an excellent job of keeping her excitement well hidden, but apparently she underestimated how perceptive they were.

"You were very nice to Constable Gates," Betsy commented.

"I was simply being polite," the housekeeper protested.

"And I 'eard you laughing as you come down the stairs," Wiggins added. "Last night before we went up to bed, you looked like a right old gloomy Gus."

"Thank you very much, Wiggins," she said tartly. She wasn't ready to share her idea with them as yet. There were still one or two facts she needed to understand and get straight in her own mind before she was certain she was correct. "But as it happens, you're right. I was a bit down in the mouth last night."

"I'm sorry, Mrs. Jeffries," he said contritely. "I didn't mean to say anything disrespectful. It's just you look so much more chipper this mornin'."

"That's because I am," she confirmed. "I have had a few ideas about this case, but I'm not certain I'm right. There are a few more things we need to find out."

"I knew it, I knew," the cook cried gleefully. "I just knew you'd figure it out. Who is it? Who's the killer?"

"Gracious, I only said I had a few ideas," she fibbed. "I didn't say I'd come to any conclusions as yet."

"Are you sure?" Luty asked suspiciously.

"Of course I'm sure," Mrs. Jeffries said. "Please, I'm not trying to be mysterious. I do have some ideas about this murder and how it was committed, but there is still much we must learn."

"But you've got a good idea who the killer is, don't you?" Ruth pressed. "I'm so glad. Gerald was getting quite depressed about the whole matter."

"As was I," Mrs. Jeffries replied honestly. "And you'll be pleased to know that I had a quick word with the inspector before Constable Gates arrived this morning. I hinted that he really ought to speak to Pamela Humphreys again and ask her about her late husband's inventions."

"What do the man's gadgets got to do with anything?" Luty frowned heavily. "He's dead so he couldn't have killed anyone."

"I'm aware of that," she answered. "But it's important the inspector speak to her and learn as much as he can about them."

"But who do you think did the murder?" Wiggins cocked his head.

"We might as well stop badgerin' her for the name. She's not goin' to tell us," Smythe said flatly. "She always gets like this towards the end of a case. Alright, Mrs. J., what do ya want us to do?"

"I'd like you to find out if Francis Humphreys gave his nieces, Imogene Ross and Annabelle Prescott, Enfield revolvers. We know he gave them to the men in the family, but did he give them to the women as well as the men?"

"That's not a very nice present for a young lady," Mrs. Goodge commented.

"I don't think it's a very nice gift for anyone," she agreed. "But nonetheless, if you'll recall, Leo Kirkland told the inspector that both the nieces and nephews used to go shooting with their uncle at Kirkland's country house back when the two men were still friends. I think it's important we find out precisely how many guns there were in the house on the day Humphreys was shot. Whoever killed him had to acquire a weapon from somewhere, and if the conspiracy theory is correct, what better place than from one of Humphreys' relatives."

"That's a tough one, but I'll do my best." Smythe grinned broadly.

She turned to Betsy. "I want you to go back to Acton and see if you can speak to Agnes again. Find out a bit more about everyone in the household's movements on the day of the murder."

"Alright." Betsy looked doubtful. "But I'm not sure I'll have a chance to speak to her."

"Just do your best."

"What would you like me to do?" Ruth asked.

"Find out if Leo Kirkland was as devoted to his late wife as he claimed. The inspector has more or less dismissed him as a suspect, but Estelle Collier jilted him for Francis Humphreys."

Ruth nodded and got to her feet. "You're thinking he wanted a bit of revenge? He waited a very long time."

"We once had a case where the killer waited thirty years to get back at his tormenters," she reminded everyone.

"Yes, of course. I shall be pleased to help." Ruth smiled. "And I know just the person to see. She knows everything about everyone in London."

Mrs. Jeffries turned to Luty and Hatchet. "I'd like the two of you to find out what you can about Collier's real financial situation. I want to know if he was being pressed by any creditors." Finally, she looked at Wiggins. "And I want you to go have another chat with Johnny Cooper. See if you can get a look at that coal box he used to take coal to Mrs. Humphreys' house on the day of the murder."

"Inspector, I'm not really sure why we're here," Constable Gates whispered to Witherspoon as the maid went off to fetch her mistress. They were standing in the foyer of Pamela Humphreys' home.

The inspector wasn't sure, either, but he didn't intend to admit it to this young man. Trying to explain about his inner voice was difficult at the best of times, but he'd learned to trust it when it guided him in a certain direction and this morning, it had led him here. "I've thought of several other questions that really ought to be asked."

"What questions, sir?" Gates pressed. "Err, I mean, you were very thorough in your previous interviews with Mrs. Humphreys."

"One can never be too thorough," Witherspoon stated.

The maid stuck her head around the corner. "Mrs. Humphreys will see you in the morning room, sir. If you'll just step this way."

"Thank you, miss," the inspector said politely. He and Gates followed the girl down a hallway the length of the house. She paused at the door, knocked, and opened it for the two policemen. "Go right on in, sir." She grinned at Witherspoon. "She's expecting you."

Gates was right behind him as he stepped into the room. Pamela Bowden Humphreys rose from a small secretary in the corner and waved them closer. She was dressed to go out in a navy and gray plaid traveling suit with a tight-fitted jacket and long, flared skirt. A dark blue hat with a veil that trailed to the floor and a fur muff were sitting on the top of the tiny desk. She did not appear pleased to see them. "Come in, Inspector, and state your business. I've not much time."

"We'll be as brief as possible," he replied. "I do have several more questions for you, Mrs. Humphreys."

"All right, get on with it," she ordered irritably. "I'm very busy today."

"So you've said, ma'am. I understand your late husband was an inventor."

Her eyebrows rose in surprise. "He was. Why do you ask? My husband has been dead and buried for some time now. His occupation couldn't possibly have anything to do with Uncle Francis' death."

He noticed she used the word "death," not "murder." "Did the late Mr. Yancy Humphreys have an apparatus commonly referred to as a 'bird scarer'?"

"Oh my God." She rolled her eyes. "Has someone been complaining about that stupid contraption again? I don't care what anyone in the neighborhood says, I've not used the wretched thing since Yancy died. It's upstairs in the attic and now that Francis is gone, I shall burn it."

Witherspoon was startled by her reaction but didn't allow his expression to change. "No one has complained, ma'am. I'm merely asking if your husband had invented such an apparatus."

"Yes he did, and that particular invention of his has caused me no end of grief, Inspector." She laughed harshly. "Do you know how many times the neighbors called the police that last summer he was alive? They were here half a dozen times." She began to pace in front of the tiny fireplace, taking two or three steps before whirling around and going in the opposite direction. "It was maddening, absolutely maddening. But would he listen to me? No, I was nothing more than a mere wife and the silly man just kept right on with his experiments, not caring in the least that none of the neighbors would speak to me and we hadn't received any social invitations since he'd been testing that stupid thing." Her eyes filled with tears and a red flush crept up her cheeks. She whirled around, put her hand on the fireplace mantel to steady herself, and took a long, ragged breath as she fought to compose herself.

Beside him, the inspector heard Gates shifting his feet. He glanced at him and saw that the constable was staring at the carpet, obviously uncomfortable. The interview was awkward for Witherspoon as well. His questions had apparently opened an old wound. But he had no choice. He had to keep at it.

"Mrs. Humphreys," he said softly. "Please forgive me for intruding on what must be a very private grief, but there are a few more questions I need to ask you."

She said nothing for a moment, then she straightened her spine and turned to face him. "What do you want to know?"

"This bird scarer." Witherspoon chose his words carefully. He wanted to make sure he asked just the right question and that he fully understood her answers. "Was it mechanical with a clockwork mechanism?"

"That's correct."

"And did this clockwork mechanism act, in effect, as a timing device as well?"

"Yes." She frowned in confusion. "At least that was what Yancy was trying to achieve. You see, he thought that by having a timing device on the apparatus, it would be much more effective in getting rid of birds. That's why he was always testing it, you see. He had it out there blasting away with the most terrible noises and he'd play about with the mechanisms so it was impossible to know when the silly thing was going to go off." She suddenly smiled. "As much as I hated what it did to our social standing in the neighborhood, the scarer did work. The noise it made kept the birds out of the currant bushes and the herb garden. Of course, it also terrified the local horses and had our neighbors filing complaints with the police that we were disturbing the peace."

"May I see it?" Witherspoon asked.

"It's in the attic somewhere, Inspector," she replied. "With all of his other contraptions. It'll take ages to find it, and right now I simply don't have time. You're welcome to come back tomorrow, but Imogene—Miss Ross—is coming for morning coffee and after that, I'm going to Southend to look at a house."

Witherspoon hesitated. He sensed that the apparatus was important, but for the life of him he couldn't think of a logical reason why he felt so strongly about it. Yet something was pushing at the back of his mind, something important. He frowned and tried to grab the thought before it completely escaped. But it was too quick for him and was gone in the blink of an eye.

"Inspector," she said impatiently. "Unless you've more questions for me, I really must ask you to leave. I'm on a very tight schedule today."

Witherspoon had no grounds for insisting she delay her social engagements. "I've no more questions, ma'am. But perhaps we'll come back tomorrow to see your husband's invention. Thank you for your time, Mrs. Humphreys."

Betsy leapt in front of the young maid with all the grace of a two-year-old tumbling out of bed. "I thought that was you," she exclaimed with an enthusiasm she didn't feel. Trying to make contact with Agnes Wilder was no easy task. She'd spent the last two hours trotting up and down Linton Road pretending to look for her mistress' lost spaniel. Luckily, there'd been very few people about and she'd not had to actually use that pathetic story to explain why she'd been hanging about the neighborhood.

Agnes had finally appeared and Betsy had breathed a huge sigh of relief. She had come out the side entrance of the house with a shopping basket slung over her arm and walked in the direction of the High Street. Betsy dawdled behind her, taking care to stay out of sight until she could arrange an "accidental" meeting as Agnes came out of the greengrocers.

"Mary." Agnes smiled uncertainly. "What are you doing here? It's not your afternoon out, is it?"

Betsy laughed. "It is, that's why I was so happy to see you. I've been chasing you for the last quarter mile. I was hopin' we could have tea again." She felt bad. She knew that Agnes was lonely and there was part of her that felt it was wrong to lead the girl on, to make her believe they were becoming friends. She struggled with her conscience for a split second and then shoved the matter to the back of her mind. Murder was serious business and she'd do whatever was necessary to help catch this killer. Besides, after the case was solved, she'd be sure to invite Mary to Upper Edmonton Gardens. She liked her.

"Oh, I don't know." Agnes glanced at the beets and carrots, their tops poking out the newspaper wrapping, in her basket. "Cook is waiting for these vegetables to finish her soup for the ladies' supper tonight."

"That's too bad." Betsy pouted prettily. "I wanted some company. But I don't want you getting into trouble with the cook. Tell you what, why don't I walk you back to the house."

"That would be lovely." Agnes smiled broadly.

Betsy took her arm and they started off. "Have they said what's going to be happening to the household now that your master is gone?" she asked. They stopped at a busy intersection as a four-wheeler and a cooper's van loaded three barrels high came hurtling around the corner.

"Mrs. Eames says for us not to worry." Agnes made a face. "She thinks we'll all have our positions but she can't say for certain. Mind you, I overheard her tellin' the cook that if Mrs. Prescott inherited the house, she'd need us to stay." They stepped off the curb and crossed the road. "But I'm not sure Mrs. Eames knows much more than the rest of us."

"Maybe you'll learn more once the will's been read," Betsy said.

"That's supposed to be tomorrow." Agnes giggled. "I know because when I was clearin' up the drawing room after the reception, I overheard Mrs. Prescott havin' words with Mr. Collier. She was goin' on and on about how disrespectful it was that Mr. Francis' solicitor wasn't at the service. Mr. Collier called her a hypocrite and said the only reason she'd wanted the lawyer to come see the old man buried was so the will could be read as soon as the guests left the reception. Mrs. Prescott stomped off in a huff and then Miss Ross came over to Mr. Collier and told him they'd already made arrangements for the reading and he shouldn't upset Mrs. Prescott, that she was suffering more than the rest of them over Mr. Humphreys' death."

They turned the corner and came to Linton Road. Betsy knew she'd not have much more time. She needed to know who had been where on the day of the murder.

"Mind you, it'll be nice to be away from the house tonight," Agnes continued.

Betsy stared at her in surprise. "Are you goin' somewhere?"

"We are." Agnes laughed. "Just after breakfast, Mrs. Eames told the staff we're all to have the evening off. The family is so grateful for everyone's hard work that they're actually payin' for us to go to a real restaurant and the music hall . . ." She broke off and bit her lip.

"What's wrong?" Betsy asked.

"I wasn't supposed to say anything." Agnes looked worried. "Mrs. Eames said the family wanted our outing kept quiet. The neighbors might think it disrespectful to be going out to such places when there's been a death in the household. You won't tell anyone, will you?"

"Of course not," Betsy lied.

"It's ever so thrillin'." Agnes giggled happily. "Imagine, we're goin' to a real restaurant. Mrs. Eames said we're to wear our best clothes and we're to be ready at five—that's when the coach is comin' to fetch us. Even cook was excited and bustlin' about the kitchen makin' sure everything was ready for the ladies' evening meal. That's why I got sent to do the shopping. Mrs. Eames said the ladies wanted a vegetable soup for supper."

They were almost at the house and Betsy knew she'd

failed. There wasn't enough time for her to ask her questions.

"It's a good thing that Mr. Joseph is going to have his meal with one of his friends. I don't think he'd be happy with just some soup and a tray of sandwiches for dinner. But it's nice that the ladies will have some time to themselves tonight. All the comings and goings since Mr. Humphreys died has been difficult for both of them. You know, always havin' to smile and be polite to all his friends and neighbors. I heard Mrs. Prescott asking Miss Ross if she'd been sleepin' well and Miss Ross said she hadn't. Mrs. Prescott said she'd not been sleepin', either."

"It's not surprising people have trouble resting when there's been a death in the family," Betsy murmured politely. "It's hard on the nerves." She felt like screaming in frustration.

"Maybe that's why Mrs. Eames got the laudanum down from Mr. Francis' medicine chest," Agnes said thoughtfully. "Maybe she was gettin' it for Mrs. Prescott or Miss Ross. I know she never uses the stuff." They were at the house. "It was nice of you to walk me back. My usual day out is Wednesday afternoon." Agnes smiled hopefully. "Do you think we can meet next week?"

Mrs. Jeffries hummed as she put a plate of buttered brown bread at each end of the kitchen table and stepped back to survey her handiwork. The tea was made, the table was set, and all was right with the world. She felt so much better about this case and now that she'd pointed the inspector in the right direction, it ought to sort itself out very quickly.

"You're lookin' very pleased with yourself." Mrs. Goodge took her seat. "I think it's right mean of you not to tell us who did it."

"Now, Mrs. Goodge, don't look at me like that. You

know I'd tell you if I was sure. But I'm still not one hundred percent certain my theory is correct," Mrs. Jeffries explained. "I should know more after our meeting. Provided, of course, that everyone was successful in their tasks today."

The back door opened. They heard several voices speaking at once and then footsteps pounding up the hall. "Looks like we'll be finding that out right quick," the cook commented. "Sounds as if everyone's back."

Not quite everyone returned on time. Lady Cannonberry, usually the soul of promptness, didn't appear, and after waiting for fifteen minutes Mrs. Jeffries reluctantly concluded she must have been unavoidably detained. "I do hate not waiting for Ruth, but we've no choice. We must get started, we've much to talk about this afternoon. Who would like to go first?"

"Madam had a bit of good fortune today." Hatchet gave his employer a sour look. "She accomplished her task with ease."

Mrs. Jeffries decided to ignore the glares passing between the two of them. She smiled at Luty. "What did you learn?"

"Go on, madam, tell them what you did," Hatchet challenged.

"Oh don't be such an old stick," Luty snapped. "I ain't the only one around here who's reached into their purse to grease the wheels a bit. So I passed a bit of silver over the man's hand. It got us what we needed to know."

"You didn't just pass a bit of silver, madam," Hatchet yelled. "You promised that broker you'd give him your future business."

"No, I said I'd come to him if I ever wanted to buy any shares in copper mines, but if you'll stop and think a minute, I don't buy mining stock these days. I don't approve of how they treat the native workers. But that's neither here nor there. We ain't got all day so we'll just have to argue about this later." She turned to Mrs. Jeffries. "I had a word with Michael Collier's broker. Collier's in debt up to his neck, but two or three of his investments have started to go up in value and one of them is a goodly amount of money. Collier instructed the broker to cash him out when the stock reached a certain price. It hit it last week and the broker sold. Collier told him he was going to use the money to pay off his creditors."

"Maybe he'll pay his grocer now," Betsy murmured.

"Thank you, Luty," Mrs. Jeffries said.

"I'll go next," Smythe volunteered. "Mine won't take long. I did my best to find out if the girls in the Humphreys family were given revolvers, but I didn't have any luck. None of my sources knew that much about the family's past." He looked at Mrs. Jeffries. "Was it important?"

"I'm not sure," she replied honestly. "Perhaps not, but it would have been useful to have the information. But I know you did your best, so don't fret over it. Sometimes, no matter how much we try, we simply can't find out certain facts."

"Don't worry." Betsy patted his arm. "My day wasn't much better than yours."

"Neither was mine," Wiggins added. "Johnny Cooper and I had just gone into the garden shed when Miss Ross comes flyin' down the shortcut and he hares off back to weeding the flower beds. He asked me to leave, said he didn't want to get into trouble for larkin' about. I told him she'd been rushin' so fast she'd not noticed me, but he'd have none of it so I had to go. But that lady was in a 'urry, all right. She were runnin' down that path like the 'ounds of hell were chasin' her. Johnny was right put out about it and kept mutterin' that the family never used the shortcut between the houses, that it was for the servants. The family always walked down Linton Road."

"So you didn't get a look at the coal box?" Mrs. Jeffries asked. She tried not to be disappointed. After all, it was only a theory. If the idea she'd planted in the inspector's mind this morning blossomed as she hoped it would, he'd figure it out and he'd be able to look not just at the box but at the coal bin as well.

"I got a quick look before Miss Ross come," he said. "It looks like a wheelbarrow with a tiny wooden house over the bed. He didn't have time to show me how the thing worked, but he told me about it. There's a lever on each side of the wooden frame. Johnny told me that the one on the left opened the top so the coal could be poured straight in from the coal wagon, while the lever on the other side opened a door on the front so the coal could be chucked directly into a coal chute. Mr. Yancy Humphreys invented it so he could have his fuel put directly into his cellar. He even fitted out the cellar with an opening just a bit bigger than the front of the coal box so none of the coal would spill on the ground and be wasted. It's a right clever gadget if you ask me," he concluded.

Mrs. Jeffries tried to imagine it in her mind. "Considering you were so abruptly interrupted, you've done very well. I wonder why Miss Ross came rushing back to the house?"

Wiggins shrugged. "Johnny didn't know. He thought maybe Miss Ross and Mrs. Humphreys might 'ave 'ad words, but then he seemed to dismiss the idea. Seems like them two ladies are friends and he knew Miss Ross had gone there for morning coffee. It was Mrs. Prescott that didn't get on with Mrs. Humphreys."

"That doesn't mean they didn't have words," Mrs. Goodge pointed out. "A death in the family can bring out the worst in people, especially if there's a bit of money in the offing."

"That's what Agnes hinted at." Betsy nodded her head

for emphasis. "She said that both Mrs. Prescott and Miss Ross were having trouble sleeping and that everyone's nerves were a bit frayed."

"You were able to make contact with her, excellent," Mrs. Jeffries said approvingly.

"But I didn't have a chance to ask her about anyone's movements on the day of the murder," Betsy grumbled. "So my trip to Acton was a waste of time. Agnes didn't let me get a word in edgewise. All she talked about was how the Humphreys family was so grateful for everyone's hard work, they were sending all the servants off to a restaurant and then to the music hall for the evening."

"That's very strange." Mrs. Goodge frowned in confusion. "I've never heard of any household sending the staff to a music hall two days after there's been a death in the family. It simply isn't done."

"Agnes told me the housekeeper said they were to keep quiet about it because it sounded disrespectful," Betsy replied. "I thought it was a bit odd as well."

Inside Mrs. Jeffries' mind, the pieces of the puzzle fell into place and she knew with absolute certainty not only what had happened but what was going to happen next. It wasn't a pretty sight, either. She shoved back from the table and leapt to her feet.

Alarmed, everyone stopped talking and stared at her.

Images, snatches of conversation and ideas, were careening through her brain so quickly that it took a moment before she realized the others were looking at her. "We've got to find the inspector," she cried. "Does anyone know where he is?"

"I do." Ruth's soft voice took them by surprise and everyone turned to see her standing in the doorway. "I knocked on the back door," she explained, "but no one answered so I let myself inside. I hope that's alright."

"But of course it is." Mrs. Jeffries finally came back to

the here and now. "But we've got to find the inspector and we've got to find him right away if we want to save an innocent life. Do you have any idea where he might be?"

Ruth moved toward the table. "He told me he was going to spend the day at the Acton Police Station. He said that after he interviewed Mrs. Yancy Humphreys again, he was going back there to go over all the interviews and make a timeline. He said his timelines had always helped him in the past. I think he was having very grave doubts as to his ability to solve this case."

"But he will solve it," Mrs. Jeffries vowed. "He'll solve it tonight if we're not too late. But we've got to come up with a reason to get him to Humphreys House right away. There's no time to lose." She looked at Smythe. "How fast can you get the carriage ready?"

"Bow and Arrow are the fastest horses in London." He got up. "I can be there within the hour."

"You've got to go get the inspector first." Mrs. Jeffries began to pace. "And we must come up with an excuse for getting him to Acton that sounds logical."

The silence was deafening as everyone tried to think of a reason without giving the game away. Mrs. Jeffries stalked back and forth across the kitchen floor with such energy that Fred got up, albeit with a slightly confused expression on his face, and kept pace with her steps. He was nothing if not loyal.

"Tell him that I said I've heard gossip that Imogene Ross is responsible for Estelle Collier Humphreys' death and that she's going to kill again tonight," Ruth stated.

There was a brief, shocked silence and then everyone spoke at once.

"What?" Smythe and Wiggins both said at the same time.

"Excuse me, but did I hear you correctly?" Betsy rose to her feet.

"Nells bells, that's a good one." Luty laughed approvingly.

"Lady Cannonberry, are you sure about this?" Hatchet clucked his tongue.

"That would get the inspector to Humphreys House," Mrs. Goodge agreed.

Only Mrs. Jeffries remained quiet. She stared at Ruth for a moment and then held up her hand for silence. "Are you certain you wish to do this? If I'm wrong and we use your name to get the inspector to Acton, it could do great harm to your friendship with him."

"Nothing is going to harm my relationship with the inspector," Ruth replied calmly. "And I've great faith in your abilities. Now stop worrying about me. You said we've no time to waste."

Mrs. Jeffries hesitated for the briefest of seconds and then turned to Smythe who was already moving toward the coat tree. "Do as Ruth says," she directed. "And take Wiggins with you."

Wiggins leapt up and raced for his jacket and cap.

As the two men headed for the back door, Ruth called out, "If something does go wrong, I don't want the household held responsible. Make certain you tell the inspector that you got this information directly from me. Tell him, I came running into the kitchen half hysterical and insisting that you take action immediately."

CHAPTER 11

It was full dark by the time Smythe pulled the carriage up in front of Humphreys House. A cold wind whipped in from the north rustling the leaves of the small shrubs by the side of the road. Smythe glanced to his right as he yanked the brake, bringing the rig to a stop. The house looked dark and sinister, with only one or two lights gleaming through the windows of the ground floor. Now that they were here, Smythe was beginning to have grave doubts about the enterprise. What if Mrs. Jeffries was wrong? They'd all end up in a right old mess.

"Place is quiet as a churchyard," Wiggins whispered. "I hope Mrs. Jeffries is right about this one. If the inspector goes bursting in there, even Lady Cannonberry's tale won't save his career if Constable Gates decides to make trouble."

"I know." Smythe wrapped the reins around the metal seat guard. "I've been thinkin' the same thing myself. My feelin' is that Gates is cut from the same cloth as his uncle Nigel, so I don't trust the man an inch. Let's hope Mrs. Jeffries knows what she's doin'." He climbed down to the ground.

Wiggins got down the other side just as Witherspoon and Gates stepped out of the carriage. "I don't quite understand what we're doing here, Inspector," the constable whined.

Witherspoon didn't understand all that much himself, but he certainly wasn't going to offend Lady Cannonberry by ignoring her information. He didn't see all that well in the dark, so he moved carefully up the small incline to the stone pathway and started toward the house. "I received some information that needed my immediate attention."

"But it's very late, sir." Lionel fell into step behind him. "Couldn't this have waited until tomorrow?"

"You didn't need to accompany me, Constable," Witherspoon said irritably. "I didn't ask you to come along." He'd done his best to keep the constable at the station, but Gates had insisted on tagging along.

Smythe and Wiggins waited till the two policemen were halfway up the walkway before they began to move themselves. Both men tread lightly, not wanting their footsteps to alert Gates that they were following him.

"Yes, I know that, sir," Lionel replied. "And I don't mind coming along. It's just I don't quite understand your thought process . . ." He broke off as the most horrendous bang blasted the quiet night.

Witherspoon, knowing immediately what the sound meant, charged for the front door of the house. "That's a gunshot," he cried.

Lionel froze.

Smythe stuck his arm out as Wiggins started after Witherspoon; he grabbed his arm and whirled him around to face him. "Run get the constable on the corner. Have him blow his whistle and bring help."

"But what about you and the inspector?" Wiggins looked frantically toward the house and then back at Smythe, his expression anguished. "You might need me . . ."

"Go, get help," Smythe ordered. "We need you to hurry."

Without a word, Wiggins turned and raced for the corner, moving faster than he'd ever gone in his life.

Smythe sprinted for the house, dodging around Lionel just as the constable got ahold of himself and started to move. Another shot rang out. Lionel went completely still, sobbed, and flopped down on the walkway.

Smythe raced up the stairs and pushed through the partially open front door, down the hall and into the drawing room. He skidded to a halt. At the far end of the couch, Inspector Witherspoon was locked in a silent dance of death with a woman. One of his arms was straight up in the air, trying to wrest the gun that was pointed at his head out of her hand. Another woman was lying on the couch. Her torso was covered with blood.

Smythe hurled himself into the fray, grasping the woman from behind and trying to jerk her backward, away from Witherspoon while simultaneously grabbing for the gun. But she was strong and agile, twisting slightly, and banging her head against his jaw.

"Let me go, you bastard," she cried, kicking backward with her foot directly into Smythe's shin. He stumbled, and somehow she managed to turn the barrel a fraction of an inch. She pulled the trigger and Smythe yelped in pain as a bullet whizzed past his ear and skimmed his shoulder and arm.

Witherspoon renewed his efforts, yanking her arm down with all his might and grabbing at her hand, clawing hard at her fingers until she dropped the gun. Smythe fell to his knees and only then noticed there was another body, that of a man, lying on the floor on the other side of the loveseat.

The man moaned, caught Smythe's eye, and struggled to get to his feet. Blood was running down his right leg onto the floor and seeping through the fabric of his gray trousers.

Witherspoon gave the woman a most ungentlemanly shove, causing her to fall to the floor. She scrambled away, moving on all fours toward the drawing room door. The inspector rushed to Smythe, knelt down, and tugged at his coat, pulling it to one side so he could look at the wound. "Are you bleeding badly? Lie still. Don't move until help arrives. Where on earth is Constable Gates? Gates!" he yelled. "Get in here! We need help."

Annabelle Prescott gained her feet and started for the door. Witherspoon hesitated, not wanting to leave Smythe. "Don't let her get away," the coachman cried. "I'll be alright. You can't let her escape."

"Imogene, Imogene," the man called softly as he finally found his footing. "For God's sake, speak to me." He stumbled toward the couch, which brought him directly in the path of the fleeing Annabelle. "If Imogene dies, I'll kill you with my bare hands," he snarled at her.

Annabelle laughed, pushed him away, and kept right on going. She'd reached the doorway when Wiggins and two constables came hurling into the room. She leapt to one side, grabbed a straight-backed chair, and whirled it about as the men rushed into the room.

The constables, seeing bodies and blood everywhere, raced toward Witherspoon. Wiggins, seeing Smythe on the floor with blood seeping out onto his shirt, ran toward him. "I'm fine," he yelled. "Help the inspector. Don't let her get away." The footman veered off, leapt over an ottoman, and turned back toward the door.

The inspector waved the constables off. "Stop her," he

called. He tripped over a rug, went down on his knee, and righted himself just as Annabelle flung herself through the door and down the hallway. He charged after her, followed by the constables and Wiggins.

"Halt in the name of the law," Witherspoon ordered. Annabelle yanked the door and rushed through, directly into Lionel Gates. The sound of their skulls colliding made a horrible noise as they crashed head-on and both of them went down. Annabelle sprawled backward onto the tile floor of the foyer while Lionel fell back out the front door.

"Oh, that hurts," he moaned as he pulled himself up to a sitting position half in and half out of the doorway.

Witherspoon, breathing hard, reached his quarry just as she was scrambling to her feet. He grabbed her arm and pulled her up. "Annabelle Prescott, you're under arrest for the murder of Francis Humphreys and the attempted murders of Michael Collier and Imogene Ross."

Things happened quickly in the next hour. More policemen and a doctor arrived. As soon as Annabelle Prescott was led off to the police station by Constable Gates and two other policemen, Witherspoon dashed back to the drawing room to check on Smythe.

The coachman was sitting on a chair with his coat off. "I'm fine, sir," he said. "The bullet just grazed my shoulder and my arm, but it didn't go in so I'm in no danger. The doctor said it's only a flesh wound." His arm and shoulder was bandaged. He kept casting worried glances at the pale-faced woman on the couch. "She's trying to come to, sir," he said to Witherspoon.

A balding doctor, his bag open on the floor next to the couch, was examining her wounds. He glanced at Witherspoon, nodded, and turned his attention back to his patient. "The bullet passed through her side but luckily, it went through flesh and not any important organs. She's bled quite a bit, but I think she'll be alright."

"Thank God." Michael Collier, his coat off and his arm bandaged, dropped to his knees next to the couch. "Imogene, can you hear me? It's Michael."

She moaned faintly and opened her eyes. "Michael. I thought I heard your voice, and then I thought I must be dreaming. I think Annabelle put something in the wine. It tasted odd so I didn't drink much of it. She was annoyed about that."

"Laudanum," the doctor said flatly. "I do wish people would realize that stuff is dangerous."

"If she's been drugged, perhaps I ought to wait until tomorrow to take her statement," Witherspoon said.

"That would probably be best," the doctor agreed.

"I can make a statement." Collier straightened and turned to Witherspoon. "Annabelle Prescott tried to murder Imogene and myself. She wanted Imogene dead because Imogene had realized she'd used cousin Yancy's bird scarer to make everyone believe he'd been murdered when we were all together having tea, but that's not what happened. Annabelle had killed him an hour earlier, when the train to Bristol went past. No one heard the shot because the whistle blows for a good ten seconds and it's so loud you can barely hear yourself think."

"How do you know this, sir?" Witherspoon asked.

Collier laughed harshly. "Annabelle told me. She's spent the last half hour holding a gun on us while she bragged about how clever she was, how she'd never get caught and was going to get it all. She said she deserved it."

"Deserved what, sir?" The inspector sat down on the loveseat. "Why don't you sit down and tell me everything, Mr. Collier," he suggested. "You look very tired."

Collier pulled over the straight-backed chair Annabelle had hurled at the policemen, turned it around, and sat down. "Uncle Francis' estate," he replied. "She said she deserved every penny of it because she'd had to put up with him for the past two and a half years. I think she's quite mad, Inspector. I couldn't reason with her, couldn't make her understand you were bound to catch her, if not for Uncle Francis' then for our murders. But she just laughed and said she'd never get caught, because she'd make it seem as if Imogene had murdered Uncle Francis and then tried to murder me to get a bigger share of his estate for herself. But she didn't count on the police turning up, did she?" He closed his eyes briefly. "I don't know why you turned up, but I'm eternally grateful that you did."

The room was silent for a moment except for the striking of the clock and Witherspoon realized how late it was. He looked at Wiggins, who was sitting pale faced on a stool, staring at Smythe. "Go on home, Wiggins. There's no reason for you to stay here. The household must be very worried."

"I want to make sure he's alright." He jerked his chin toward the coachman. Seeing the blood oozing through Smythe's clothes had scared him witless. Truth to tell, he'd die if something happened to Smythe.

"The doctor's already said mine is just a flesh wound," Smythe replied. "But he wants to have another look when he's finished with Miss Ross. Now get going, you know how the women worry."

Reluctantly, Wiggins got up and left. It was only after the front door closed that Smythe realized he'd not told the lad to say nothing to Betsy about his wound.

"What took you so long?" Mrs. Goodge asked as Wiggins hurried into the kitchen. "You've been gone for hours."

"Where's Smythe?" Betsy demanded. "Why isn't he with you?"

"Is everything alright?" Mrs. Jeffries asked, her expression concerned. Wiggins was as white as a linen serviette. "Were we too late?"

He shook his head and flopped into his chair, grateful to be able to sit down again. His knees were still just a bit wobbly. "We got there on time. No one's dead, but Annabelle Prescott had done a bit of shootin' before the inspector and Smythe managed to get the gun away from her. She shot Miss Ross and Mr. Collier—they're both goin' to be fine—but that's what took so long for me to get back. We 'ad to wait for the doctor and the inspector wouldn't let Smythe move so much as a muscle until the doctor examined his wound."

"What wound?" Betsy cried, her face wild eyed with fear. "What happened. Was he shot? Is he alright?" She leapt up and started for her coat. "I must go to him. Where is he, where have they taken him?"

"He's fine, he's fine," Wiggins cried. He looked imploringly at the housekeeper, wanting her to help. But there was no relief from that quarter. Mrs. Jeffries stared back at him as an expression of absolute horror spread over her features. "Oh my God," she murmured. "What have I done?"

"Cor blimey, he'll 'ave my head for blurtin' it out like this and scarin' everyone to death." Wiggins looked frantically from the housekeeper to Betsy. "Come sit back down and I'll tell you everything. He's fine, Betsy. Just fine. The doctor said it was only a flesh wound."

Betsy stopped halfway across the room. "You swear he's alright?"

"I swear it, Betsy. I'd not lie to you about something important like this," Wiggins said.

Betsy searched his face intently for a moment, then something seemed to satisfy her. She sat back down. "What happened?"

"Is Gerald alright?" Ruth asked quietly.

"He's right as rain, but it'll be late before he gets home." Wiggins took a deep, calming breath. He had to keep his

head here and say just the right thing. Betsy was still pale,
Mrs. Goodge and Mrs. Jeffries both looked as if they were
going to cry, Ruth's hands were balled into fists so tightly
the knuckles were turning white, Luty chewed on her lower
lip, and Hatchet's mouth was set in a thin, flat line. He
desperately wanted to say something to cheer them up.
"You'll all be pleased to know that Constable Gates made a
fool of himself. When the shooting started, 'e was so scared
he just stood outside the house doin' nothin'. And 'e was
still standin' there, chewin' 'is fingernails when I got back
with the constables."

They were on their third pot of tea by the time the inspector and Smythe arrived back at Upper Edmonton Gardens.
Betsy rushed over and threw her arms around Smythe as
the two men came into the kitchen. He yelped in pain as
she squeezed too hard on his wound and she jumped back,
terrified she'd hurt him. "I'm alright, love. It's just a bit
tender."

She examined Smythe from head to toe and only then
was satisfied he was in one piece. "Go sit down," she ordered. "You need tea. Tea with sugar, lots of sugar."

Lady Cannonberry had risen as they'd come in and she
smiled tenderly at Witherspoon. "Are you well, Gerald?
Young Wiggins told us how brave you all were."

Witherspoon beamed happily. He wasn't in the least put
out that his kitchen was filled with people. "I'm fine, and
more importantly, two innocent lives were saved by your
good sense. But I'm afraid your gossip was a bit off the
mark. It wasn't Imogene Ross who was committing murder, it was Annabelle Prescott."

"Goodness, Inspector, it sounds as if you've had a very
exciting evening. We happened to stop by when we saw the
lights were still on here as we were on our way home from
the theater," Luty explained. "And of course, as soon as

Lady Cannonberry told us what she'd heard and that the men had all gone to Acton, we had to stay and find out what happened."

Mrs. Jeffries, who'd quietly risen from the seat at the head of the table and gone to the sideboard, put a clean cup down in the spot. "Do sit down and have a cup of tea, sir," she said. "We'd love to hear the details if you're not too tired."

"I believe I can manage a few moments." He slid into the chair while the housekeeper poured the tea. "Where to begin? Hmm, I suppose it started this morning when I suddenly realized I ought to ask Mrs. Humphreys a few more questions about her late husband's inventions." He grinned at Mrs. Jeffries. "I think that conversation we had at breakfast must have inspired me. You mentioning all the wonderful devices you saw at the Crystal Palace Exhibition made me think. Of course, once I spoke with Mrs. Humphreys and got confirmation about my theory, I knew I was on the right track, so to speak." He broke off and laughed. "I will admit though, I didn't quite expect things to move quite so quickly, rather like an express train. Which"—he stopped and took a gulp of tea—"was really part and parcel of the murder."

"Huh?" Mrs. Goodge said. She was confused and she wasn't too proud to admit it. "I don't understand."

"It's very simple really," Witherspoon explained. "Mrs. Prescott wanted her uncle dead. Like the others in the family, she thought his selling off all the American Railway stock and buying into the one in South America was foolish. She was afraid that by the time he died of natural causes, there'd be no estate left. So she decided he had to die, but as she was one of his main heirs, she'd naturally come under suspicion, so she came up with a plot that made us think the murder was committed at a few minutes past four, while she was playing hostess in a roomful of people, when the reality was she murdered her uncle at 3:09 when the express train to Bristol went past."

"How on earth did she do that?" Luty asked.

Witherspoon took a quick sip of tea. "She used her cousin Yancy's bird scarer. It's a rather unusual device. It fires a cylinder, much like a bullet only, of course, it's not a bullet. The cylinder is geared to a mechanical timer that was set to fire at a few minutes past four, making everyone think that was the time the murder was committed. She wanted us to believe the killing had been done by an outsider. She helped invent the contraption so she knew precisely how to work the thing. She had it set up in the attic, and she set the mechanism so it would fire when she was safely downstairs in a room filled with witnesses. Afterwards, she slipped back up to the attic, took off the firing cylinders, and covered the contraption with a cloth. The constable, searching the attic, had no idea what the gadget actually was and simply thought it an odd household contraption. It never occurred to anyone that it was capable of firing a cylinder that imitated a gunshot."

"Why was she trying to murder Imogene Ross?" Betsy asked. She kept glancing at Smythe, reassuring herself that he was genuinely fine.

"Because when Mrs. Humphreys mentioned to Miss Ross that I'd been there asking questions specifically about the bird scarer, Miss Ross realized what could have happened and rushed back to the house. By this time, Mrs. Prescott was suspicious about Miss Ross because she'd come running into the house and gone straight up to the attic. That's where the bird scarer was stored. Mrs. Prescott had stolen it from Mrs. Humphreys." He picked up his tea and took another long drink. "But she hadn't had time to sneak it back to Mrs. Humphreys' attic. When she saw

Miss Ross go up there, she knew someone else had figured out what she'd done. She went to Mrs. Eames and told them she was giving the servants the night off."

"Why did Miss Ross stay in the house alone with her if she was suspicious of her?" Luty asked.

"She thought she was safe. She'd sent a note to the station to me, asking me to come see her. She had no idea that Annabelle Prescott was on to her. By the time she realized everyone was gone and she was alone in the house with a murderess, it was too late."

"What happened to the note?" Hatchet asked. "Was it at the station? Is that where you found it?"

"It never got there." Witherspoon shook his head in disgust. "Miss Ross gave it to the maid to take to the Acton Police Station, but Mrs. Prescott waylaid the girl and said she'd take the note. The girl had no idea what was in the note, so she's not to be blamed." He suddenly yawned. "Oh dear, forgive me, but I am dreadfully tired."

"Then I'd best go home and let you get your rest." Ruth got up.

Witherspoon rose as well. "I'll walk you across the garden."

"But Gerald, you're exhausted and you've a very full day tomorrow," Ruth protested.

"Nonsense, no gentleman would allow a lady to see herself home." He took her arm and pulled her gently toward the back door, stopping just long enough to grab her cloak. As he draped it over her shoulders, she glanced back at Mrs. Jeffries and gave the housekeeper a look that plainly said she'd be back the next day to hear the rest of it.

As soon as the door closed behind them, Luty said, "Okee dokee, we ain't got much time, tell us how you sussed it out."

"I woke up early this morning with something Miss

Ross had told the inspector running through my mind," she replied. "Imogene Ross told him on the day of the murder she'd come to her uncle's door and knocked because she wanted to apologize for the terrible row they'd had. But he didn't answer. She assumed that it was because he was still angry at her, but all of a sudden I realized the answer was right under our noses all the time. He didn't answer because he was already dead. I'm sure that's one of the reasons that Imogene Ross figured out what had happened when she heard the inspector was asking about the bird scarer. She realized he'd been lying in his room dead as well."

"We should have known." Luty shook her head. "Everyone said that Humphreys liked tellin' his family what to do and makin' 'em dance to his tune. Men like that, they don't miss a chance to make you kowtow and humble yourself. If he'd been alive, he'd have answered that door and let her say how sorry she was."

"Which is precisely what Miss Ross was prepared to do when she went to his room to apologize," Hatchet finished. "I say, Mrs. Jeffries, it was very clever of you to figure it out."

"Not really, the clue was there all along and I don't think I'd have ever realized the significance if Annabelle Prescott hadn't made a fatal mistake."

"What was that?" Wiggins asked. "I mean, other than tryin' to murder half her cousins."

"She sacked Rachel, the upstairs maid," Mrs. Jeffries said. "If she'd left the girl alone, she might have gotten away with multiple murders."

"But Rachel was sacked because she was lazy," Betsy reminded them. "Even Agnes said that was the reason."

"I don't see the connection." Mrs. Goodge stared at the housekeeper over the rim of her spectacles, which had slid down her nose.

"I'm not explaining it very well, but something Wiggins pointed out kept running through my mind," Mrs. Jeffries replied. "He reminded us that a death in the family causes the household a huge amount of extra work. No one in their right mind would fire a housemaid right at that moment in time. I couldn't get that notion out of my mind, and once I started thinking about it everything suddenly made sense. Rachel was the upstairs maid. She told us she'd seen Mrs. Prescott taking something up to the attic on the day of the murder but more importantly, she mentioned that Mrs. Prescott sent her down to clean the drawing room right after the murder. That in and of itself was odd; there were still guests in the house so cleaning up after a tea that hadn't actually happened shouldn't have been anyone's priority. So I asked myself, why did Annabelle Prescott send the girl downstairs when she still had guests, and suddenly the answer was very simple: Rachel was cleaning something on the top floor landing." She paused to take a breath. "In most houses, that landing is the last one before the attic. Once I realized that fact, I understood that Rachel was sent downstairs so that Annabelle Prescott could get to the attic without being seen. She had to dismantle the cylinders from the bird scarer so that the police wouldn't understand how it had been used to fool everyone."

Wiggins frowned in confusion. He thought he understood what had happened, but he wasn't sure. "So Annabelle Prescott rigged up this bird scarer to fire a cylinder of some sort right when everyone was havin' tea, right?"

"That's right," Mrs. Jeffries said. "But the real murder took place at 3:09 when the express train to Bristol went past. Tommy Parker told me that the whistle blast was particularly loud that day, but I didn't understand the significance until I began to put it together."

"So what he heard was both the whistle and the real gun

going off," Hatchet murmured thoughtfully. "Sinister, but very effective."

"Why go to all that trouble?" Luty muttered. "Why not just wait till the old feller was out taking a walk and shoot him then? Why have a houseful of guests, all of which could be potential witnesses if something went wrong? And let's face it, they don't call the GWR "God's wandering railway," because the trains are always on time. She was takin' a terrible risk. What if the 3:09 had been late?"

"It was usually not more than ten or fifteen minutes late," Mrs. Jeffries pointed out. "I'm sure she'd simply have adjusted the time. All she cared about was making certain she had an alibi for the time of the murder. It made no difference to her whether he died at 3:09 or 3:15. All she had to do was step into his room, point the gun at his forehead, and shoot. If you'll recall, Constable Barnes noticed the wound didn't look right when he first saw it, but he couldn't determine what made it appear unusual. Now we know it was because the wound wasn't, er, well, how shall I put it . . . freshly made. She was actually quite lucky the blood hadn't dried around the hole."

"It was raining and wet that day," Hatchet said. "Nothing dries in that sort of weather."

"All in all, she was bloomin' lucky." Wiggins yawned. "But why did you want me to look at the coal box? What's that got to do with the murder?"

Mrs. Jeffries smiled wryly. "I'm not certain about how she managed this part, but my guess is that she used the coal box to get rid of the gun. Annabelle Prescott is a very clever woman. She knew that if she committed the murder while the house was full of guests, that it was likely the police would be called straightaway and she'd not have time to get the weapon she used off the premises before the house was searched. So she used the coal box. She'd been acting as the mistress of the house for two years, so she knew when the coal was delivered and, more importantly, that several boxloads were then taken down to Pamela Humphreys' house." She leaned forward. "She committed the murder at 3:09 and then slipped out to the garden when Johnny Cooper was busy elsewhere or in the kitchen having a cup of tea. She put the gun in the coal box and then probably watched while he trundled it down the shortcut to Linton Road."

"And no one would ever know because it's at the bottom of the coal cellar," Betsy added excitedly. "So even if it was found, it would be Pamela Humphreys who would take the blame for the murder. She had a motive and it's her house."

"Correct." Mrs. Jeffries sank back in her chair. "My guess is Annabelle didn't think the weapon would be found. As a matter of fact, I imagine if we check with Mrs. Eames, we'd find that it was Annabelle who gave her instructions that Johnny Cooper "should go about his business" and take the second load down to Mrs. Humphreys' house after the murder. That was just a bit of insurance."

"Because the second load would go in on top of the first one and would probably hide the gun." Luty nodded enthusiastically as she saw it all in her mind's eye. "Nells bells, it might take years before the gun was dug out. Even if it was found later, the police could never say for certain how long it had been down there and if they managed to connect it to Francis' murder, they'd be looking at Pamela, not Annabelle."

"Which was precisely what she intended all along," Mrs. Jeffries said.

"What a diabolical woman." Hatchet pursed his lips.

"Evil cow," Betsy muttered. She glanced at Smythe. "Are you alright? Are you in pain? Maybe you ought to go up and lie down."

"I'm fine, love," he assured her, though the wound hurt like the devil. "I want to hear the rest of it and then I'll go up and rest."

"You know most of it," Mrs. Jeffries said quickly. "Annabelle Prescott's motive was simple. She didn't want her uncle selling all his assets to buy into an enterprise that might not be successful."

"And apparently Mrs. Prescott was of the opinion that her uncle investing in a Trans Andean Railroad was so risky that she was prepared to kill to keep him from doing it," Hatchet said quietly.

"She put her plan into action after she found out that Francis had gone to see both his solicitor and his banker," Mrs. Jeffries reminded them. "She wasn't about to let him fritter away a fortune she felt was partially hers."

"I wonder what 'appened to Joseph Humphreys' gun?" Wiggins asked as he reached for his tea.

"I'll bet she stole it," Betsy suggested. "You know, to muddy the waters a bit or make the police think he was the guilty one."

"But she didn't know 'e'd be leavin' the gun case in the hallway on the very day she was plannin' on murderin' her uncle," Wiggins argued, waving his cup dangerously for emphasis. Some of the tea slopped over the side of the cup, spilling onto his sleeve.

"She hadn't planned to do it," Betsy speculated. "But I think she's the sort of person who seizes opportunities and is willing to take a risk. Joseph Humphreys said he left the gun case in the hallway for the maid to take up to his room. I think Annabelle Prescott saw it there, opened the case, stole the gun, and slipped it into her pocket. For all we know, she might have even used it to commit the murder."

"I agree she probably stole Joseph's gun," Mrs. Jeffries said. "But I don't think she used it for the actual killing. She acted impulsively in stealing the weapon, but I'll wager she had her own at the ready for the murder. Remember, we know she knew how to shoot. Leo Kirkland verified that fact."

"His other relatives didn't like the idea of him sellin' off his good stock, either." Wiggins pursed his lips. "But they didn't commit murder."

"Maybe they weren't smart enough to come up with a plan that would keep them from hanging," Betsy suggested. "You've got to admit, Annabelle Prescott thought most of it through pretty carefully. She almost got away with it."

"Almost, but not quite," Mrs. Jeffries said. "There were lots of places where her plans came undone. She hadn't counted on Michael Collier arriving at the house tonight to see Imogene Ross."

"I don't think she realized they'd fallen in love," Betsy interjected.

"She wasn't as clever as she thought she was. Not only did we figure out what she'd done, but Imogene Ross came to the same conclusion, and I have a strong suspicion that Michael Collier might have even begun to think along those lines as well."

"And both of them almost lost their lives because of it," Hatchet reminded them. He looked at Mrs. Jeffries. "What was it that made you realize Annabelle Prescott was planning on murdering Miss Ross tonight?"

"The moment Betsy said that Agnes had told her the house was going to be empty, I knew something had happened and she planned on killing again," Mrs. Jeffries said thoughtfully. "Mrs. Goodge's comments set me to thinking as well. No matter how eccentric a household might be, it simply isn't done to send all the servants off to the music hall three days after there's been a death in the family. Then when Betsy made those comments about the housekeeper getting the laudanum out of Mr. Humphreys' medicine chest, I knew she had something fiendish in mind."

"Imogene Ross and Michael Collier owe you a great debt of gratitude," Hatchet said to the housekeeper. "If not for you, they'd both be dead."

"They owe *all of us* a debt of gratitude," Mrs. Jeffries corrected him. "Without everyone's contribution, especially Smythe's, those two would be lying on mortuary tables as we speak."

"Any of you would have done the same thing." Smythe blushed, embarrassed by the praise.

"He's a brave one, my man." Betsy patted his arm gently. "But I'll not have you doing such a thing again, you hear me."

"I hear you, love." He laughed in delight. He was glad to be alive and glad to have her sitting beside him.

"Good," Betsy replied. "Next time, let someone else grapple with the crazy killer lady."

Fred suddenly jumped up and ran for the back hall as the door opened.

"The inspector's back." Luty got up. "We'd best be on our way. We'll be back tomorrow morning to hear the rest of the details," she whispered as Witherspoon came into the kitchen.

"We're just on our way out, Inspector." Hatchet rose and grabbed Luty's cape off the back of the chair. He draped it over her shoulders. "Madam has had enough excitement for one night."

"Fiddlesticks." She snorted delicately and then looked first at Wiggins and then at Smythe. "And as for you two, don't you be scarin' me like that again. But you're both right brave and we're real proud of you. Come on, Hatchet, let's go before we wear out our welcome."

As soon as they'd gone, Mrs. Goodge started to get

up, but the inspector waved her back to her chair. "I've something to say," he said. "I want you all to know how much I appreciate all that you've done for me."

Alarmed, the cook looked at Mrs. Jeffries, who gave a barely imperceptible shake of her head, indicating that Mrs. Goodge wasn't to panic. Not yet. They'd wait until they heard the rest of what he was going to say before they assumed he'd figured out just how much they helped on his cases.

"But I must say, even though Smythe and Wiggins acted properly tonight, I was so frightened for both of them when all the shooting started. Please, please, don't ever put yourself in danger like that again."

"That's what I said, Inspector," Betsy replied pertly. "And they've both promised me they won't."

Betsy stood at the window of the third-floor sitting room, staring out into the night. She was very proud of herself. She'd done an excellent job of keeping the others, especially Smythe, from seeing how horribly upset she'd been tonight.

Tears sprang into her eyes and she hastily brushed them away. She'd already had one good cry in the privacy of her room and she didn't need another. But my Lord, when Smythe'd walked in with that bandage peeking through the opening of his shirt and she'd seen the bloodstains on his clothes, she'd almost died.

"Betsy, are you alright?" Smythe stood in the door, hesitating before coming fully into the room. He knew she'd been crying, he knew she was barely hanging on to her emotions, and he didn't want to push her over the edge. Dignity was important to his Betsy.

She brushed her cheeks quickly and quietly tried to clear her throat before she spoke. "I'm fine. I just needed a few moments to myself. You know, let some of the excitement wear off before I go to bed. Otherwise, it'd take ages to fall asleep."

He moved farther into the room, coming up to stand behind her. Her back was still to him, so he put his hands on her shoulders and stared out the window with her.

When he'd come into the kitchen tonight, he'd seen her expression as her gaze took in the bandage and his bloodied clothing. He'd seen the horror, the anguish, and the fear she tried so hard to hide. She'd done a fine job of pretending she was just fine, that the terror were gone, and that she was as right as rain. But he knew better. He knew she was putting on a brave front for his benefit. She thought she'd lost him and that had scared her to death. Now he desperately wanted to do something to take the fright right out of her and give her something wonderful. He decided to tell her about tracking her sister to Canada.

They had plenty of time to get her whole family here before the wedding. He'd spare no expense to make sure all of them, even the little ones if her sister had had children, were in the church and watching her walk down that aisle.

"Let's just stand here a moment and enjoy the peace of the night," he whispered. He'd tell her in a moment and she'd be so happy the fear in her eyes would vanish in a heartbeat.

"Alright." She leaned back against him, delighting in the solid feel of him next to her back. She'd almost lost him. She couldn't get that thought out of her mind. If that bullet had been another inch or so either way, he'd have been killed and she'd never have seen him again. Life was short and precious; she of all people should have remembered that.

"Betsy," Smythe said softly. "I have a surprise for you."

She turned and threw her arms around his waist, taking care not to jostle his shoulder. "I've got one for you as well. Let me go first." She didn't wait for him to reply but simply plunged straight ahead before she lost her nerve. "I want us to get married right away. I want to do it as soon as the banns are read. I don't want a big wedding, I don't want a lot of fuss, I just want you to be my husband. I almost lost you tonight, my love, and I don't want to wait a second more than necessary. This time nothing—and I mean *nothing*—will stop us from getting married."